THE DEMONOLOGISTS' DAUGHTERS

By K. Scott Culpepper

Jacket art: Brandi Doane McCann
Author Photo: Josiah Culpepper

www.kscottculpepper.com

Hardcover ISBN: 979-8-9916850-0-9
Paperback ISBN: 979-8-9916850-1-6
Ebook: ISBN: 979-8-9916850-2-3

For Ginger, who makes every step in all my journeys better because she walks alongside me. There's no one I'd rather share love and life with than you.

CHAPTER ONE

"DINAH? DINAH?"

She turned a clammy face toward me. Her eyes were filled with terror. Even in her distress, my sister was still beautiful. *The prettiest of us by far*, I thought.

"Debbie! Help me! Help me!"

Blood poured down the legs of the kitchen table.

I felt a rough jerk on my arm.

"Deborah! What are you doing in here, Child?" My mother's voice was rougher than her hand. She started pulling me away.

"I'm not a child! I'm thirteen. I can help!"

Except I was and then I wasn't. I was morphing back and forth from my thirteen-year-old self to a tiny five-year-old. And I seemed to have the strength of that smallest persona, unable to resist the vise-like grip of my momma.

"You are not ready to face these horrors," Lucille insisted. "You're just in the way."

"Dinah!" I screamed.

"Debbie! Oh God, don't leave me! Please, don't leave me! They're killing me!" A loud thumping sound drowned out her voice.

"Dinah!"

It took me a moment to realize that I was screaming out loud. I sat up in my bed, sweat pouring down my body, tears streaming down my cheeks. I looked down at my damp pillow; I looked around my darkened room. And then I heard it again. The thumping sound from my dream. It was coming from my living room. And there was something else, soft but growing louder. A voice.

"You will not defy the will of the living God. Leave her!"

It's my father's voice!

"Burn in hell, old man." The voice was guttural and unearthly, demonic. "Like Dinah. She's burning in hell. Roasting like a pig."

"Stop your lies and come out of her! In the name of the Father and the Son ..."

"And Scooby and Shaggy and all those other meddling kids," the spirit cackled with malevolent mirth.

I shook my head and tried to propel myself out of the dream. But it wasn't a dream. Those sounds were flooding my ears. They were getting louder. And definitely coming from the next room.

"Maybe I should kill the rest of your kids before they start meddling. Gut them one by one, all those screaming girls."

"No! Leave her, you bastard!"

My father's scream jerked me out of my frozen trance. I'd never heard him shout like that. He was controlled and firm, loud, but never unhinged.

The more pressing problem that demanded action was why I was hearing him at all. I threw the covers off and jumped to my feet, not having fully decided what I intended to do. My mace was nestled in the pocket of my blazer, but my blazer was hanging on a rack by the front door. I reached over to my bedside table and came up empty. The only thing there was my book. Literally throwing the book at my intruder would make for a great story, but I opted for self-preservation over humorous icebreaker. Besides, it was a paperback.

A strange squeak echoed from the living room, barely audible under the sounds of the exorcism. Gathering my courage, I tiptoed to the door.

I glanced at my sweats on the floor and wished I had time to throw them on. Grisly images of my dead body being photographed in just a t-shirt and panties by the CSI ran through my mind. *That's what you're worried about?* I eased the door open and slid noiselessly into the living area.

I looked across the room, and my blood ran cold. The squeaking sound came from the hinges of my front door. I'd told the landlord six weeks ago that they needed to be oiled. Just last week I'd made a note to buy some WD-40 and do it myself. Now the door swung on those squeaky hinges, propelled back and forth by the rising wind. I could scarcely breathe. As a gust blew the door wider, I saw something white on it and slowly walked toward it.

"The power of Christ compels you to leave!"

Before I could read my door, my father's shout drew my gaze to the coffee table. I slid over to my couch and picked up a phone sitting on it, never taking my eyes from the darkened doorway. An MP4 file was playing the exorcism on a loop. It was only audio, loaded with a plain red background for the visual image.

Silence settled for a moment in the room. Assuming the recording was over, I reached down to press the pause button on the phone. Just as I leaned toward the phone, a woman's scream echoed through the speaker, sending a chill down my spine. My limbs went numb as it continued for a full minute.

"What have you done?! Mia! Mia! My God, you've killed her! She's dead!"

"Mia! Mia! No, no, no!" a man said, his voice breaking into sobs.

"I ... I'm not sure what happened. I didn't touch her. I didn't mean to hurt her," my dad said. He sounded unsure. Denny Hebert never sounded unsure.

I thought I heard movement behind me. Still keeping an eye on the door, I tapped the red button at the bottom to stop the video. Silence filled the apartment, broken only by the whirring sound of the wind. And then the door banged again, causing me to jump. I scanned the room around me, but there was only darkness and the silhouettes of my furniture. Just beyond the small dining area, I could barely see into the kitchen. It was only about 70 square feet, and there didn't appear to be anyone there.

I crept toward the door with the phone still in my hand. A gust of wind struck the door again and blew it inward. A message was emblazoned with bright white paint, more easily seen against my dark brown door. I caught an involuntary scream in my throat, muffling it before it could emerge. The paint was fresh. Small streaks were still dripping down the door. My legs gave way, and I sank to my knees, reading the message on the door:

THEY KILLED ME

WHY DID YOU LEAVE ME DEBBIE

WHY DID YOU LET THEM DO IT AGAIN

I rose, slammed the door closed, and locked it. There was no sign of damage to the lock. *How did they get in?* I stumbled to the kitchen and poured myself a full glass of wine to steady my nerves. It was only when it had started coursing through my system that the obvious finally hit me. *They knew Dinah's final words!*

"Debbie!" I was hearing her again. My sister's voice pleading with me, but this time I was wide awake. No one in Nashville called me "Debbie" or "Deborah." One mischievous student tried my first year of teaching and learned quickly why most people respected my wish to distance myself from the Hebert legacy.

I moved to my balcony, stopping to retrieve the mace from my blazer pocket on the way just in case. A full moon spilled bright light across the Vanderbilt quad across the street. My gaze flicked down to the opposite edge of the street, and I saw her. Her slender figure stood in the shadows just beyond the streetlight. Her face was obscured, but there was no mistaking the long black tresses, white skirt, and purple shirt. She died in those clothes. Dinah slowly raised her arms toward me as if she were pleading with me.

"Why did you leave me, Debbie?" she whispered. The words echoed in my head.

"Dinah, I'm so sorry." I felt heat on my cheeks as salty tears streamed down my face again. I closed my eyes for just a second. When

I opened them, my older sister was gone. I leaned against the balcony's iron rail, wrestling to assert control over my emotions. More than one colleague referred to me as "incredibly stoic" under pressure. The roller coaster I was experiencing tonight was unwelcome for someone who tried to build her life on analytical precision and focused reasoning. Now I was beginning to doubt my sanity. Had I really seen and heard Dinah? My parents would believe I had.

Most parents fill their little girls' lives with cute dolls, frilly pink dresses, and dance classes, but mine filled our crowded Louisiana home with darkness, death, and demons. They pursued dark powers as self-proclaimed "demonologists." Denny and Lucille Hebert, pronounced "A-Bear" in good Cajun French style, rejected ivory tower intellectual demonology for active reality television style exorcisms and ghost hunting. Demonologists' daughters learn early that the fairy tale is a sham while the wicked witch hiding in the woods is very real. For my sweet sixteen, I received a silver cross necklace. Not so different from other girls' except that mine came with a printed ritual prayer for casting out evil spirits attached with a miniature rosary. We weren't even Catholic. My parents liked to have all their bases covered.

After a few minutes, I knew what I needed to do. It couldn't wait, even though it was three in the morning. I returned to my bed and plucked my phone from the nightstand. My text notifications revealed that Dorcas had contacted me first:

Momma and Daddy in trouble! NEED YOU NOW!

Deliverance session went wrong! Murder charge!

My blood ran cold. The last time they had faced that kind of investigation was after ... that night.

Dorcas had included Delilah in her texts too. A good twenty minutes had gone by before our other sister's reply arrived. The middle finger emoji proclaimed how done she was with us all. A further text from Delilah rammed the point home.

SERVES THEM RIGHT. LET JESUS TAKE THE WHEEL. STOP FILLING MY PHONE UP BITCH!

The desire to stay wrapped up in the alternate universe I had built for myself in Nashville was strong. No, I had to remind myself that the alternate universe was "down there." Vanderbilt University represented the real world, teeming with life and possibility. South Louisiana, for all its attractions, came at me like a vacuous black hole exerting incredible force to suck me back into its orbit. Like Michael Corleone said in *The Godfather III*, "Just when I think I'm out, they pull me right back in." Could I ignore all of this and forget it happened? I didn't need to get tangled up in their mess again after fighting so hard to break free.

But the image of the four of us together flooded my mind, breaking my resolve. It hadn't been all bad. My sisters and I had stayed close for so many years, but time, Trey, and death broke our little circle and chipped away at our bond. But now I could still see us splashing in the waters of the river, happy and together. I remembered little Dorcas stumbling along behind us, fighting to keep up with us when we ran up the big hill on the ridge overlooking our wood-framed house. Her cute little pigtails would wave in the wind as she called for us to slow down. That little sister was handling everything alone now.

I swallowed and pushed the button on my phone. Dorcas picked up instantly.

"Debbie! Oh, thank God!"

My sisters and Trey called me Debbie. Not many others did. I tried to get everyone to call me Debbie as a form of mild rebellion when I was thirteen. Lucille refused to allow it. "Deb-or-ah! Deborah led God's people to victory over his enemies. Debbie sounds like a stage name for a stripper at an I-10 truck stop."

"What the hell is going on, Dorcas? How is Dad?"

"I'm sorry. He kept asking me to wait because he hoped it would blow over. You know him. He's trying to be strong for Momma and me. But he's scared, Debbie. People just keep asking them to do more. They see those characters in the movies, and they think the Heberts can do anything."

My parents had dug their own graves in that regard. They insured creative input into every *Demonologists* film that was produced when they signed the contracts. Lucille spent a lot of time on set when the films were in production, and Dad traveled over to New Orleans to join her when his expanding roster of "deliverance appointments" allowed. I knew when they started down that road ten years ago that it would come back to bite them in the ass. Fame moves like water; you can't control the cracks and crannies it seeps into. Sooner or later, it invades those places you wanted to keep dry and out of sight.

"What happened, Dorcas?"

"I don't know," Dorcas said. I could hear the tears in her voice. "It started out normal. We were working with this young woman. She was about twenty-five. We spoke scripture over her and commanded the demon to come out."

I rolled my eyes and reminded myself to be patient. Dorcas could never just tell you what you wanted to know. She had to set the scene and bring the drama.

"She spoke to us with another voice. Cursed us, blasphemed, spat on us. She broke one of the ropes tying her hands to the chair. Her parents were with us. When her father tried to step forward and grab her hand, she ... she knocked him across the room!"

Sounded like pretty typical Hebert fare so far.

"Then she looked at Dad. And in that guttural demonic voice, she said ... she said ..."

I waited for Dorcas to regain control.

"'You think if you help this girl God will forgive you for killing your daughter?'"

A chill rippled through me.

"What did he do, Dorcas?"

"He threw everything at her for hours. Prayers, incantations, sleep deprivation. He kept going. Long after he should have. She screamed, thrashed, and fought. And then, she just went limp. We thought the demon was gone. Thought we had won. When we checked, she was dead. Debbie, Daddy wasn't himself. He went at her like a man ..."

"Possessed," I finished. I'd received an unwelcome front-row seat to the audio version.

"I need you here. Momma needs you."

"I'm sure Lucille is eager to see her disappointment return at this desperate hour." Actually, I was what we called her "quiet disappointment." My M.O. emphasized asking forgiveness rather than permission. I quietly rebelled bit by bit until I was too far out for the consequences to catch up with me. Delilah was the "loud disappointment." She went nuclear often and with gusto. Lucille and Delilah screamed at one another until both of them were hoarse. Then they screamed some more. Alongside her hit songs, Delilah published racy pictures of herself with men, women, and all other available categories on her website. Part of it had to do with the pop star persona, but I guessed she also thought about Lucille watching that site religiously and reacting to each scandalous photo. You almost thought Denny and Lucille sensed something wild about Delilah from birth. They named all of us after virtuous women of the Bible except for Delilah. She was named after a Philistine whore with a hair fetish. I felt the familiar stab of pain that always came when I thought about Delilah. Images of her were always followed too fast by thoughts of her and Trey. But those thoughts were better left in the past.

"Debbie ..."

"Diana!" I snapped. Regret seized me immediately. Thoughts of my rocky past with Delilah always caused me to get irritable. "I'm sorry, Dor."

"It's okay. I actually need Diana Chambers instead of Debbie Hebert right now."

"Why?" I was curious for the first time. My family, especially Dorcas and Lucille, never understood why I had chosen to be known by the professional name "Diana Chambers." For them, my adopted name and blonde hair dye represented a rejection of them instead of what it really was, a rejection of the dark, closed, and guilt-ridden world my parents built for us. Dorcas must really have been desperate if she was so willing to call on my professional persona for help.

"Something's not right. All of it was weird. There are more details I don't want to tell you over the phone. I need a skeptic. Someone who has the knowledge and experience to cut through what happened and see if there is any way that we can prove Dad is not responsible."

"Dor, I can do that," I began carefully, "but we might not like what I find out. What if Dad really is responsible for that woman's death?"

"If that's the case, then so be it." Dorcas was channeling her guru voice now. It creeped me out how quickly Dorcas could shift from hysterics to stoic robot mode. Just like Lucille. Our youngest sister had always been Momma's girl.

There was no way I wanted to get involved. I had developed an international reputation for disciplined intellectual engagement with religious questions and phenomena. My colleagues and I were often called in to test supernatural claims and testify in cases where religious questions or spiritual abuse was involved. Investigative work was not uncharted territory for me, but I was too close to this one. Would I be able to maintain my objectivity and focus with the churning emotions sure to be kicked up by a return to Picardy? Was I ready to see my parents again? Was I ready to see Trey? I left Picardy in 1999. It was the summer after my high school graduation. Was twenty-three years long enough to still the voices of the past raging inside me? Was there any amount of time that could?

"Dorcas, I don't know."

"Please, Deb-- Diana!"

"Surely Lucille has worked out her story already. Dad will be free by the end of the week, and the next book will be half written, primed for adaptation into a hit film." I tried to sound more confident than I was.

"Please don't talk that way about Momma," Dorcas said. "She really does love you. Why do you hate her so much?"

"I don't ..." I caught myself before I shouted at my little sister again. Not the time to rehash old arguments or to try making Dorcas understand something she never seemed able to grasp. For her, being the heir to the Hebert legacy came easily. It gave her meaning and mission. For Delilah and me, it became a chain to shake off. Especially after Dinah had died.

"I'm sorry, Dor," I finally said after a long silence between us. "I'm going to have to think it over and get back to you."

"I love you, Debbie," I could hear her voice quavering. My own eyes misted.

"Love you too," I whispered and quickly hung up before my resolve could crumble. *Why didn't I tell her about seeing Dinah? Or about the phone?* I still wasn't sure about Dinah, and I needed to find out more about the phone first. Besides, how would it sound for the voice of reason in the family to start telling ghost stories?

The sun was going down, and the shadows were lengthening the next day as I made my way to our … *my* … small apartment on the edge of the fan-shaped original campus. I passed several groups of students I knew and tried to disengage from my inner turmoil enough to give a nod and a word of greeting. My feet were aching from my heels. I was longing to slip into slippers or, better yet, feel the soft carpet with my bare feet. A good glass of wine was in order, too. I hadn't had much at the post-conference reception, so I was due.

I'm not sure what sets one shadow apart from the others. They all look the same until suddenly one sends a chill down your spine. It sounds ridiculous to feel like you're being watched on a crowded college campus. Of course, you're being watched. But I was starting to notice that the groups of students were thinning out the closer I got to my apartment, and the shadows were only getting darker. I glanced behind me and saw nothing. Scolding myself for being paranoid, I tried to rehearse the lecture I was crafting for my graduate seminar next week.

Just when I thought my nerves were steadied, I caught a movement out of the corner of my eye. I glanced right to a mass of thick bushes nestled up against an administrative building. Had I seen someone there? I debated whether to look closer and decided against it. No way I was going to commit rookie horror movie mistake number one.

I quickened my pace across campus, trying desperately not to break into a full run. My feet were killing me now. I had gone about three yards when I thought I heard the distinct sound of shoes pounding the pavement behind me. They were coming fast. I reached into my pocket and wrapped my fingers around the little canister of mace hidden there. A hand reached from behind and grasped my arm. I gave a shout and whipped out the mace.

"Wait! What the hell?!"

I gasped and stopped myself from pressing the button just a second before the searing spray was released into my ex-boyfriend's face.

"What are you doing?" I yelled, still panting.

"What am I doing? I came to check on you. I didn't realize you were so tired of my company that you were willing to unleash weapons of face destruction," Pedro Silva said.

I blushed, suddenly embarrassed at my panic. But it had seemed so real.

"I'm sorry. I was just ..."

"Seeing demons behind every bush?"

I started to reply and decided not to bother. We knew each other too well for lies.

"Let me walk you back to the apartment," he said gently. "If you're not going to call the police about last night, at least let me make sure you get inside safely."

I wondered again if I should have told him, but I'd had to share it with somebody.

"I don't think that's a good idea."

"I promise to behave like a perfect boy scout," he said, fingers raised in mock salute.

I glanced around the darkening campus. The wind was starting to pick up. Strange noises filled my ears as it tossed branches and rolled trash around the sidewalk.

"Okay."

We walked the rest of the way in silence.

The boy scout decided to stick around for a glass of wine. He knew where it was, so I excused myself for a few moments to remove my bruising shoes. I slipped out of my skirt and blouse, donning a Vanderbilt sweatshirt and jogging pants. I pulled my blonde hair, dyed that color since I slipped away from Picardy for the last time in 1999, into a ponytail. Pedro cast an eye over my informal appearance as I returned.

"Don't get fancy on my account."

"A woman always appreciates such generous feedback," I said with a grimace.

"You know I like it when you do the coed look," he said. He was trying for light banter, but there was a familiarity and hunger behind the words that reminded us both that we needed to be careful.

Two of these spontaneous encounters this spring had resulted in Pedro staying over again and both of us insisting the next morning that this should be the last time. He offered me a glass of wine as we settled into two chairs on the small balcony overlooking the campus. The moon was up now; it was full and cast a brilliant glow across the street. I sipped the wine and felt it burn the back of my throat with pleasure. What would Lucille say? I looked across at Pedro, who was sipping his own wine and staring across the campus.

Moments like these caused me to question why we had decided to break things off. We both agreed that if we couldn't move forward, we should look elsewhere. Every time we talked about an engagement or marriage, I found a way to put it off. I was never quite sure why. But there was something so comfortable about being with him. I loved spending this time with him in comfortable silence like we had countless times before in the five years we shared this apartment.

"So, are you going?" Spell broken.

"Going where?"

"You know where. Your sister asked, didn't she?"

"Yes. She said something went wrong with an exorcism. A girl died. Dad's been accused of causing her death."

Silence settled between us for a few moments.

"I think you should go."

"What!? Why?"

Pedro cleared his throat and took a long sip of his wine. I could see the wheels turning in his head and the calculation in his eyes.

"Maybe going back is what you need. Facing all those demons. The metaphorical ones, I mean."

"Is this about fixing me or about fixing us?"

He winced. Pedro had been a psychologist before he came to Vanderbilt to teach and then ascend to the role of administrator. Attempts to bring his expertise to bear on our relationship never ended well.

"You know I would not presume to psychoanalyze you."

"Like hell."

"It's not about us, Diana. Maybe if you could face the past, face why you became who you are, maybe then you could have some closure and maybe ..."

"Move forward," I snapped. "I have moved forward and then some, Pedro Silva. Just because I don't choose to do it with you does not mean I'm not capable of doing it."

Pedro raised his hands in mock self-defense.

"I'm sorry I brought it up. Look, let's talk about something else."

But the spell was shattered. I rose angrily from my chair and headed for the door.

"You can show yourself out," I called over my shoulder.

I strode to the bedroom and slammed the door. About thirty minutes later, I heard him softly close the door on his way out. *Took time to enjoy that drink*, I thought bitterly. Honestly, I was more angry at myself than Pedro. My whole career was focused on careful analysis and critical detachment. It seemed like I excelled at that in every area except when it came to my family. *Go back! How could he even suggest that when he knows what it could cost?* I knew the answer to that one. He was desperate. Frustration had turned to desperation, and the only means he saw of securing some kind of future for us lay in reckoning with my past.

There was more to learn in Picardy than just the truth about my dad's last exorcism. Pedro was right when he said I had unfinished business in my hometown. The mystery of Dinah's death hung over my life and my family like a dark cloud floating on the periphery of everything. Maybe I didn't owe my family anything anymore, but I owed Dinah everything. She would want me to help them. I picked up the phone planted in my apartment and considered my options. I had no explanation for it. It was time to get help. And maybe to give some.

CHAPTER TWO

THE SUNNY OUTSKIRTS OF HATTIESBURG, MS gave way to the tree-shaded lanes of I-59. My Toyota Corolla sped along at a barely legal seventy-five miles an hour while my mind wandered. I had finally called the police. I described the sounds I heard and gave the police the phone. A quick check revealed that it was a burner, as generic and vanilla as a phone could get. Another twenty-four hours had yielded no new leads. Pedro had come over again and tried to insist on staying with me for a few days, but I vetoed that offer and sent him on his way.

And then I had considered my next move. It was November, and Thanksgiving Break was only a week away. After that, there were only two weeks left in the semester. We had just returned to a semblance of normalcy after Covid, so I still had all my online materials and hybrid learning tools at the ready. More importantly, I had Pedro's help in securing permission to go online for the last two weeks. If I wanted to head home, I could.

"You're coming! Thank God! I can't wait to see you," Dorcas had gushed when I called to tell her I'd come.

"Slow down. There's more." I'd described the home invasion, deciding not to omit a single detail. Silence had followed for a few seconds.

"I'm actually not surprised. I told you earlier there were other things I didn't want to discuss over the phone."

"Yes," I'd said, concerned by Dorcas' solemn tone.

"All of this feels like more than an accident or a tragedy. A lot of things have been happening. Taken together, it all feels orchestrated, like some sort of attack."

"Lucille would say Satan is always prowling like a roaring lion," I'd quoted.

"Yeah ..." That silence again.

"Dorcas?"

"We can talk more when you get here. When can we expect you?"

"I have a few details to iron out here. I'll try to do that tomorrow and head out on Friday. Dorcas ..."

"Yes?"

"Not a word to anyone outside the family. I want to keep it quiet that I'm coming home if I can."

"No worries, Dr. Chambers, we appreciate you coming down to help us poor folk out." Dorcas exaggerated her already thick Southern accent.

"Dor, I ..."

"See you soon." The line had gone dead.

Orchestrated. An attack. Those words ran through my mind now on a continuous loop as the miles fell behind me. Dorcas held the undisputed title of family drama queen. Even Lucille, ever her champion and defender, got frustrated with her embellishments and paranoia sometimes. But she hadn't sounded carried away over the phone.

I did need to consider that there was a lot of bad blood between my family and many citizens of Picardy. My parents' determination to hunt down the persons responsible for Dinah's death, driven in part by the fact that they were the most logical suspects, had resulted in a full-fledged satanic panic. Allegations that satanic cults were meeting in the woods and organizing to take control of the town had gripped Picardy for almost two years. In the end, it owed more to Frank Peretti's fictional *This Present Darkness*, read religiously by Lucille at least once a year, than to any real satanic activity.

No one was ever arrested in connection with Dinah's death, nor was any real evidence ever produced linking anyone to either the official Church of Satan or any home-grown group. It did result in the dismissal of a beloved teacher, Aaron Francis, whose homosexuality was revealed during the course of the investigation. Francis was outed and fired due to the potential for "negative influence on minors." He had served as one of the best teachers in the school for ten years, even earning an award for "Teacher of the Year." It also earned me glares and rude comments from my classmates about how my family cost them their Marilyn Manson albums. It had gotten so bad that Lucille took the three of us out of school and briefly homeschooled us during the fall of 1996.

That was a hard year made even harder by the distance I felt between me and Trey for most of it. I wondered what it would be like to see Trey again now. *Will it be comfortable or awkward? Will he even want to see me after all this time?* My left hand left the wheel and wandered to my locket.

My journey from traumatized Demonologists' daughter to tenured professor and Demonologist-debunker started, like so many things in my early life, with Trey. Trey spotted me sitting alone in the lunchroom in third grade. I was sitting in my tattered hand-me-down dress vacated by Delilah only a year before. It had once been a bright red but had faded to a dull pink after so much time in the sun hanging on the clothesline. I was staring through my lunch as if my gaze could penetrate the table itself. My cheeks burned and my ears stung with the sounds of muted laughter coming from behind me. The words "freak" and "sackcloth" hissed from Crissy Hines' mouth two tables away as her prissy little posse giggled at my expense. Trey's shadow fell over my sandwich, and I looked up to see a boy my age with messy brown hair tousled beyond control.

He eased himself into the chair across from me and reached out a hand. In his palm were three M&Ms, two brown and one green. The Heberts weren't supposed to have candy because sugar was "stimulated artificially," and artificial stimulation was the work of ... you guessed it ... Satan. I looked up at the boy suspiciously. He smiled and stretched his hand out further. I regarded the bright candy shells like Eve must have examined the shimmering skin of forbidden fruit. Finally, I took them and popped them into my mouth. The sugar produced a sweet rushing sensation on my taste buds. My eyes widened slightly as I savored the synthetic sweetness, so different from the dull fare of fruit and nuts we got at home.

"Thank you," I said. My voice, so subdued and shy back then, was barely audible.

Trey smiled again and wordlessly brought his other hand up from below the table. He held a large black sleeve with M&M emblazoned on the side in big white letters.

"You want more?"

Momma's voice rang in my head for a moment like one of those little angel figures that appears on the shoulders of cartoon characters when they need to make a decision. A devil figure usually shows up too in the cartoons, but Daddy and Momma said the devil doesn't need to show up because he's always there, waiting like a hungry lion. I pushed my long jet-black hair behind my shoulders and gazed at the package.

"Yes."

The story of our friendship. Whether it was chocolate candies or MTV videos, over the course of our formative years Trey offered new experiences that opened worlds my parents never wanted me to see. I sneaked home with Trey in the afternoons when I was supposed to be at 4-H. We would eat Doritos and sit in Trey's living room watching TV, where I discovered there was more out there than endless misty bayous and tiny towns. A whole world was waiting to be experienced. I never got to watch TV at home. My parents forbade it. Lucille always said, "That box is the devil's portal. It's a window into all the twisted lies he wants you to believe."

Lucille Hebert was nothing if not colorful. She wrote horror well. All the Heberts' "cases" were chronicled and written with each lurid turn described in vivid detail. Lucille wrote like Stephen King, if Stephen King actually believed his own bullshit.

Diane was the sophisticated but silly blonde on the bar show we watched. I felt a wicked thrill watching a show set in a bar. "Spirits lead to spirits." "Alcohol is the devil's door." A Lucilleism existed for every occasion. Diane had friends. It looked like fun. She was pretty and funny. There was also this man named Sam. They fought sometimes. Then they were friends. Sometimes they kissed. I started to wonder what that was like. It looked like the most amazing thing.

Maybe those were the lies Satan wanted me to believe? The ones Momma and Daddy said would get me in the end if I wasn't careful. Sitting in Trey's living room, it didn't look like lies to me. It looked like life. Life away from the noise of our crowded home, free of the fear that a demon was lurking around every corner or a ghost was waiting to tear your heart out at a moment's notice. No screaming voices from the "office" while you were trying to sleep at night or strange people showing up at all hours of the day or night waiting for your parents.

Diane Chambers lived in a magical place called Boston. Everyone knew her name and was always glad she came. I looked over at Trey one day and said, "I want to be like her."

"You want to work at a bar?"

"I want to dress nice and say smart things. And have friends. Be normal. And never hear anybody talk about the devil again."

When I left Picardy for Princeton, I started using Diana Chambers as my alias. I tweaked the first name to keep it from being completely derivative. *Cheers* and Shelly Long might come looking for royalties after all. The "ah" sound at the end represented one of many personal tributes to my oldest sister. Pedro would say that spending my days teaching religious studies courses on exorcisms and keeping a "D" at the beginning of my professional name owed more to my childhood influences than I would like to admit, but now all those childhood influences were waiting for me at the end of this drive, including Trey.

I suddenly passed the sign that announced: PICARDY: PARADISE ON THE BAYOU. Louisiana was enamored with the notion of paradise. License plates had proclaimed the state a "Sportsman's Paradise" for decades. That claim rested much closer to the truth than Picardy's questionable bid to crown itself a little slice of heaven. Not that it was a terrible place to live. Picardy boasted a population of about nine thousand, not counting the folks who lived outside the city limits on the edge of Bayou Mystère. There were enough businesses and fast-food joints to hold you over until your monthly or, in the case of the Heberts, biannual, trip to New Orleans about an hour away.

Skipping the town for now, I steered toward Rural Route 15 and passed through the series of fields that bordered our humble two-story house. I should have been prepared for the storm that awaited me, but naively, I'd expected all to be quiet like normal. Instead, the front yard was filled with vans bearing the logos of familiar news organizations. In addition to the local network affiliates, national news channels like CNN and FOX were present as well. I saw the throng of reporters waiting as I pulled into our little driveway. *Great!* I was afraid I would run over one of them as they swarmed the car. A wicked part of me thought it would be fun to bump one of them just lightly enough to teach them not to play chicken with moving vehicles.

They mobbed me as soon as I emerged from my Corolla.

"Dr. Chambers, what convinced you to come home after all these years?"

I bit my lip in frustration. For a while, I'd enjoyed freedom from public connections to my Louisiana roots because most people never thought to connect the rising young scholar from Vanderbilt with the demon-chasing family from Picardy. The *Demonologists* films had changed all that.

"Did your father kill Mia Jordan?"

"Are you here to prove your parents are con artists?"

"Diana ...!"

"Dr. Chambers ...!"

Every bad martial arts movie features at least one fight scene where the hero takes on five ninjas at once, but with each ninja graciously choosing to attack one at a time rather than rush the hero as a group. Dealing with the press offers the best opportunity to kill that myth forever. Press ninjas all attack at once, more like a swarm of hungry piranhas. Those questions didn't come one at a time. They came all at once and so fast I could barely comprehend what they were saying.

"No comment! Please let me pass." I struggled to elbow my way through the crowd. It took forever to get to the front porch. As I climbed the steps and opened the porch screen door, the front door opened to reveal Dorcas' wide brown eyes surveying the crowd. She was slightly heavier than I remembered, but her hair was still jet black like mine used to be. It was her face I saw but another voice rang from behind her.

"Get out of her way! I'll call the police on all of you if you don't step back!" We often said that Moses would not have needed his majestic rod if Lucille Hebert had been standing on the banks of the Red Sea beside him. Her commanding voice alone could divide seas and shatter mountains. The media mob stepped back, and I slipped inside.

Dorcas enveloped me as soon as the door slammed shut. She had filled out a little and the lines of care were etched on her face, but she still seemed to channel an eternal childlike quality. There were seven years between us. Daddy often referred to her as "our little surprise" and always quickly added that it was a pleasant one. As we separated, I was struck by her resemblance to Dinah and found myself wondering how much I still favored all of them.

As my eyes adjusted to the dimly lit front parlor, I made out the second figure waiting expectantly in the entryway. Lucille Hebert's striking dark brown hair and sharp aristocratic profile was compared by friends and family to a young Katherine Hepburn. Looking at the older version, I saw that she had grown into a more matronly figure who still resembled the famous actress in her mature years. Her hair was streaked with gray now and pulled into a tight bun rather than flowing down her shoulders, but beyond that she looked so ageless that I was tempted to believe all the tales of immortal vampires that terrified us as kids.

"Lucille," I said tentatively.

Dorcas' eyes revealed her disappointment at my lack of respect, but she kept silent.

"Hello, Deborah. It's been a long time." I could see her daring me to insist that she call me Diana behind her otherwise placid eyes. No point in butting heads so soon over something so basic.

"Yes. It has. How are you? I mean, besides the obvious."

"I've been better. We've all been better."

"Of course."

"Your hair is so blonde."

"Yes."

"I have supper waiting in the kitchen. Dorcas can help you get your things settled. I thought we would sneak down to the jail and see your daddy after we eat. Fewer people around then. He'll be very happy to see you." She offered a nod and a half smile before turning toward the kitchen. I'm not sure what I was expecting or wanted, but I found myself feeling disappointed all the same. Dorcas seemed to sense my uncertainty.

"Let's get you settled," she said, taking my bag with one hand and squeezing my hand with the other. As she led me to the stairs, I noticed the white door leading to the storage room. I felt a chill despite the unseasonably warm day. Eerie voices pricked the edge of my consciousness, filling my mind and, for an instant, I thought my ears as well.

"You okay?" Dorcas paused on the stairs when she noticed I hadn't followed.

"Yeah ... it's just ... How do you live with all that creepy crap in here?"

"It's safe. It's all been blessed and surrounded by a hedge of protection." She sighed at my skeptical look and raised an eyebrow. "They put most of it in the barn outside anyway, so the sightseers don't try to tramp through the house."

I followed Dorcas up the stairs to the rooms we once shared with our sisters, trying to ignore the thought of the haunted items and the ghosts of the little girls we once were haunting every corner of the house.

Our drive to the local jail revealed how much my hometown had changed in the years since I left.

"Oil and gas jobs have been slipping away for years," Dorcas explained from the back seat. I was driving my Corolla in the hopes that reporters were less likely to recognize my car than my sister's 2010 Impala. Lucille sat in the front passenger's seat gazing out the window and tossing in a comment every few minutes.

"I thought the cities around Lake Pontchartrain were experiencing some growth after Katrina," I said.

"The financial crisis in '08 slowed all that down. Plus, we're too far away to really benefit from that. Lots of young families have been moving closer to New Orleans or to Texas."

As we rounded the corner of Fifth and Main, I saw the most prominent casualty of those demographic changes. Picardy High School stood where it always had, the long main brick building connected to a sidewalk leading down to the massive gym that hosted Picardy's small-town heroes on the hardwood. A small shed for the school's ag program rested at the bottom of the hill, and the football stadium could be seen rising behind the main building. Like the town itself, Picardy High School was now just a shell, shuttered and empty. The parish had decided to consolidate a number of public schools with declining enrollments ten years ago, and Picardy didn't make the cut. The buildings now stood empty, used only for the occasional public event.

"Your Daddy will be out tomorrow," Lucille said as we drove around the back of the jail, avoiding the media parked across the street.

A hearing had been held while I was driving throughout the day. Bail was set at $55,000, close to the minimum for the charge of involuntary manslaughter. Lucille had immediately started working her network of "partners," the quirky televangelist term for donors. Combined with the cash my parents had stowed away from their publications and films, bail was secured and ready for delivery the following morning.

We parked two blocks from the jail and walked the rest of the way. Deputy Jim Gorman's slim profile greeted us at the back door. Gorman had attended my parents' Assemblies of God church for years and been one of their most ardent defenders when the authorities got frustrated with their intervention in cases. He tipped his hat at Lucille and Dorcas. Jim eyed me with a questioning glance and nodded.

"So, you decided to come back. Well, I'm sure your daddy will be glad to see you. Right this way."

He led us through the dim supply room into the only slightly better lit cell block. There were only four cells in the small facility, and I was surprised to see that my dad was not in any of them.

"He's in here."

Gorman opened the door to a room that appeared to be some sort of guest bedroom. It was furnished with a twin bed, and a door on the side led to a private bathroom. My dad was lying on the bed reading a book. He set it aside when he saw us. His smile broke out wide and stretched his thick gray beard. He leaped forward and scooped me up into a tight bear hug. He was all muscle and sturdy bulk on a scale that could compete with any grizzly. My dad could literally crush the life out of someone, but he was always a gentle giant with his girls. I felt warmth on my neck and realized it was his tears. The thought of my tough as nails dad crying made me tear up too.

"You look so beautiful, Di," he said when he finally broke our embrace. Lucille shifted uncomfortably, but she let it pass without comment.

"Thanks, Daddy. You look pretty good yourself. Better than I feared. This place looks more like a hotel than a prison."

He gave us all the rakish smile that Lucille claimed had first drawn her attention at the parish fair. "It's the room they use to house visiting law enforcement. I haven't spent a second in a cell."

"And here I thought you were suffering in the big house," I said with a relieved smile.

"I'm an Hebert in a Louisiana big house. Membership has its privileges," he said with a wink. *Which is one of many reasons why Louisiana has such a sterling reputation for public integrity,* I thought with a grimace. I was glad that my dad had it so good, but it was disconcerting to think of all the more dangerous offenders who benefited from the Louisiana "good-ol'-boys'" clubs.

"Jim, thank you so much, old buddy. Could you leave us for a little bit?"

"Sure thing, Denny. You folks need water or soda? Okay, then. Let me know if you do."

Gorman closed the door, and we heard his footsteps moving toward the front office.

We sat on the bed and two chairs Gorman had obtained, talking about general safe topics for a little bit. Lucille sat beside my dad, her hand linked with his the whole time. There flowed a gentle affection between them that could only be forged by time and shared sorrows. I could criticize Lucille for many things, but her love and support for my dad was unwavering.

Finally, I said, "I need to tell you something." I told them about the intruder in my apartment and the recording of the exorcism. I left out the ghostly apparition of Dinah. Dorcas and Dad looked shocked while Lucille seemed lost in thought. She was the one who spoke first.

"Do you have this recording?"

"No. The police kept the phone to try to trace it and dust for prints. Nothing so far."

"It sounds like the Mia Jordan exorcism," Dad said with a glance at Dorcas. She nodded.

"Who was there?"

"Me, Dorcas, Mr. and Mrs. Jordan, and Pastor Dixon. And Tio was running the audio and video as usual."

"So, you do still record the exorcisms?" I tried to sound neutral. The look in his eyes told me he detected the distaste that lingered below the surface of my question.

"It's for everyone's protection. And so that we can learn to help others. Tio is good at the job, and he's trustworthy."

"And so you can try to convince other people they need the same services?"

Denny Hebert's eyes flashed with deep hurt, but he remained quiet. Lucille shifted beside him and said, "Maybe we need to just stick to the facts and not bring your particular little brand of worldly judgment and earthly philosophies into this."

Here we go. Lucille could cite sticking to the facts one minute and then talk about how the pyramids were created by aliens after they got bored probing the asses of cattle in the next.

"I'm trying to ask some logical questions to get to the bottom of what happened here. A woman is dead. Saying a few freaking incantations and shibboleths is not going to bring her back or tell us why she died."

"You need to show some respect for the things of God." Lucille started to rise but stopped when Denny's hand grasped her arm. He shook his head. She slowly sank back beside him. While her body complied, her eyes stated clearly that the argument was not over.

"Yes, we recorded the exorcism," Dorcas said.

"Audio and video?"

"Audio and video."

"And who is this Pastor Dick?"

"Pastor Dixon, Eric Dixon."

"Though the first name you used matches his character more," my dad muttered. Lucille shot him a disapproving look.

"Who is he?"

"He's the pastor at Grace Bible Church in Picardy."

"I don't remember that one."

"It's a new church plant. Been here about five years. Dixon grew up here. He was the same age as your sis ..." He stopped. We all knew from his hesitation which sister he meant. He would have been about four years older than me then. The same age as Dinah. He recovered and said, "Dixon has really been preaching hard against the notion of deliverance ministry and spiritual warfare. Says the passages in scripture telling us to wage war with the powers of darkness are allegorical."

"You might find him something of a kindred spirit, Deborah."

I ignored Lucille's attempt to bait me.

"So why was he there if he's so against the practice?"

"We invited him," Dorcas said. "He told us during a public debate on spiritual warfare at New Orleans Baptist Seminary that he was willing to be convinced if we would let him witness an exorcism first-hand. It was one of the those point-counterpoint conferences where they invite people with different perspective to debate dueling theological views. We saw it as a great opportunity to convince all the skeptics in the audience. Plus, we couldn't afford to back down in front of all of them. We took him up on it."

"Obviously not the best one for him to attend." No one reacted to my weak attempt at humor.

"Diana, I pressed her hard. Maybe harder than I should have. But we didn't do anything different from what we've done for fifty years. The only difference was that your momma wasn't there."

"Where were you?" I asked.

"I didn't feel well," Lucille said. "I had bad stomach cramps. I thought I was going to have to go to the hospital, but they got better later that night."

I frowned. Those cramps must have been severe for Lucille to miss an exorcism.

"Everything else was the same. Until the end."

"Can I see the video?"

"I think that could be arranged," Dorcas said.

I didn't voice the thought, but I was wondering why the version left at my apartment was audio without the video. Maybe viewing the video would help answer that question as well as fill in some of the other missing pieces of the puzzle.

We talked with my dad for a few more minutes and then hugged him goodbye with promises to see him tomorrow. We sneaked out the back door again and rode home in silence. At home, Lucille excused herself and went to bed. Dorcas and I talked for a few more minutes downstairs, mostly her asking questions about my life in Nashville. At about eleven we started up the stairs to our shared bedroom, the same bedroom Delilah and I had shared from five to seventeen.

As we settled under the covers of the twin beds on separate sides of the room, I remembered something Dorcas said in our phone conversation.

"Dor, you said there was more to tell me about the circumstances around Mia Jordan's death."

She chewed her lower lip and furrowed her brow. "Let's wait until tomorrow. We can grab some time before Dad gets home."

"Okay," I said.

"Good night," she said, blowing me a kiss across the room. I felt a little silly returning the air kiss, but it was the least I could do after neglecting Dorcas so much over the years.

I rolled over and tried to sleep. Some people complain about noise at night. My problem was the silence, the utter stillness, of our rural homestead. The sounds of the night were crickets and frogs out in the nearby marsh, not cars driving by or the hum of conversation floating from campus. I fought to sleep for about an hour.

I suddenly snapped awake, not even aware for a moment that I had been asleep. I looked at the clock on Dorcas' nightstand and saw that it was about 2:00. It was about 2:00 the night Dinah died when I woke up, wandered downstairs, and stepped straight into a living nightmare. I had left my bed that night because I heard voices and furniture bumping around in the kitchen. I heard it again in the present. Voices and the sound of bumping furniture.

"Dorcas," I whispered.

She mumbled something in her sleep and rolled over.

Surely, I'm imagining it. The words had barely sailed through my mind when a distinct audible thump sounded from the kitchen.

I threw my covers off and grabbed my jeans from where they hung over the black desk chair. No waiting this time. I looked at Dorcas again and almost woke her. *No point in bothering her if it's just my imagination running wild.*

I threw on a green t-shirt and slipped on my tennis shoes. Slipping out of our room, I paused to pull my phone out and turn on the flashlight. I tiptoed down the stairs. When I reached the ground floor, I peeked into my parents' room. Lucille was sleeping soundly. Her comforter was pulled up around her neck. Their king-sized bed looked very empty without my dad's solid frame beside her.

Assured that she wasn't making the sounds I'd heard, I panned my little light around the living room and then stepped into the kitchen. All was silent and dark. I flipped the light switch on. My breath caught in my throat. Two of the five table chairs were stacked on top of each other on the tabletop. They were facing each other, one turned upside down. I knew for sure that none of us left them that way. As I approached the table, I thought I heard a whimper from somewhere behind me. Someone was crying softly.

I backed out of the kitchen and surveyed the living room once again. The sounds stopped the moment I entered. Chill bumps erupted on my arms as I stepped toward the curtains that hung over the huge picture window framing the center of our living room. Those curtains were the only place someone could conceal themselves. I took a deep breath and ripped the curtains aside. Nothing but the still night and a bright moon greeted me through the window. I exhaled, not realizing until then that I had been holding my breath.

Footsteps sounded behind me. Once again in the kitchen. This time I chalked it up to overactive imagination. Then they started running. I whirled around in time to see a brief flash of white as the outer kitchen door leading to the barn slammed open. Curiosity overcame fear, and I raced through the kitchen and out the door.

A light flashed in the barn. I ran across our lot and entered the two-story structure. Ours was painted light blue instead of bright red. The Heberts never bowed to custom.

"Hello!" I called. "Whoever you are, come out! Why were you in our house?"

I was greeted by the sounds of crickets and tree frogs. I stumbled around the barn by the light of my phone, wishing now that I had taken the time to grab a proper flashlight. I almost tripped over a wood splitter.

Finding nothing on the first floor, I climbed the ladder to our hay loft. The smell of hay reminded me of summers spent jumping from the loft to the loose piles on the floor below. I had just stepped off the stairs and turned to check out the loft when my light fell on a horrifying face; unnaturally large black eyes framed with red hair gazed back into mine with stern malevolence. The mouth was pulled back into a smile meant to be endearing but which could only accurately be described as sinister. I screamed and jumped so far back that I bumped into the ladder and teetered on the edge of the opening below. My heart was racing so fast I thought it would tear through my chest. It took a minute or two for me to recognize the figure.

"Well," I said, wishing my voice didn't sound so shaky. "This is where they keep you these days, Bitch?"

Christine, as always, didn't speak. Now that my eyes were adjusted, I could make out the wooden frame of her case with the printed sign carrying the words: *DANGER, DO NOT OPEN UNDER ANY CIRCUMSTANCES.* Christine could be the antique doll version of Laura Ingalls Wilder if Laura had woken up one night and decided to murder Ma, Pa, Mary, and Carrie in their sleep. Her porcelain face reflected the moonlight while her eyes seemed to be watching every move you made. Denny Hebert had recovered the supposedly possessed doll during a series of exploits in the early 80s that you could read all about in *Christine's Revenge* by Lucille B. Hebert.

There were multiple origin stories for Christine, with one alleging that she was cursed by none other than the legendary voodoo queen Marie Laveau herself. Another story attributed Christine's malevolence to Delphine LaLaurie, the infamous early nineteenth century French Creole socialite and murderer of slaves. Lucille went with that version.

In her book, Denny discovered the doll in the LaLaurie Mansion at 1140 Royal Street, said to be the most haunted house in New Orleans. Lucille believed the dark powers that drove LaLaurie and her daughters to torture and kill so many were housed in the doll. I tended to believe it was more likely that Christine belonged to a LaLaurie daughter than to Laveau, mainly because she looked more like the kind of doll a rich white girl would have owned. It was even more likely that the doll belonged to no one special at all and Denny picked it up at an antique store for much less than Christine had earned them from sightseers over the years. I hated Christine with a passion and always had. She creeped me out more than any of the other "artifacts," and that was saying something. To be fair, Christine seemed to hate all of us too with her perpetual sadistic smile plastered on for the general discomfort of all.

As I played the beam of my flashlight around the loft, I could see that many other exotic items were housed here too. Marble gargoyle statues, an allegedly satanic altar with goat horns carved into the side, and an iron maiden.

"You still keep bad company, Christine," I muttered. I got the distinct impression that she would have given me the finger if she could. "Yeah, love you too."

I stepped past her and tried to ignore the other artifacts to focus on the task at hand. There had been no more sounds of any kind since I entered the barn. I was just about to start downstairs when I thought I heard a voice.

"Why?"

It came softly at first, but then got louder with each repetition.

"Why? Why? Why?"

It was coming from outside. I started walking slowly toward the window of the loft.

"Why did you let them kill me?"

I reached the window and looked out, seeing nothing but the vacant yard between the barn and the house.

"Why, Debbie?!"

My blood turned to ice. The voice seemed to be coming from all around me and inside my head all at the same time. I leaned out the window, looking toward the slope of the hill that framed the place where the woods met the edge of our property. I almost lost my grip and had to recover before I plunged to the ground below sans hay. I steadied myself and blinked to assure myself that I was really seeing her.

A figure in a purple top and long white skirt stood on the hill just at the edge of the woods. A slight wind rippled through the leaves and tossed her long dark hair. She looked just like she did the last time I saw her alive and when she stood across the street from my apartment. I couldn't make out the details of her facial features, but the hair, her slender frame, and the clothes were all the same. Slowly, both her arms rose from her sides and stretched imploringly toward me.

"Why? Why did you leave me, Debbie?"

I couldn't find my voice. As I stared in horror, drops of red suddenly appeared on her white skirt.

"They're killing me, Debbie!"

For the second time, I screamed. In seconds, Dinah went from prim and proper to covered in blood and gore. It stained her clothes, covered her face, and matted her hair. I closed my eyes.

I tried to tell myself she wasn't real. That at best she was an illusion and at worst an imposter. My guilt and grief overwhelmed my logic.

"Dinah, I'm so sorry! I wanted to save you. Dinah!"

When I opened my eyes, she was gone. The hill was empty. A gentle breeze tossed the trees, and the sounds of the night continued as if nothing had interrupted them. I sank exhausted to the floor of the loft and sat there for what seemed like hours.

I finally returned to the bedroom where Dorcas lay miraculously still sleeping and realized I had only been gone about thirty minutes. As I settled back into my bed, my mind was swirling with questions and fears. I didn't believe in ghosts. Nor in demons. Although having to forcefully remind myself of these facts didn't really do a ton to support my claim to scientific rationalism. Were there mysteries in this universe? Sure. But I had seen enough with my parents before I was seventeen to convince me that so many "supernatural phenomena" were simply smoke and mirrors. My years of study and teaching only added to that conviction.

So what do I make of tonight? Was it really Dinah? And, if not, how could she know what Dinah said the night she died? There were only a handful of people there that night. Most of them members of my family. I decided after talking with Dorcas the next morning that I would do some research on Dinah's death. I had never looked into official reports of her death or even seen her death certificate. I had read *Devil's Circle*, the book Lucille wrote six months after Dinah's death telling the family's version of the story. The book was filled with the same embellishments and outright lies Lucille told in her other books.

I suppose writing the book provided some sort of catharsis for Lucille, but it was hard for me not to see it as just another attempt to cash in on the Hebert brand. This time at the price of disrespecting my sister's memory. Lucille insisted that there were lingering suspicions and that people needed to read the real story.

The "real story" alleged that Dinah was the victim of Satan worshippers, whose nefarious plots she had uncovered at the local school. They cursed her and targeted her. All the Heberts' efforts were not able to save her. That was the Cliff's Notes version.

Despite the fact we were living by that time at the end of the Satanic Panic wave, Lucille's book reignited fears of occult activity in our little town. Suspicion ran rampant. What had caused the gushing blood running down the kitchen table that I had seen that night? The family said her death was due to "supernatural" causes. I wanted to know for the first time what the coroner had said. I plunged into a restless sleep. Dreams of Dinah screaming my name haunted the rest of my night hours.

The next morning, Dorcas was nowhere to be found. Lucille said she had left early to run some errands in town before she picked my dad up. I quickly ate the eggs and bacon Lucille laid out on the table and washed it down with orange juice.

"I think I'm going to run into town too if that's okay," I said.

"You don't seem to need my permission any other day, so I don't know why you need it today."

"I'll be back in the early afternoon."

"That will be fine. Your daddy will want to spend some time with you this evening."

"Sure," I said, rising and pulling my keys from my pocket.

"Deborah?"

"Yeah?"

"I thought I heard someone in the barn last night. You know anything about that?"

I swallowed. "No. I didn't hear a thing."

Lucille raised her eyebrow and stared me down with skeptical eyes. "No matter how long we go without seeing our child, a mother always knows when one of her own is in danger. I got up to check on you when I heard you scream and saw you walking back from the barn through your bedroom window. I want to help, Deborah."

Something in her tone almost pushed me to tell the whole story. But what was I going to say? *Christine scared me and then I saw my dead sister on the hill.* Instead, I said, "Thanks, but I'm fine."

She shook her head and said, "Be careful." Lucille sipped her coffee at the table while I gathered my laptop and headed for my car.

Fifteen minutes later I was rolling through the quiet streets of Picardy. The local police had managed to impose a media ban for my dad's release, but I doubted it would last long. Hopefully long enough for us to have a peaceful Thanksgiving the next day. I saw a couple of their vans in various parking lots, but they didn't seem to notice me driving by; maybe they would take the holiday off and leave us alone. One could hope!

There was a new coffee shop in town just off Main Street. I thought it would be a good place to get free wifi and send out inquiries about Dinah without being interrupted by family. I parked at *Coffee Corner* and checked to see if the drug store was still across the street. My head was throbbing after last night's terrors and poor sleep.

Sam Dearman was still perched at the counter he had occupied for fifty years.

"Hello, young lady, how are you today?"

I would be flattered, but anyone under sixty was a "young lady" to Sam. I'd just turned forty and was glad to take any "young ladies" I could get. Sam was a town favorite, an African-American man who kept strong ties to the community despite years of racial strife and battles over segregation. He had been one of the first black students to attend Picardy High School.

"Fine. Thanks," I said as I hurried past him.

I felt a stab of remorse at my rude response. Sam was sharp and too likely to see the dark-haired little girl who bought cinnamon sticks from him once a week in the middle-aged blonde buying ibuprofen. He also could have seen news of my arrival on TV. Maybe I would stop by again and catch up later, but I wasn't ready yet. I surveyed the variety of options and chose a generic brand. As I looked at the labels, I got the impression that someone was watching me. I looked down the aisle and saw only an elderly woman I didn't recognize looking at toothbrushes. A glance the other way revealed a brown-haired man standing at the far end of the aisle looking at a magazine. His back was turned to me. He wore a pair of gray slacks and a blue polo. The man didn't seem to be taking any particular notice of me. Still, I couldn't shake the feeling.

I hurried to the counter. Sam had gone to help another customer; a young woman with dark skin and long curly hair was running the cash register in his place. I breathed a sigh of relief and paid for my drugs.

I ordered a café au lait at *Coffee Corner* and settled into a booth located, appropriately, in the corner. I had started to catch up on email when the bell over the door dinged. A group of six women walked in and started ordering. They were chattering like a group of high school girls, but most of them looked about my age. One of them, a woman with short blonde hair and a sharp pointed nose, was louder than the rest.

"I don't know. I've said for years that those people do nothing but bring down the reputation of this town. Really, hunting ghosts and chasing demons. Nobody believes that crap in this day and age. At least, nobody with any sense."

"I don't know, Christine," a tall woman with red hair said. "Lots of folks watch their movies and all those ghost hunting shows on TV."

The loud woman's identity had come to me an instant before her friend identified her. *Crissy Hines! Picardy's Queen Bitch.* She I had not missed at all.

"Those people are just plain white trash. Always have been."

Crissy tossed this comment into the discussion as the six women settled into a booth across the room. A couple of them looked my way. I gripped the edge of the table and lowered my head over my laptop, turning it slightly in the hope that my hair would obscure my profile. The women turned back to their conversation seemingly satisfied that I was unknown to them and not worth their precious time. I tried to block out their conversation. Thankfully, it turned to other local gossip.

As I worked, the bell over the door sounded again. I expected to hear the person order, but instead it sounded like the steps were coming my direction. *Keep your head down and don't look.* As the person approached, I could see out of the corner of my eye that it was the man from the drug store. I fought to keep myself from looking until he had passed. Instead, he stopped beside my table. Before I could look up, something dropped onto the table beside my computer. I gazed at the package of M&Ms and smiled despite my determination not to react.

"Fancy a sugar high?" asked a familiar voice.

CHAPTER THREE

NOVEMBER 21, 1995

"I want the blue ones."

"No way, Debbie. Blue's brand new, and I bought the pack."

"Whose birthday was this month?"

"Two weeks ago."

"Birthday month rules."

"That is not a thing."

"Is absolutely a thing. I'm older, I make the rules."

Trey rolled his eyes. "I'll be thirteen next month. Enjoy being ahead while you can."

"Normally I would let you have it because we should be kind to short people, but it's my birthday month," I said as Trey scowled.

My growth spurt had hit two years ago. I now stood a full foot over Trey. My momma assured me that the boys would catch up with me one day. For now, I was enjoying holding my height over my friend, pun intended.

Trey counted out several blue M&Ms, keeping two for himself. I smiled and decided not to contest the two outliers. The folks at Mars had held an election in good democratic fashion to decide what their new

M&M color would be. Blue, which happened to be Trey's favorite color, won. So, 1995 became the year of blue.

"Hey, Losers," Kevin Quan called from the bleachers. "You interested in coming over to play *Doom* later?"

Trey looked at me with questioning eyes. I shook my head. "I have to go home. I promised Dinah I would help her pick some wild holly for our Christmas decorations. Daddy loves it."

"And when Dinah calls ..."

I shook my head, pretending to be annoyed. It pleased me that Trey got jealous of Dinah sometimes. She was the one person who could pull me away from his company. And I liked for him to be reminded how much he enjoyed mine.

"I'll be there, Kev!" Trey called. "Hebert's ditching us for bushes."

"Bush? The president?"

"No, holly, man."

"Oh, Holly Pratt. I'd ditch both of you freaks for her."

"No man, the plant."

"You kids having communication issues again?" a familiar voice asked.

I turned to see two blue eyes just like my own surveying us with mischievous glee. The long black hair matched mine as well, though it was permed in curly ringlets instead of hanging straight like mine. Momma freaked when Delilah came home like that two weeks ago. She insisted that beauty was fleeting, and it was a woman who feared the Lord whose beauty was unfading. Delilah shouted back that Darcy's Mom's offer to give her a free perm was fleeting too so she took it while she could.

"Hey, Delilah," Trey said.

It annoyed me that my friends treated Delilah like she was so much older. There were only thirteen months between us, and I ran circles around her as far as real maturity was concerned. Well, inner maturity. I was reminded that she was ahead of me in some respects by the noticeable bulge of her ample breasts barely covered beneath the Lucille-banned low-cut top she wore. As she often did, Delilah slipped out of the house with one shirt on and discarded it at her locker as soon as she arrived in favor of skimpier attire beneath. I was keenly aware that Trey was noticing her physical assets as well.

"You ready for break, Delilah?" he asked.

"Hell, yeah. This place blows."

"Randy meeting you this afternoon?" Randy Sparks reigned as Delilah's latest love interest. I gave it about six weeks. Randy was just a sophomore. Delilah had her sights set on a junior or senior in time for prom.

"No, he's got basketball practice."

"I'm going with Dinah to gather some holly if you want to come with us," I inserted.

"Gather holly? You girls think you're little women on the prairie?"

"I think those are two different books," Trey said.

"You think so, T?" Delilah knew she intimidated Trey sometimes and relished it.

"Pretty sure."

"Well, what would I do without you to keep me straight?"

Trey didn't have time to reply. A brown station wagon rolled around the corner and pulled up to the Picardy High School common area. My oldest sister waved to us from the driver's seat.

"Dude, your sister is so hot, Hebert," Kevin had wandered over to render his vote for most appealing Hebert.

"Shut up, Creeper," I said. "You better invite me over to play *Doom* later this week."

"Maybe I will if you set me up with your sister."

"Gross," Delilah said as we left them and headed for the car.

I expected to take shotgun but when I opened the door I was greeted by a ball of boundless energy.

"Debbie, I got to ride shotgun! Dinah said I'm the best coprolite ever."

Dinah laughed at my confused expression. "Co-pilot, Dor. You're the best co-pilot."

"Yeah, I'm that."

I looked imploringly at Dinah, who shrugged as if to say, "What do you do?"

Delilah snickered as I took my seat in the back next to her.

"Got demoted, huh, Hot Shot?"

I stuck my tongue out at her.

Dinah eased out of the parking lot and headed toward our place.

"Your arthritis affecting your foot, Grandma?" Delilah asked.

"School zone," Dinah said, giving Delilah a sharp look through the rearview mirror. "You have somewhere to be?"

"I'm excited to get to be a pioneer girl today. De-Bore-A invited me." She glanced at me to see if her dig hit home.

"I'm so happy we'll be blessed with your uplifting commentary the whole time." Dinah read all the time, and her vocabulary reflected her habits.

"She's Debbie now," Dorcas piped up, her little black ponytail flying as she shook her head back and forth.

"How long do you think that's going to last?" Delilah asked me.

"As long as I want it to."

"Momma's going to shut it down. She already said you couldn't do it. Ain't that right, Diner?" Our Grandma on Daddy's side always pronounced her name "Diner." Delilah liked to use it on occasion to poke fun at Dinah.

Dinah gave her an eye roll through the rearview.

"Debbie's getting old enough to decide what she wants to be called. Leave her alone."

We pulled into our front yard, and Dinah reached out the driver's side window to retrieve the mail. I noticed her cheeks flush a little as she studied the stack of letters.

"Dinah, are Momma and Daddy coming home tonight?"

"I don't know, Dor. I hope so."

We never knew when Momma and Daddy were coming home when they left on one of their "trips," code for a paranormal investigation. They used to bundle us off with them and expose us to some truly terrifying phenomena. As their cases got wilder and Dinah got older, they started leaving us in her care. "Older" was relative. Dinah was all of twelve years old the first time they left us in her care with a cross, instructions for using prayers for laying a spiritual "hedge of protection" around the house, and Daddy's Saturday Night Special in his bedroom for unwanted visitors of less supernatural persuasions.

Dinah served more as a mother figure for us than Momma did for the next six years. She had completed high school in the spring of 1995 with excellent grades after being homeschooled through most of elementary school and junior high. While most of her classmates moved on to university and jobs, Dinah stayed in Picardy throughout the summer and early fall doing the same thing she had done for years, serving as our surrogate mother while Denny and Lucille Hebert chased the devil and his minions.

Lucille often emphasized how important their work was. "Satanists and Secular Humanists have been working to take control of our culture for many years now. We are fighting a war to make people free of the devil's control. Free to live for Jesus." She always praised us for being "good little soldiers" in that conflict.

Unlike Dinah, Delilah and I had attended public school most of the way through due to both financial reasons and the increasing demands of "the ministry." I got the benefit of a more mainstream educational experience, but the cost was my sister usually tucking us in at night instead of Momma. Even on the nights when they were there, my parents often had "clients" downstairs. Dinah usually read our bedtime story punctuated by the sounds of someone losing their mind and raging at all things holy in the "office" below.

We entered the living room, and Dinah directed us to get some buckets from the storage room to hold our festive bounty. I grabbed a bucket and headed back to the living room while Delilah and Dorcas wrestled over a particular green bucket they both preferred. As I reentered the room, I noticed Dinah reading a letter. It looked formal from the style and typeset. Her hands were trembling. When she looked at me, her face and eyes were practically glowing. She quickly folded the letter up and stuffed it in the pocket of her jeans.

"What's that, Di?"

"Nothing, Debbie. Just junk mail."

My oldest sister never lied to me. The few times she did, I could see right through her. This was one of those times.

"Come on, Girls!" she called, shooting me a quick reassuring smile and heading out the door.

A soft breeze stirred the holly bushes as we gathered some choice branches festooned with berries. It had been a crazy weather year. Flood waters had caused extensive damage throughout Louisiana and Mississippi in May and June. Hurricane season was mercifully mild with the last storm of the season, Hurricane Tanya, weakening to a tropical storm.

We collected our buckets full of leaves and berries as dusk began to fall. Dinah and Dorcas arranged them in the back of our station wagon while Delilah and I walked along the little stream that ran west along our property line. Delilah took her shoes off and waded in the water despite the temperatures starting to move down into the fifties. I walked beside her on the bank.

"So ... Trey."

"What about Trey?"

"I think he likes you."

I glanced at her. "Well, of course, he likes me. He wouldn't put up with you all the time if he didn't like me."

She snorted and eyed me with a condescending look that was almost pitying.

"You really need to grow up, De-Bore-A. Lighten up and get a little more interesting. There are more things you could do with Trey than watch TV and play video games. Or Dungeons and Dragons."

"You promised, Delilah!" I said, realizing that my face was turning white.

"I'm surprised Momma couldn't see the little devils perched on your shoulder after you cast all those spells in Trey's basement."

"You played too!"

"I was just an innocent victim of peer pressure."

I reached over and pushed her. Not hard, but enough to make her lose her balance. Delilah cried out and tumbled backwards. The water rose to only two feet by the bank, but it was enough to wet Delilah's pants and the bottom of her shirt when she landed on her butt.

"Bitch!" she cried.

My mouth dropped. "Momma would freak if she heard you say that."

Delilah rose to her feet and charged toward me. Before I realized what she was doing, Delilah grabbed the front of my shirt and pulled me forward. I tried to hold on, but she was strong in her anger. I fell face forward into the water and just managed to stop myself from burying my face in the muddy bank with my outstretched arms. Cool water saturated my jeans, the front of my shirt, and my bra. I jumped to my feet angry as a drenched cat.

"Hey! I'm soaked all the way through to my bra!"

"No problem. It's not holding much up anyway."

I screamed and grabbed her by the arms. We went down in a jumble of arms and legs, rolling on the edge of the bank. I felt a sharp pain as she went for my long hair. Mud squished into every crack and cranny of our clothing as we struggled.

"What are you doing?!"

We both froze and looked at the bank, where Dinah was standing in barely contained fury. Dorcas stood beside her, laughing and pointing.

"Debbie and Delilah are dirty." The kid had a point.

"What are you? Three?" Dinah's hands rested on her hips, and her narrowed eyes conveyed absolute disgust. Sometimes my sister scared me more than Momma.

"Debbie's being a bitch about Trey!" Dinah also looked shocked at Delilah's newly acquired favorite word.

"Delilah, do you know how Momma would flip out if she heard you say that?"

"Do you think I care? Debbie's just jealous because she wants Trey all to herself."

"Trey is everybody's friend, and he's a person," Dinah said. "No one owns him."

Trey had become a family favorite with everyone except Lucille, who still viewed him as a potential bad influence. He always ended up hanging out with all of us when he came to see me. Delilah spent more time with us than she would like to admit to her "cool" friends.

"She's telling stuff she has no business telling," I shouted.

"Like what?" *Oops, didn't think that one through.*

"Nothing," I muttered.

"Where am I supposed to put the two of you?" Dinah lamented. "You're filthy and you reek!"

"I think the beach towels are in the back seat still from our trip to Lake Pontchartrain," I said in a subdued tone, finally having the decency to realize I should be embarrassed for the trouble we'd caused my sister.

"Good," she said. "Now, apologize to each other."

I looked at Delilah, who was still glaring at me.

"I'm sorry," I mumbled.

"Screw you!" Delilah yelled. "And you too, Grandma Di! You don't do anything but act like a glorified babysitter! Are you ever going to get a life of your own?"

Dinah's reaction surprised me. My usually stoic oldest sister's eyes widened. Her lower lip started to tremble. I could see tears forming in the corners of her eyes. She furiously wiped them away. When she spoke, her tone was even but filled with rage.

"You ... have ... no ... idea! No clue what I have given up for this family. You ungrateful little ...!"

I could tell that Delilah regretted what she said the moment she said it. But Delilah land was a world of no apologies.

"You always take her side," Delilah screamed, pointing at me and starting to cry. "She's your favorite. She's Trey's favorite. No one gives a damn about me!"

Delilah's language was becoming a new revelation every minute. We were all too upset by this point to be shocked. Dorcas was hearing new words for sure. Her eyes were two gigantic brown saucers. Delilah gave us one final defiant look and turned to run through the brush and up the hill.

"Delilah!" Dinah yelled.

No response followed, just the sound of Delilah crashing through the brush in the gathering darkness. Dinah threw up her hands and looked back at us. Dorcas and I both instinctively shrank under her gaze. A line from one of the movies Trey and I watched, *Lethal Weapon,* flashed through my mind. I imagined Dinah saying in Danny Glover's voice, "I'm too old for this shit!" More profanity would probably not be a welcome addition to the night, and I doubted Dinah would appreciate the joke given the circumstances.

As I looked at my beautiful sister, I suddenly realized how tired she appeared. The more I thought about what she had said, the more I realized that she looked tired a lot. Never complaining, often smiling, but always with that slight hint of weariness beyond her years. She wasn't too old for this shit, apologies to Momma; she was too young for it. I saw her in a new light that night. It was the first time I seriously considered how much Dinah must be wishing there were someone to tuck her in every night. *We're so selfish. I'm so selfish.* I wanted to grab her and hug her, but my filthy condition made that an unwelcome gesture. My vision clouded as I watched her trying to decide what to do.

"What's wrong, Debbie?" she asked, pausing in her deliberations to notice my tears.

"Nothing. I ... I'm sorry. Thank you, Dinah. For everything."

She understood. Dinah smiled despite her frustration and reached for me. She took my hand and squeezed it hard.

"I would hug you if you weren't so filthy," she said, but with a little twinkle in her eyes.

We pushed forward by the light of my Daddy's flashlight, which Dinah had retrieved from the glove compartment of the station wagon. The three of us walked single file with Dorcas safely sandwiched between us. It was dark, but we had the advantage of knowing the area well. We'd played along the banks of the river and roamed these woods since we were old enough to walk. Delilah was never one for subtlety. Her trail was hard to follow in the dark, but not impossible due to the way she had ripped through the brush with utter abandon.

We finally encountered her about a mile from where she had left us. She was coming toward us and fast. Dinah and I exchanged a confused glance. Delilah reigned as the ultimate fickle pickle, but this swift change of mood was remarkable even for her.

"Turn that light out and follow me," she hissed, barely speaking above a whisper. As usual, no apologies. We were just supposed to forget her explosion and get on with it.

"I don't think so," Dinah said. "Stop acting like a child, and let's get Dorcas home. She's starving."

"I've got a candy bar in my pocket. She can have that." Delilah reached into her pocket only to remember that her candy bar was now a soggy mass of swamp chocolate.

Before Dinah could insist again, Delilah grabbed my arm, "Debbie, you've got to come see this. There are real freaking Satanists out here."

"What? Where? How do you know?" I said in total confusion.

"I saw them, Di. They're in that little grove on the other side of the hill. Just like all the rumors going around school. Freakin' Geraldo was right. They are real. I thought Momma and Daddy were just full of ..."

"I think we've introduced enough new words tonight!" Dinah said with a sharp nod toward Dorcas.

"I don't want to see Sanists, Dinah," Dorcas whimpered.

"Satanists, goofball."

"Delilah! Give it a rest."

"Come on, Debbie," Delilah said, tugging at my arm. "I need somebody else to see so I know I'm not crazy."

"Dinah?" I asked.

"If it will speed our trip home, let's get it out of the way."

We continued up the hill, taking care to avoid stray twigs. Twice we had to remind Dorcas to keep quiet. When we reached the summit of the hill, I looked down and saw the ghostly light of a bonfire flickering through the trees. We moved slowly down the hill, skirting along the edge of the tree line. When we reached the edge of the grove, Dinah motioned for us to get low.

Sounds were coming from the grove. Drums were beating. Against the backdrop of the bonfire, I could see bodies moving, dancing along the edge of the fire. A woman dressed in white stood near the edge of the circle. I stifled a gasp as I saw a diamond-back snake slither around her neck. The fire flickered and reflected her ebony skin. She was chanting. It sounded like the call and response that we witnessed in black churches we had visited with our parents. I remembered liking the way the crowd had responded to the pastoral call, almost as if they were having a conversation.

"Voodoo," Dinah whispered, "or Hoodoo. I'm not sure which."

Dinah was apprenticed in homespun demonology as part of her homeschool education. The rest of us had received some of it as well, but she was the one with the deepest knowledge of the occult world our parents inhabited.

Everything my parents taught me told me that I should be terrified at this moment. But I was fascinated. Entranced even. The people were energetic and somewhat frenzied in their movements, but no more so than the congregation at our local Pentecostal Church, the folks Daddy called "holy rollers." I even remember hearing about some churches in the Tennessee mountains who worshiped with snakes too.

"We come to this place, where black bodies were broken and bleeding for so many years, to honor the dead and raise up the living," the priestess intoned.

The crowd responded with a chant in words I couldn't understand. While the dancers wore ceremonial robes, the crowd around the dancers were dressed in regular garb. They clapped and chanted along with the dancers. There were about fifty people total. I didn't recognize the dancers or priestess, but I did recognize many faces in the crowd. Most were from Picardy. Predominantly African-American, but there were several white people there too.

I was taking it all in when I heard an intake of breath beside me and the inevitable windup to a massive sneeze. Dinah and I both tried to cover

Dorcas' mouth, but it was too late. She sneezed louder than I would have thought any little girl could. Most people in the crowd were oblivious, surrounded as they were by the pounding of the drums and the tramping of feet, but a couple of people on the edge turned and looked our way.

Delilah panicked. She grabbed Dorcas' hand and started running. There was no hiding now. Dinah and I glanced at each other, rose, and ran. As the bonfire receded behind us, I looked back to see if anyone was chasing us. I saw only one lone man who had emerged from the grove to watch us. I couldn't tell for sure because of the distance, but I thought that he was smiling.

Delilah made it up the hill in record time. We heard Dorcas protesting and demanding that she slow down. Once we reached them, Dinah threw her arms around us like a mother hen and ushered us in the direction of the station wagon. We sat twenty minutes later in our car panting and looking around to be sure no one had followed us. Dinah cranked the car and gunned the engine. Delilah actually looked impressed as we bounced onto the dirt road on what felt like two wheels.

As we approached the house, Dorcas squealed, "Momma and Daddy are home!"

Daddy's black Ford F150 stood parked on the side of the house. Momma was waiting on the front porch with her arms folded and her long hair blowing in the wind. She only left it free like that at home. Usually, it was bound up in a ponytail or bun.

"Where have y'all been? I was about to send your Daddy looking for you."

Before anyone could speak, Dorcas said, "We were watching Sanists, Momma!"

Lucille Hebert turned pale. "What? Dinah, what's she talking about?"

Delilah glared at Dorcas. Dinah tried to explain.

"We were gathering some holly for Daddy for Christmas decorations. There were some people in the grove near Moreau's Ridge. It looked like some kind of Voodoo or Hoodoo ceremony."

Momma subconsciously gripped the little cross necklace that hung around her neck.

"You should know better than to get near such things. Why would you even go over that far?"

Delilah stiffened and waited for the inevitable shoe to drop. Dinah chose not to look her way.

"I guess we just lost track of time and where we were. Sorry, Momma."

"Really, Dinah? I expect you to be the responsible one."

"Yes, Momma."

My heart broke as I saw the slightest slump in my oldest sister's proud shoulders. She didn't deserve the criticism, but she bore it well. I shot Delilah a nasty look that she returned in equal measure.

Momma sighed and shook her head. "Well, thank the Good Lord that you're all okay. Your Daddy and I will investigate that circle you saw tomorrow. Do not go back there until we've said it's clear. Understood?"

"They didn't want to hurt us," I said.

"What?" Momma asked.

"They didn't want to hurt us. No one even followed us when we left. And they weren't really doing anything scary. They were just dancing and singing like we do in church."

Even by the pale light of the porch bulb I could tell the color had drained even more from Momma's face.

"You do not understand these things yet, Child. That dancing has summoned dark powers since the days when those people's ancestors were living in Africa. Those people are dangerous. You stay away from them. Do you understand?"

I nodded slowly. There were a million more questions in my mind about the whole experience, but it was obvious that further inquiry was not welcome. We tramped into the house at Momma's direction. Daddy was hanging his long brown duster up on the peg by the stairs when we entered. He wore it more for effect than warmth when he wore it at all. The duster was a gift from his sister that he mainly kept around in case she asked about it. He usually just wore a plaid shirt and jeans. Combined with his peppery black beard, he cut a figure easily recognizable around town and in the deliverance ministry circles he frequented.

"There are my little angels," he laughed, scooping Dorcas into one arm and throwing the other around my shoulders. We chatted with him about what we saw in the grove while Momma quietly went to unpack. Daddy listened intently and oohed and aahed at all the right moments. He seemed concerned, but he never worried over things quite as much as Momma did.

"You just stay away from there for a while like your momma said. No worries. We'll take care of it. Now head up to bed."

As the rest of us filed upstairs to brush our teeth and get ready for bed, I noticed that Dinah lingered behind.

"Daddy, can I talk to both of you? In private?"

"Sure, Angel. Let me get your momma, and we can go into the office."

I brushed my teeth and hurried back to the top of the stairs. The office was beside the kitchen, and you could just make out the top of the doorway from where I was stationed. I saw my parents walk in and close the door. A few minutes later, Dinah appeared at the foot of the stairs. She could see me if she looked, but she was too focused on the office door to glance up the stairs. Dinah took a deep breath and reached into her pants pocket. She removed the letter I had seen her reading that afternoon before our adventure at the grove. Dinah squared her shoulders and seemed to prepare herself. She walked to the office door and entered, softly closing it behind her.

I returned to the room I shared with Delilah. She was already snoring. I jumped into my own twin bed and covered my head with my fluffy pink comforter. I wasn't sure how long it was until I heard Dinah coming up the stairs. She paused at the door to Dorcas' room across the hall. After a few moments, I heard the door to our room open slightly. I could feel her looking at us, but I pretended to be asleep. After another minute or two, she eased the door closed but not completely shut. I waited until I heard her move on to her own room. About five minutes later, I heard sounds I couldn't quite identify coming from Dinah's room. I slipped out of my bed and tiptoed to our door.

I stepped into the hallway. Dinah's bedroom door was shut tight. As I stepped closer to it, I could make out the sound of deep throaty sobs coming from Dinah's room. I'd never heard Dinah cry like that. My heart ached, and I wanted to go in and comfort her. At the same time, there seemed something forbidden about this moment, as if I were trespassing in a time and place where I had no business. I stood rooted to the spot, listening to my sister weep until she drifted off to sleep. I returned to my own bed, wondering what happened downstairs. *What was in that letter?* The questions lingered, but sleep came before any answers arrived.

CHAPTER FOUR

An Excerpt from

DEVIL'S CIRCLE (1996)

by Lucille B. Hebert

Deborah saw the flickering flames first.

"Dinah, what's that?"

Dinah peered down the hill toward the familiar grove.

"I don't know, Deborah." She gripped the silver cross in her pocket. "Maybe we should go get Mamma and Daddy."

"I want to go see," Delilah insisted. "We'll be careful, Dinah."

Dinah nodded. "Okay, but stay close to me and do exactly as I say."

The girls snuck down the hill and skirted the edge of the woods until they were near enough to see inside the grove. Deborah stifled a scream as the horrific scene unfolded before them.

About two hundred people were gathered in the grove. All African-Americans, they danced around a large bonfire roaring in the center of the circle. A naked young woman stood at the center, her ebony skin reflecting the flickering fire as it played across her exposed breasts and buttocks. A diamond-headed snake slithered around her neck as she voiced incantations.

"We call upon the power of darkness! We call on Papa Legba, Prince of demons and Father of chaos!"

"We call on Papa Legba, Prince of demons and Father of chaos!" the crowd responded.

The dancers around the circle began to shake uncontrollably, their eyes glowing with a feral yellow light.

"They're possessed," Dinah whispered.

"How do you know?" Deborah asked.

"The yellow tint in their eyes. And, well, look how they're acting."

"Can you cast 'em out, Dinah? Like Daddy?"

"Maybe for one or two of them, Dor. But there are a lot of them. We need to go back and get Daddy."

Delilah gasped and tried not to scream. The other girls looked to where she was pointing.

A tall dark figure in a black cloak had produced a human skull and approached the high priestess. He raised the skull to her lips and tipped it. She paused in her rhythmic movements and drank deeply. Red fluid dripped from the corners of her mouth.

"Is that ... blood?" Deborah asked.

"I think so," Dinah said, pulling Dorcas closer. "We need to get out of here."

They started to ease backwards. Just as Dinah thought they were home free, a shout went up from the circle. The music stopped. The abrupt interruption caught everyone's attention. Dinah looked back to see the assembled worshippers all looking their way. Her eyes met those of the young high priestess. Their gazes locked for a moment. The high priestess licked her lips, slathering up a few stray driblets of blood.

"Run!" Dinah commanded.

The Hebert girls threw caution to the wind and broke into a run. Dinah scooped Dorcas into her arms as she started to fall behind. A roar of frustration erupted from the crowd.

"They're coming!" Deborah screamed.

A flurry of torches bounced in the air behind them, held aloft by a band of enforcers who had detached themselves from the circle.

"Are they going to drink our blood, Dinah?" Dorcas wailed.

"No, Sweetie," Dinah panted, wishing she were as sure as she sounded.

The girls reached the top of the hill, but they could hear the pounding feet of the cultists behind them.

"I can't go any faster, Dinah," Delilah said.

It was over. There was no way they could outrun the mob behind them. Just as Dinah was considering where to make a stand, the clouds cleared, and she saw a figure ahead by the light of the full moon. The shadow of a Stetson and billowing duster filled her with new hope.

"Daddy!" She called, a cry taken up by the other girls too.

"Get up here and stand behind me, Girls!" Denny shouted. They reached his side and gathered in a cluster behind him. Denny produced his silver cross in one hand.

"Will that stop them, Daddy?" Deborah asked.

"If that won't, this will," he said dryly. Denny eased his duster back to reveal the sawed-off shotgun he was gripping in his right hand.

Denny raised his crucifix and shouted, "Stop in the name of God the Father, Jesus Christ the Son, and the Holy Spirit!"

The band of cultists halted halfway up the hill. Their menacing eyes shot hostile venom, but their bodies wilted before the power of the cross. Denny took a step forward, and they moved back. A few of the younger men among them looked at each other. Denny noticed their glances and prepared himself. As two particularly aggressive young men started forward, Denny raised the shotgun and fired a blast at their feet. The girls shrieked, and Dinah covered Dorcas' head.

The cultists got the message. They slowly retreated down the hill. Denny watched them until they had returned to the edge of the grove.

Denny pulled his pistol out of its holster and handed it to Delilah. "You girls get back to the truck. I'll be right there."

Delilah took the weapon.

"Be careful, Daddy," Dinah said as they hurried away.

Denny watched them go. He turned to scan the hill and the grove. The cultists were standing at the edge of the grove, peering up at him.

They were silent, but he could feel the menace even from a distance. Denny tipped his hat in their direction.

"You think you've won."

Denny jumped and raised his shotgun. The Voodoo priestess stood a few feet away. She had thrown on a white robe. It matched the white paint forming striped lines on her face. Her gaze ran up and down Denny, measuring him inside and out from head to toe.

"We are visitors here from New Orleans, but there are other circles here in Picardy. Powerful circles. Circles that will aid us in defeating you."

"You're welcome to try," Denny said. His eyes never left the priestess, watching for any sudden movements.

"You will pay a price," the priestess intoned. Her eyes flamed with a demonic light. "The ones you love are not safe."

Denny's anger got the better of him. "You threaten my family, and you will feel the wrath of God Almighty like you never dreamed you could."

The priestess grinned, exposing a mouth filled with yellowing teeth. "We'll see. You can't protect them forever."

An eerie mist enveloped them. Suddenly the priestess was gone. Denny looked around, but there was no trace of her. She was spirited away by the dark forces driving her. Denny tried to dispel the foreboding her words had raised, but he couldn't shake a sense of dread. He had always believed there were active Satanist groups operating around Picardy. Now the Voodoo priestess confirmed his fears. As Denny began the trek to meet his girls, there was no way he could have predicted the devastating conflict ahead or the tragic price it would exact.

CHAPTER FIVE

I SKIPPED A BEAT BEFORE LOOKING UP.

"I don't suppose it would do any good to say I don't know what you're talking about, Sir."

"None at all," Trey said. "You could fool the world, but you can't hide from me. I'd know you anywhere." He looked good. Trey had never been breathtakingly handsome, but he had nice green eyes and a full mop of curly brown hair which still held its body and color. His cheeks were a little fuller and his forehead higher since I had last seen him.

"You've aged well," I said. Probably not the best icebreaker after twenty years.

"Ditto," he said, sliding into the booth across from me.

"So, you stalk women in the pharmacy now?"

He laughed. I smiled at the sound of it. That was one thing that hadn't changed a bit.

"I knew it was you when you greeted Sam. You've changed your accent and made it airy and aristocratic now, but I'd know that voice anywhere." Trey feigned a *Steel Magnolias* Southern lilt as he did a poor imitation of my accent and moved his arms in sweeping motions for dramatic effect.

I laughed so loud that Crissy and the other women looked over at us and frowned. It felt good to laugh like that. I'm not sure how long it had been. I found myself wondering if Pedro and I had laughed that way and, if we had, when we had stopped.

"You're still a nut."

"Always your nut, Sweetheart," he said, doing a perfect Humphrey Bogart impersonation.

A shadow fell over my heart for just a second, and he saw it on my face as well.

"Hey ... I didn't mean ..."

"It's okay. You were just having fun, and I shouldn't be so sensitive."

"De ... I don't even know what to call you. You know I never meant to hurt you. That's the last thing I ever wanted to do."

"I know." I pushed the memories away. "It was a long time ago. I'm very happy to see you."

He nodded. "Me too. It's been too long."

"Diana."

"Huh?"

"Diana is my name now. Diana Chambers."

He paused for a moment, and then a huge grin broke out on his face.

"Of course, it is. Because making your way in the world today takes everything you've got."

My face flushed. He leaned in a little closer with a mischievous smile on his face.

"And, you know. Taking a break from all your worries sure would help a lot."

"Stop," I insisted, trying to sound angry. My smile betrayed me.

Trey broke out into full song. "Wouldn't you like to get away?"

Crissy looked up in irritation. Several members of her posse whispered to one another.

"When are you going to grow up, Trey Laurence?" Crissy called, "Leave that poor woman alone."

"You're just jealous because you never got a serenade, Crissy," Trey said. My mouth fell open. Trey would never have been so bold back in the day. I had to remind myself that we weren't kids anymore.

"As if I would ever give you the time of day," Crissy rose from her seat and her crew followed suit. As they left, she looked back and said, "I guess once a dork always a dork."

"If bitch rules apply to dorks too, then that's probably true," Trey said.

She shook her head in exasperation, letting the door slam behind her.

Trey shifted his internal playlist. "That's just the way she is, some things will never change."

I'd made the mistake of taking a sip of coffee while they sparred. It dribbled down my chin and threatened to soak my shirt as another wave of laughter shook my body. Trey watched as I caught it with a napkin.

"So why are you here now? Your dad's beat accusations like this before."

I told him about my experiences in Nashville and how they compelled me to come down. *Why am I trusting him so much? I haven't seen him in years. Can I be sure he's still the same person?* Despite my questions, I rattled off the whole story, skipping only the part about seeing Dinah in the distance last night. I wasn't ready to say that part out loud. Not yet. Still wasn't sure I believed it.

"Trey, what do you remember about the night that Dinah died?"

He shifted uncomfortably in his seat. "Not much. We'd been fighting some, so I was glad we got to see each other the night before. Then the next morning I remember getting your call. You were so out of it that I couldn't even understand what you were saying. I didn't know what happened until I got there and saw ..." Trey's voice trailed off.

"It's okay," I prompted.

"Saw them carrying her body out on the stretcher. There was a white cloth over her. But you could still see the stains ..." He got quiet again.

I nodded.

"I have to say I'm more than a little worried about you. Breaking into your apartment and going through the trouble to secure that recording doesn't sound like the actions of someone who's playing around."

"You really think someone is out to hurt us like Dorcas said?"

"Picardy is a small town, and people have long memories. Some people consider your parents local heroes who hit the big time. Just as many, maybe a few more, see them as hucksters preying on the gullible. The most antagonistic see the Heberts as two abusive parents who killed their daughter and tried to frame half the town for it."

"Please don't whitewash it for poor little me."

"I'm serious, Diana. Have you never considered the possibility that your parents might actually have done something, either accidentally or on purpose, that led to her death?"

I paused. The truth hovered somewhere in the middle. The thought crossed my mind on occasion, but I knew I had never seriously considered it. There was never any reason to doubt that my parents loved Dinah. They loved us all in their own imperfect, sometimes twisted, way. But they also believed in a higher calling. Jesus himself told his disciples they could not follow him unless they hated father and mother, son and daughter, in comparison to their love for him. *Is it possible that a situation could arise where my parents thought they had to put the "ministry" ahead of Dinah?* I thought of the *Akedah* recorded in Genesis 22 where God commanded Abraham to sacrifice his son, Isaac, to prove his love. God spared Isaac, and Abraham, by providing an alternative sacrifice at the last minute. *Could my parents have endured a similar test with a darker outcome?*

"I honestly haven't, Trey. Maybe not as seriously as I should."

"There are a lot of people very upset about Mia."

"Mia? Mia Jordan?"

"Yeah."

"What can you tell me about her?"

"Not much. She was in my class her senior year."

"Are you still teaching at the consolidated high school?"

He looked surprised. "You've been keeping up better than I expected."

"I do my research," I said, trying to sound mysterious.

"Is that Professor-speak for social media stalking?"

"Social media stalking and updates from Dorcas," I said.

"Little Dor," Trey said with a fond smile. "She was always rooting for us. Yes, I've taught at the consolidated school for about five years. It's a thirty-minute drive one way, but I got to be one of the lucky few still employed after Picardy High shut down."

"I'm not surprised you're a natural teacher. You were solely responsible for getting me through freshman composition and Shakespeare."

"Mia Jordan did well in school. It looked like she would be valedictorian until she got wrapped up with a rough crowd her junior year. Drugs, drinking, two pregnancies; she really went into a tailspin. She'd go to rehab on occasion and get straight again only for things to fall apart within months. The kids were adopted, one by a family in Slidell and the other by some folks in Baton Rouge. Working with your parents was her idea. Her mom and dad, Janice and Ed, resisted the idea for a while, but they were desperate."

"Her parents weren't part of my parents' church?"

"No. They attended Grace Bible Church." The second time I'd heard that name in as many days. It was their pastor who attended the exorcism.

"Do you know Eric Dixon, the pastor of their church?"

"Only a little. We've bumped into each other a few times at athletic events and community meetings. As you know, I've never been much of a churchgoer. Erin dragged me to church a few times."

I swallowed and searched for the best way to tackle the awkward elephant in the conversation. Deciding the direct approach was best, I said, "I heard about the divorce from Dor. I'm sorry."

Trey waved a dismissive hand, "Thanks, but I'm fine. We had a good fifteen years. Then things kind of fell apart."

He reached into his back pocket and produced his phone. "We have two kids, a son and daughter. This is Brandy, and the youngest is Chip. Brandy's thirteen, and Chip is eight."

The boy had cute freckles and red hair, clearly taking after his mother. Brandy wore long brown hair, and her face carried a strong resemblance to my friend's.

"They're cute. It's weird to think of you as a dad. Do they live with you?"

"We have joint custody. They're here on weekends usually. What about you? Ever get married? Any kids?"

"No," I said. "I had a few relationships in college and grad school, but I was too focused on getting through to devote much time to them. A couple after college came close to marriage, but they never quite worked out. I lived with a colleague for five years. We just broke things off a few months ago."

"I'm surprised," Trey said. "I thought someone would have snatched you up by now."

"Just me." I glanced at my phone. "I need to go. Dad is probably home by now."

"Give him my best," Trey said.

"I will. It was really good to see you, Trey."

"Ditto, Dr. Chambers."

I exited *Coffee Corner* and walked down the block to the Picardy Public Records Office. I didn't know the clerk, and she didn't know me. But that didn't stop her from whistling when I said I wanted to see a death certificate for Dinah Lucille Hebert. She pushed her pointed spectacles up the bridge of her nose and ran her hands through her curly gray hair.

"That's a live one." Then, realizing the irony of what she said, the clerk covered her mouth and giggled. "Sorry. Dinah L. Hebert? I can already tell you I don't have it."

"Don't have it?"

"Yes, Ma'am."

"You mean it's stored somewhere else?"

"I mean it's not there at all. Anywhere, as far as we can tell. People would come by on occasion working on books or trying to do a feature story, and we would always come up short."

"Are you saying one was never filed? Isn't the coroner required to file one by law?"

"He was, and he did. We have a record that Ron Thibodeaux filed the death certificate, but when we looked for it five years later, it was nowhere to be found. Hasn't turned up since."

Ron Thibodeaux attended Trinity Assembly of God with my parents. Another of my dad's faithful friends.

"Could you give me a number to reach Mr. Thibodeaux?"

"Honey, you're not talking to him without a séance. Ron's been dead about ten years now."

I cursed inwardly, but outwardly thanked the clerk and wished her a good day. Back on the street, I wandered in a fog back to my car. My sister's death remained the best-known case of death under suspicious circumstances in our town, probably the whole parish. How could her death certificate just not be there? So many questions swirled through my mind. *Had there been an autopsy? What were her exact wounds?* At this point, my best option was to ask my parents. But how would they react?

Dad was sitting on the front porch in his favorite rocking chair when I drove up. Dorcas emerged from the house with a couple of lemonades as I joined them. Dorcas offered to get me lemonade and then sat down in the other rocking chair when I declined.

"How are you, Daddy?"

He smiled at me and said, "Better now that I'm back home and with my girls."

Dorcas smiled and winked at me. I wanted to share their joy, but just the three of us sitting there reminded me too much of our two missing sisters. I heard Lucille moving something in the house.

"She's not coming to join us?"

"You know your momma," Denny said. "She never slows down."

After a few minutes, I said, "Daddy, I need to ask you something. It might be hard for you, but I need to know."

He and Dorcas both looked apprehensive.

"Sure, Angel. What?"

"Daddy, how did Dinah die?"

Dorcas shot me a look that would make all the hosts of heaven and hell tremble. I ignored her and stayed focused on my dad. His eyes were haunted with images of that tragic night. When he finally spoke, his voice was shaking.

"The Satanists cursed her. She came home that night bleeding and saying that someone was trying to kill her. We laid her on the kitchen table because she was hurting too much to be moved. I called the doctor and then tried to lift the curse every way I knew how." He stopped and wiped his eyes.

"She was bleeding? So, she was stabbed?"

Dorcas shook her head at me.

"No, she was bleeding from the inside. Something was wrong in her intestines and stomach."

"I saw her for a few minutes, Daddy. It was a lot of blood."

"I ... I ... sorry, Deborah, I can't!" He covered his face with his hands. My dad was always careful to honor my wishes and use my pseudonym. The fact he forgot in that moment revealed how distracted he was.

"It's okay," I said, wrapping my arms around him. "I'm sorry. I just have to know."

"Why?" Dorcas asked. Her frustration had been replaced by curiosity and anticipation. I experienced a momentary flash of memory, Dorcas bounding out of the station wagon like a little ball of energy. She was charged with that same intensity as she leaned forward in her chair.

"Well, I've always wondered."

"And now, after all these years, you decided to go down to the public records office and check out her death certificate?"

I completely failed to hide my surprise.

Dorcas laughed. "You may have a Ph.D., but you still can't outsmart your little sister. Annette called me after you left. She's in my Sunday School class."

I guessed Annette was my conversational clerk.

"Okay. Yes, I wanted to check the death certificate. But it wasn't there. I guess you know that given your connections."

"Yes," Dorcas said. "It's been gone for a while. I'm more interested in why you're looking."

"Like I said …"

"You've seen her."

Daddy looked very uncomfortable with the direction the conversation had taken. "I told you that was just your imagination, Dor."

"No. Diana saw her too. Didn't you?"

I was trying hard to keep up. "Yes. I guess there's no use lying to you, Dor."

"It's what I wanted to tell you about. But I sure didn't want to say it over the phone. Momma answered the phone the day before the Jordan exorcism. Someone was saying they were Dinah and wanted to know why Momma let her die."

"Just a sick prankster."

"Yes, but why, Daddy? And what if it isn't?"

"And what do you think it is, Dor?" I asked.

"I think it's a spiritual attack. We know that demons manifest as the dead all the time. That's where 'ghosts' come from."

That, at least, was the view my family took of the matter. I knew plenty of people steeped in supernatural beliefs who disagreed, but I decided to let it go for the sake of argument.

"You don't think we're really seeing Dinah?" I asked the question with relief. Part of me was afraid that Dorcas would latch onto whatever was happening and interpret it as some sort of angelic visitation from our sister.

"No," Dorcas said. "I don't remember Dinah as well as all the rest of you. But I don't think she would ever try to make us feel guilty or harm us in any way. She just let things pass."

"She did," I agreed. "Sometimes even when she had good reasons to stand up for herself."

My dad raised his eyebrow. We had never talked about the night I watched Dinah go into the office with them or how I heard her heartbreaking sobs afterward.

"Were there more contacts with this ... whatever?" I asked before my dad could inquire further.

"Yes, the phone calls came daily and then twice a day just before you arrived. You may notice that Momma doesn't answer the phone now. I only do it because I want to keep up with how often they or it calls."

"And you saw her too?" I leaned forward.

"Yes," she said, her usually large eyes getting bigger. "It was the night we got back from the Jordan exorcism. Daddy was exhausted and broken up about Mia's death. I helped him inside and then took our equipment to the barn. While I was in there, I heard ..."

She paused and shivered despite the warmth of the day. Her complexion lightened a little. *This encounter must have been insane to spook Dorcas.*

"I was against the far wall rifling through the toolbox when I heard someone crying. Lightly at first and then with greater intensity. I looked at the doorway, and there she was. She was covered in blood from head to toe. She didn't speak. Just stretched her arms toward me."

"What did you do?"

"I had our duffle bag with the crosses, holy water, and weapons beside me. Hadn't finished unloading it yet. I bent down to get the cross, and when I straightened up, she was gone."

I described my own vision of Dinah, similar in some ways to Dorcas' but with a personal touch.

"Someone is attacking us," Dorcas said. "They're using some kind of curse or Voodoo enchantment to summon a spirit that manifests as Dinah."

I knew I needed to tread carefully. "Dor, how close did this vision of Dinah get to you?"

"As far as from the back of the barn to the doorway. Three or four yards, give or take."

"And there was no illumination at all? No light?"

"Just moonlight. And it wasn't that full that night. In fact, it was pretty much a dim crescent."

"Is it possible," I said, "that this could be someone impersonating Dinah? A real flesh and blood person with a vendetta against our family?"

"What person would have a vendetta against our family?"

I couldn't believe what I was hearing, especially from Miss Drama Queen Picardy. "Take your pick! We literally turned this town upside down trying to hold someone responsible for Dinah's death."

"That was a long time ago. You haven't been here in too long. So many people who hated us back then have apologized and moved on with their lives."

"Some of them didn't have the luxury of moving on," I said. "Their lives were in shambles because of us."

"Okay. It's very possible that some person could be orchestrating all this. But how? Did someone sneak up and murder Mia Jordan with some of us in the room and the rest of us right outside? She was never left alone. Is someone running around playing *Carrie* by dumping blood on herself and pretending to be Dinah? And, most important of all, how did this person know the exact words that Dinah said before she died? The only ones in the house then were family. Even I wasn't in the room with her."

For all my pretensions about being the logical one, I was forced to admit that Dorcas presented a compelling rational case. *How could this person or persons know what Delilah said that night?* Dorcas had confirmed Lucille didn't use those words in *Devil's Circle*. I doubted there ever would be a film adaptation. My parents knew Delilah and I would freak. And I honestly don't think they could bear to see it reenacted themselves.

"What are you thinking?" Dorcas asked. It was only then I realized how long my silence had lasted.

"That I can't believe you've actually seen *Carrie*."

She laughed and broke the gathering tension. "I read, Dr. Skeptizmo."

"What if it is her?"

We had almost forgotten my dad was there. There was an expression in his eyes that troubled me. Guilt swam in them, mingled with a despair I had never seen in him.

"What do you mean, Daddy?" Dorcas asked, shooting me a worried glance.

"What if that demon was right? What if she is suffering right now in the fires of hell because we did something wrong? What if it really is her spirit, somehow warped and twisted, wanting vengeance on us?"

I wrestled with what to say. The ideas he was proposing ran counter to everything he and Lucille had taught for as long as I could remember. As Dorcas said, they believed that ghosts and all "false gods," deities embraced by other religions, were manifestations of demons. It was a belief circulating among the earliest Christians and a central motivation for outlawing other religious movements once Christianity acquired public influence in the fourth century Roman Empire.

"Daddy," I began. "You've taught all your life that salvation is by grace. Don't you believe that Dinah was covered by God's grace?" Dorcas nodded, grateful that I was discussing the matter on my dad's terms.

"Yes, I think. I hope so. She was so good, so beautiful, so ..." Dorcas leaned over and hugged him as tears formed again in his eyes.

I tried a different tactic. "You've also always taught that there's no such thing as ghosts. Don't you still believe that?"

"I don't know, Diana. Maybe we were wrong. Maybe we're finally getting what we deserve for putting our ministry ahead of our family."

Dorcas hugged him tighter and teared up with him. As she gripped him, she looked beyond his neck into my eyes. The message was clear. This was why she called me home this time. It wasn't because the case was so different. My dad was different. Dinah's death served as his Achilles' heel. It raised all his worst doubts and regrets. He couldn't deal with all this right now because he was questioning the very foundations of who he had been for most of his life. I always thought that this day would come, and I also thought that I would relish it when it did. There was so much about Denny and Lucille Hebert's ministry that concerned me. Especially the potential harm to people subjected to their exorcisms. But now I found myself wishing that my dad had his old confidence to help us sort through the tangled webs threatening to ensnare us.

He excused himself and went inside a few minutes later. Dorcas and I sat in silence for a long while.

"Please help us, Diana," she finally said.

"Of course, I'm going to help you. If I can. You're my sister. Despite everything, they are my parents."

"Then why don't you acknowledge that when you talk to Momma?"

No sensitive issue was being left behind today. I cleared my throat.

"You don't remember how things were before. Before Dinah ..."

She nodded, sparing me the burden of saying it yet again today.

"Lucille was around a lot more after Dinah died because she had to be. There was no way that Delilah was responsible enough to take care of us like Dinah did. She tried to look to me, but I wasn't having it."

"Why not?" Dorcas asked, truly curious.

"Because I saw what it did to Dinah. She practically became our mom at the age of twelve."

"I didn't know," Dorcas said. "I mean, if I think back to my early memories, I see that it was mostly her taking care of us. But I never realized."

"You were just a kid," I said with a sad smile. "How could you understand? There was a letter. I found it in her desk drawer when we were putting her things away the week after she died. She got it the day we all saw that circle Lucille embellished in *Devil's Circle.*"

I could see Dorcas struggling to resist her natural impulse to defend Lucille. She suppressed it in favor of hearing the rest of my story.

"What did the letter say?" Dorcas asked.

There had been far too much crying already today, but I couldn't help myself. I bowed my head slightly to try to hide the tears that were trickling down my cheeks.

"I can only paraphrase it, but I can remember a lot of it. I still have it in my nightstand. 'Dear Ms. Hebert, We are pleased to offer you a full scholarship covering tuition expenses for the 1996-97 academic year. Your application materials, test scores, and essay impressed our selection committee. We believe you are well qualified to study with us and hope you will accept our offer."

"Wow!" Doras said. "Southeastern or LSU?"

"Princeton," I said, the word catching in my throat.

Dorcas's mouth fell open. "Dinah got a full ride to Princeton!"

"Yes," I said, my tears starting to dry up. This part of the story still angered me all these years later. "They weren't going to let her go, Dor."

"Did she tell you that?"

"She didn't have to. I heard her crying that night. And saw the change in her over the next few weeks before she died. But I didn't know what it was about until I found the letter that day."

"Could they really have stopped her from going?"

"No, she was eighteen by then. She was only seventeen when she graduated high school. But she would have still needed money for room and board, books, and incidentals."

"She had to give up her dream just before she died."

"That's just it. I don't think she did, Dor. There were little clues looking back that she was working on a plan to go anyway." I stopped, hesitating to go on.

Dorcas looked at me for a moment and then her eyes widened in that trademark Dorcas expression of astonishment.

"You think it may have had something to do with her death."

"I'm not sure."

"But you don't think ... Momma and Daddy would never ..."

"I don't know. What I do know is that only three weeks after my sister died screaming in a pool of blood on our kitchen table Lucille called me into the office and told me that they were leaving to hunt down the people who killed Dinah. She told me it was time for me to take care of the other girls while they were doing the 'Lord's work.'"

"And you said?"

"That taking care of your children should be the Lord's work. That Dinah might not be gone if they had been here more."

"What did she say?"

"She slapped me."

I could still feel the sting on my cheeks. That slap was meant to break me. Instead, it ignited a feral spark within me. Delilah and I weren't so different after all; we were both rebels in our own way. Lucille wanted to say she was sorry. Even as a thirteen-year-old girl I could sense it. But she didn't. Couldn't. Instead, she insisted, "I'm your momma and I know best. You will look after these girls while we do what needs to be done."

Dorcas was crying too now. "I'm so sorry. You were grieving yourself and to be treated like that. I'm so sorry. What did you do?"

All my tears were used up. I smiled a grim smile with no hint of humor behind it. "I told her we just buried my real momma. And it was true. Dinah loved us and cared for us in a way she never did."

Silence settled once again.

Dorcas broke it a few minutes later. "That's why you call her Lucille."

"That day was the last time I ever referred to her in any way as my 'mother.' Dinah deserved that title more than she ever did."

Dorcas still disagreed with my choice, but I could tell she understood now. Lucille realized that day that she couldn't just farm us out the way she had with Dinah. My dad influenced her change too. He was devastated by Dinah's death. Lucille complained often in later years that he had "eased up" on the "other girls."

"I guess it was just a coincidence that you ended up going to Princeton?"

I smiled at my little sister. *Note to never underestimate Dor again.*

"I busted my tail for the next five years. When the time came, I had ample scholarships and money saved for incidental costs. I didn't ask for forgiveness or permission. Just announced I was leaving one week and was gone the next, as you probably remember. When I sat down in my first Princeton class on day one, I liked to think there were two of us there. I don't know if we go on after we die or just cease to be. But I would like to think, if we do continue somehow, that Dinah got to see me do it for us both."

"That's beautiful, Diana," Dorcas said softly. "I think she is with us still, and I also think she's very proud of the woman you've become."

"Thank you for saying that, Dorcas," I said sincerely.

I hoped with all my heart that it was true. Most days I considered myself a neurotic mess just trying to get through the day. Beneath the polished exterior lived a woman haunted by the past and too often afraid of the future. I struggled with a commitment phobia that my in-house psychiatrist, Pedro, said was typical for people who experienced tragedy at a young age. Ripping that veil of security away at such a young age produced lasting trauma. The need to overcome that moved me to action.

"We need to solve this, Dor. Not just for Dad. For us all. I think my friend Pedro was right. Our future lies in grappling with our past. Putting it to rest once and for all."

"Are you prepared to follow the trail to the end? Even if it leads to supernatural things whose existence you might not want to acknowledge?"

I hesitated only a second. Then I nodded my head in determination. "Wherever it leads."

CHAPTER SIX

A PLEASANT SATURDAY AFTERNOON MATINEE the exorcism video was not. Mia Jordan's shirt was covered with spit and vomit. Her bright pink hair was knotted and twisted in several places where she had tried to rip it out with her own hands. She panted and huffed like a dog after a long run.

"The power of Christ compels you!" Denny shouted. Mia screamed in agony as my dad sprinkled holy water on her.

She thrashed so hard she almost turned her chair over. Dorcas leaped forward, along with a lanky gray-haired man, Mia's father, to steady the chair. When Dorcas leaned in to put her weight on the chair, Mia brought her head forward and slammed it into Dorcas'. Dorcas yelled and released her side of the chair. She staggered back, but quickly put her hand up to signal my dad to keep going even as she continued holding her wounded forehead. Even with her father holding on, Mia tipped the chair backwards and crashed to the floor. All the camera showed was Mia's legs sticking up over the upturned chair, but the audio picked up her maniacal laughter.

I tried to watch the scene with detachment as I did with other videos like it. It was hard with the familiar faces of my dad and sister constantly moving in and out of the frame.

"You will fail, old man!" The voice was unearthly and demonic, not at all female.

I noticed a man with large glasses standing slightly to the side regarding the whole scene with horror. He looked slightly older than me.

"Eric Dixon?" I asked.

Dorcas nodded. "Here's where it talks about Dinah."

I was not entirely comfortable referring to Mia as an "it," but Dorcas saw everything in terms of the entity she believed was possessing Mia's body.

"You think if you save this woman God will forgive you for killing your daughter?"

"Come out of her, you evil bastard!"

My dad didn't curse during an exorcism, a ritual he saw as a holy act akin to worship. Mia, the demon, or whatever had gotten under his skin.

The conversation turned in the direction I'd heard in my apartment. They were right. The recording planted in my apartment came from that very session. Daddy continued chanting prayers and urging the demon to depart "in the name of Christ." He began trying out common demonic names from scripture and extrabiblical sources. The homespun theology of deliverance ministry maintained that you had power over an entity if you knew its name.

"What's your name, demon? Mammon, lust, anger ..."

"Dinah. My name is Dinah!"

My dad stopped for a moment and stared. The wicked grin that broke out on Mia's face was truly terrifying. The kind of grin you only saw at insane asylums.

"Slowed you down, didn't I, old man?"

Dad gave an enraged bellow and continued.

"Daddy," Dorcas said. "Let's take a break. Please." She looked completely frazzled in the video.

"You go, Angel. I can't stop now."

He continued for several hours. We skipped over a lot of it, running the video up to the final moments. Just before the end, they finally convinced Daddy to take a break. He staggered out of the room with

Dorcas supporting him. Mia's dad remained. Mia was slumped back in the chair, her hands still firmly tied to it. Her mortal shell looked spent. Hands and head hung limp and listless, her pink hair mixing with the vomit that stained her shirt. I could only guess her mental state.

As we sat watching, Mr. Jordan covered his face and broke down. I felt a tug of sympathy for him. Then I noticed something. It was slight and quick, but definitely there.

"What was that?"

"What?" Dorcas asked.

"Roll it back. About ten seconds."

Dorcas complied. As Mr. Jordan lowered his head, there was the slightest of jumps on the video. It reminded me of those quick edits novice YouTubers and TikTokers used when they wanted to splice sections together or omit some mistake.

"There! Did you see that?"

Dorcas nodded and rolled it back again. "I need to ask Tio, but it sure looks like there's a time jump there."

Tio's video showed the final moments of the exorcism as Dad, sweat pouring down his body, prayed the Lord's Prayer accompanied by Dorcas and the parents. Even Pastor Dixon joined them. The demon roared in anger and agony. And then something strange happened.

I saw something new on Mia's face. Clarity. She looked lucid. And she looked terrified.

"Daddy!" she screamed. This time the voice issuing from her was her own. It was squeaky and high pitched.

"It's working! Keep going!" Dad shouted.

"Baby, we're going to help you!" Mia's mother said.

"S ... S ... something's wrong! Something's gone wrong! Help me!" Those last words were horrified shrieks, all coming from Mia. With that last scream, her head slumped forward.

It took a moment for the exorcists to realize that Mia was silent. One by one they stopped praying and watched her in expectation.

"Thank God," Dad said.

"Is she okay, Denny?"

"I think so. It looks like the entity has departed."

Pastor Dixon stepped forward. "Mia? Mia, are you okay?" He gently reached down to touch her hand. I saw him hesitate and then turn her wrist.

"Pastor? Is she okay?"

The pastor slowly backed away from Mia and turned toward them. Even through the camera lens and with his large frames we could see the stricken look on his face. The Jordans read all they needed to know in that expression. Mrs. Jordan let out a bloodcurdling scream. The scene descended into chaos as everyone rushed over to untie Mia and administer CPR. Pastor Dixon could be heard over the audio calling 911. Tio recovered his own presence of mind at that point and turned off the video.

I sat in silence for a minute, shaken by what I'd seen. Even though she'd been there and knew what was coming, Dorcas was struggling. She turned away just before Mia's last seconds and didn't look back until the feed was done.

"Dear God," I finally said.

"That had nothing to do with God," Dorcas said.

Something on which we could agree.

"So, there you have it. You've seen it for yourself. Any thoughts?"

I pursed my lips and sat back on our plain brown sofa for a moment. Something kept bothering me. *What was it?*

"Toward the end there. She seems to get more lucid. Those parts were edited out of the audio version I heard."

"When the demon's grip started to weaken. That's not unusual."

"Yeah, but she seemed to get more terrified also."

"Well, she's conscious of what's happening to her for the first time," Dorcas said. "Or she'd been screaming inside the whole time, and we couldn't see it until the demon was weak enough for her own personality to manifest."

Dorcas produced a lot of answers. I just wasn't sure they were the right ones. Something about the way Mia screamed, "Something's gone wrong!" was strange. Sure, something was horribly wrong. The way she said it was like the panicked cry of a swimmer who realizes they have a cramp and they're starting to sink beneath the surface. *Why would that be a news flash to her dad or to anyone else in the room?*

"Do you think Pastor Dixon will be around tomorrow?"

Dorcas looked surprised. "It's Thanksgiving. I'm guessing he'll be with his family."

"Could we go by and check?"

"I don't guess it'll do any harm."

The next morning, we ate our breakfast in a hurry. Lucille had prepared another full feast of eggs, bacon, and toast. I reminded myself to go running soon. These heavy breakfasts landed great on the tongue but with less desirable results on the hips. I wasn't accustomed to such fare anymore, usually settling for yogurt or wheat toast and tea in the mornings. We told Lucille that we needed to run some errands in town. I could tell she was wondering what manner of errands we expected to run on Thanksgiving Day.

Grace Bible Church stood on the corner of Fifth and Main. The congregants had purchased the old Baptist church, a traditional looking structure with a long white steeple stretching toward the heavens. We rounded the corner from the parking lot and started climbing the steps when I noticed a familiar face waiting for us.

"Two girls up to no good," Trey teased.

"Trey," I said, surprised to see him.

"Thanks for coming," Dorcas said. "I thought you might be able to put in a good word for us with the pastor."

"Well, I hardly know him, Dor. But ... sure."

He held the door open for us. It had been a while since I'd experienced this form of southern chivalry. Trey winked at me and moved ahead, giving me a chance to give my sister a questioning glance with a raised eyebrow. She mouthed, "What? I thought he would be helpful." I caught a hint of the devilish little smile she always had when she'd been up to something as a child.

"So, Trey," I said. "Thanksgiving plans?"

"Yeah. I'm heading to Covington this afternoon. That's where my ex and my kids live. Mom's driving up with me."

"Thanks for taking the time for us," Dorcas said.

"No problem. Always glad to help my little partner in crime."

Trey enabled all of us, but he took particular delight in spoiling Dorcas. As the youngest of four, she was rotten enough already. Trey acceded to her every demand from rides on his back to smuggled candy from his pocket. Come to think of it, he probably was a bad influence. One we had needed.

We hoped that the open door indicated that someone was there. That hope was not met with disappointment. Eric Dixon was picking up discarded bulletins from the previous night's Thanksgiving service in the worship area. The old sanctuary of the Baptist church had been transformed into a more contemporary venue with a drum kit and only a small podium where the pulpit once loomed. Screens adorned the wall. Hillsong had supplanted that old time religion in Picardy.

"Pastor Dixon? You may not remember me. I'm Trey Laurence. I teach English at the new high school."

The pastor looked confused for a moment, but then recognition dawned.

"Yes, I remember you now. Been a tough year for those War Eagles."

"It has. At least we excel at sucking."

Dixon grinned and then noticed Dorcas.

"Well, Ms. Hebert. What brings you here?"

"Dr. Chambers wanted to meet you. She's investigating Mia's death."

"Are you with the police, Dr. Chambers?" Dixon asked as he reached forward to shake my hand.

I still felt weird shaking hands after Covid and wondered if it would ever feel normal again.

"No. I teach Religious Studies and History at Vanderbilt University in Nashville."

"We know where Vanderbilt is, even down here."

"Sorry."

"You study these sorts of things, Dr. Chambers?"

"Yes." I noticed an air of skepticism in the way he was looking at me. I thought at first maybe he doubted my credentials, but that wasn't it.

"How many sisters do you have again, Dorcas?"

"Guilty as charged," I said. "My birth name was Deborah Hebert."

He nodded, "I've heard of you. Both personally and professionally. In fact, I've read your book. Very fascinating, especially the chapters on Latin American exorcisms."

"Thank you. I have a few questions for you if you don't mind."

"Such as?" Dixon sat down on a pew and invited the rest of us to do the same.

"Did you notice anything unusual during the exorcism?"

Dixon threw back his head and laughed. "Sorry. I know it's not funny. The whole thing was unusual to me. I'm not accustomed to such spectacles and frankly think it's all a bunch of baloney. Highly suggestible people manipulated into thinking that one explosive event will cure their struggles rather than daily perseverance and prayer."

"Do you believe in Satan and spiritual warfare?" I asked.

"As a fairly conservative Christian, I believe in a personal devil. I think he's real and active in the world. I think Jesus and the Apostles did perform exorcisms as recorded in the Bible. But I don't buy the possession or oppression nonsense for today and definitely not in reported cases of believing Christians being oppressed. Exorcism may work sometimes as a placebo for people dealing with psychological or even some physiological issues, but most of our struggles are rooted in ourselves rather than our demons. I think a lot of what people like the Heberts treat are clinical issues that should be more properly handled by a trained professional."

"My parents are trained in their own way and, as for professionalism, they've been doing this since before you were born," Dorcas said. I winced. *Really not the time to get into this.*

"I know what I saw was rare and that most of the drama we see in the movies is fake," Dixon said, appealing to me. He considered Dorcas a lost cause. "But that frightens me even more. What about the more typical cases of deliverance? Young people with addictions told that an ad hoc exorcism will set them free from alcoholism? Folks with sex addictions told to just resist the demon of lust? Women trapped in abusive relationships told to pray for the spirit of rebellion to go away so they can submit to their husbands?"

"Those are extreme examples," Dorcas said.

"Let's talk about the actual exorcism event," I suggested. I really didn't want to get between Dorcas and Dixon, especially since he was making a lot more sense to me than she was.

"Were you in the room the whole time?"

"Most of it. I stepped out several times to get some air. I was there for the end."

"Pastor, do you remember when Mia screamed about something going wrong?

"I think so."

"What was she talking about?"

"I assumed the exorcism. Her life, maybe? In my experience, people say all kinds of things when the end is approaching. Sometimes they make sense, and sometimes they're just delirious. Mia went down the path she did because of terrible trauma. That's all I can say. Can't be more specific because of confidentiality."

I was intrigued but knew there was no point in trying to convince him to break pastoral confidentiality. We talked a little longer, but Dixon shared nothing I hadn't already seen in the video.

"Thank you for your time, Pastor Dixon."

"Yes, nice to meet you. And good to see the two of you again."

We were almost out of the sanctuary when he called after us, "I knew your sister."

Dorcas and I paused.

"She was ... very special. To a lot of people. I'm sorry."

"Thank you," Dorcas said. "God bless."

"And you too, Dorcas. Tell Denny I'm praying for him."

When we reached our cars, I asked, "Do either of you know what he meant by the trauma that pushed Mia down her self-destructive path?"

"I heard some students saying she was raped." Trey said. It was so unusual to see him that serious; it scared me a little. Or at least he hadn't been very serious before. I had to remind myself that I had no idea what was normal for Trey anymore.

"By whom?"

"Lots of different suspects. From another student to one of the football coaches. She hung out in his office quite a bit along with a couple of other girls. There were rumors about grooming. Never anything solid, and she never came forward to accuse anyone."

Dorcas shuddered. "That's awful. I can't imagine what that does to someone long term."

"I can't imagine the short term is a picnic either," Trey said grimly. "Anyway, I should be going if we're going to make dinner tonight."

"Bye, Trey!" we said in unison, winking at each other. The four of us made a game of standing on the porch and bidding goodbye to Trey in unison to our delight and his slight embarrassment. The game always drew a frown from Lucille. All the more reason to do it.

He bowed and grinned from ear to ear. "Music to my ears. Goodbye, Ladies. Happy Thanksgiving!"

We watched him drive away.

"You can thank me later," Dorcas said.

"Thank you or kill you? The jury's still out."

We reached our house by 3:00. I noticed the number of news vans was growing. They'd taken up residence on the old McMartin place. I guessed old man McMartin's son was charging them for the use of his land and probably power hookups too. Our troubles produced a great windfall for him. That land had been fallow for years since his dad's death.

"Supper will be on the table about 5:30," Lucille said when we entered the house. "Let's try to forget everything and have a happy Thanksgiving tonight. Your daddy really needs it."

For once, we were all on the same page.

"Dorcas," Lucille said. "Could you look in my hope chest and get Grandma's tablecloth?"

"Yes, Ma'am."

Dorcas was headed into their room when Dad called her from the living room. She looked back and said, "Diana, can you go get the tablecloth for me?"

"Sure," I said.

It was only after I entered their room and flipped open the lid to Lucille's cedar hope chest that I realized what I'd gotten myself into. I hadn't anticipated how much I would feel like a stranger in my own childhood home. I felt like a home invader.

Lucille's dad, our grandpa, had fashioned the cedar chest for her just after she married Daddy. She kept all her accumulated treasures tucked securely there. Those keepsakes included the elaborate crocheted tablecloth Lucille's mother had left us. It only adorned the table on very special occasions.

I found the tablecloth fast. It lay close to the top. Lucille had probably not delved into the chest since the last time she used the tablecloth. Curiosity overcame caution. I started to move items around, telling myself I was taking a trip down memory lane. I was really looking for any clues the chest might yield to what happened that night with Dinah. I found a stack with artifacts from our childhood. Baby books, school papers, and awkward school photos greeted me. At the bottom of the stack, I felt a larger book. I realized there were two or three of them as I continued to feel my way to the floor of the hope chest.

Let's see what you're reading, Lucille. I expected some tired popular treatise on demonology. I lifted the first book from the top of the stack and turned it over for inspection. The cover was familiar. So was the large photo of a younger me clad in a long gray blazer and leaning against a column at the Nashville Parthenon. *Yikes! What was up with that hair?* I looked like Farrah Fawcett fresh from a wind tunnel. I loved that picture otherwise, both because of the neo-classical architecture and the enormous statue of Athena Parthenos inside. The title, *Exorcisms as Religious Phenomena in Popular Cultures,* and the author's name, Diana

F. Chambers, were emblazoned on the front in silver letters. An original hardback copy, the book showed all the signs of being both carefully read and lovingly preserved. Dog-eared pages indicated one good read if not two while its careful placement in the hope chest appeared intentional. I removed the other three books, all of them mine. The newest one was autographed. I remembered how Dad asked me to sign one during one of our meetups in Jackson last year, saying it was a gift for "a friend." Lucille acted like she could care less about what I do most of the time. Yet she had been keeping up.

As I removed the last book, I felt something plastic beneath. I pulled the object out and stifled a laugh. It was a CD. *Hostile Haircut* proclaimed the album title in large font on the cover. Below was a picture of a very muscular man with abs that only a computer could produce. His torso was bare, and his long black hair was held back by my sister, clothed in just enough to make the album acceptable for display at WalMart. Her hair was still black back then, cut short to her shoulders and artificially frizzy. She held a large pair of sheers while giving the viewer/potential listener a seductive wink. Her stage name, just *Delilah*, was printed in large red letters with jagged edges reminiscent of a wrought iron fence. As I plunged deeper into the chest, I discovered that Delilah's entire discography was there. Even the cover where she was locking lips with her female backup singer.

I placed the items on the floor, lost in thought. If I didn't know better, I would almost say there was a sense of pride in the way these relics of our lives were stored. Of course, they were housed at the bottom of the hope chest rather than on a shelf in the living room. Still, the fact that she had them must mean something.

"Diana? You got the tablecloth?"

"Yeah! Coming, Dor."

I arranged the items as I had found them and hurried back to the kitchen.

No one could accuse us of being a normal family or produce enough evidence to convict us of being one, for sure. Still, Thanksgiving dinner that night was nice. We talked and laughed a lot. Even Lucille relaxed. She told stories about Delilah getting gum stuck in her hair, Dorcas nearly setting the house on fire making "macroni and cheese," and my dangerous early attempts at driving. As we scraped the plates into the trash afterwards, I thought about how this was the most normal time I had spent with my family in years. Normal was relative; you could still see the lights of the vultures up the road at the McMartin place. Still, it wasn't bad. Everyone got coffee and headed into the living room.

I hung back for a moment, struck by a sudden nostalgic impulse. I pulled out my phone and searched contacts.

"Hey," I said as the call went to voicemail. "It's me. I just wanted to wish you a happy Thanksgiving and tell you ... I ... we all miss you. Call me when you can. Love you."

I settled onto the living room couch beside Dorcas as Daddy started to tell the story of the day Dinah decided to adopt a baby goat when she was five. He was just getting warmed up when we heard it: sobs that sounded like they were coming from the porch.

"No, no, no," Dorcas said, shaking her head as if she could dispel the noises with pure force of will.

Lucille's knuckles turned white as she gripped the edge of her armchair. Daddy slowly rose from his chair.

"Why did you let me die?"

Daddy covered the distance from the hearth to the door in three quick strides and threw it open. The porch was clear. No one was there. He stepped outside.

"Daddy, wait!" Dorcas leapt to her feet with me on her heels.

"Be careful, Girls!" Lucille called.

Daddy had already made it halfway across our yard by the time we got outside.

"Daddy!" All three of us froze where we were. Slowly, we all turned toward the hill where I had seen Dinah my first night back. She stood there again. Same clothes: purple top and white skirt.

"Baby! Dinah!" Daddy called.

"Daddy! No!" Dorcas said. "It's not Dinah."

"Daddy!" the apparition called. She raised her arms in that same gesture I had seen before. She was well groomed and free of blemish from head to toe.

"It sounds just like her," Daddy said in awe.

"I miss you, Daddy."

"I miss you too, Angel."

"Don't talk to it!" Dorcas begged. I was speechless.

"Why did you let me die, Daddy?"

A sob escaped Daddy's throat. "I would have given anything to save you. I would give anything to have you back."

I slowly eased off the porch and made my way to the edge of the house. *If only I can get a closer look.*

"Daddy! Come with me!"

"Where, Angel?"

"To hell!" As "Dinah" spoke, her voice changed to a guttural demonic tone like the way Mia sounded on the video. Blood began to seep onto her white skirt and move up and down her body.

"Come on!" I shouted, "Let's get up there before she disappears again!" I broke into a run, throwing aside all subterfuge.

"Ouch!" I was conscious of Dorcas falling to the ground behind me.

"What happened?" I called back.

"Just tripped over a stump. Keep going!"

I reached the bottom of the hill. She was still there, a showcase of bloody horror.

"Daddy!"

Something about Dorcas' scream made me turn around even though I was closing in on our "ghost."

Daddy was standing in the same spot. His eyes were bulging, and his face was white. He teetered for a second and his hands flew to his chest. Then he collapsed. Dorcas tried to rise and run to him. She stumbled and fell again. She pushed herself up and started hobbling as fast as she could, evidently nursing a wounded ankle. I looked back at the hilltop and saw that Dinah was gone.

I hurried back and helped Dorcas turn my dad over onto his back.

"What's happening?" Lucille called.

She came out on the porch and screamed when she saw my dad lying on the ground. She pushed us aside as she cupped his face in her hands.

"Denny! Denny!" He didn't respond. His breath was coming in quick, shallow gasps.

"Call 911," I told Dorcas. She already had her phone out.

I looked up at McMartin's vulture camp. They would be here the second the call went through dispatch.

"What's wrong with him, Deborah?" Lucille said.

"I don't know. It could be a heart attack or stroke. Maybe just a panic attack."

New lights began to come on up the road. *Great!*

Sirens wailed. Two police cars flew down the road and positioned themselves to block off the horde of reporters. I already heard the ambulance in the distance. One of the small benefits of living in a small town was quick emergency service.

As I held my daddy's hand, I looked up the hill. There she was again. Still bloody. Just staring. Fury surged within me. *How dare she step into this night, this perfect night, and hurt us!* I saw the ambulance turning into our driveway and made a quick decision.

"Dor, go with Lucille and Daddy."

"Where are you going?"

"I'm following her to hell and back if that's what it takes to end this," I said, rising to my feet.

"What? No! You can't follow her! Who knows what she is? She'll lead you into a trap or just disappear on you!"

"I have to try," I started toward the barn.

Dorcas tried to follow me, but her wounded ankle left her in no position to give chase. I ran around the house before my resolve could fade and grabbed the flashlight from Dad's toolbox. As I ran up the hill,

I saw the emergency personnel unloading a stretcher from the back of the ambulance. From the look of things, the officers down the road were not going to be able to hold back the media much longer. I made the crest of the hill and stepped into the woods before anyone below could notice me.

Only after I reached the woods did I realize that Dinah was nowhere to be found. All that hurry for nothing. I had just about convinced myself to go back when I heard a voice coming from deep in the woods.

"Debbie, come walk with me."

I whirled. I could make out the fringe of her white skirt in the pale moonlight, far ahead of me. I crashed through the underbrush, fighting my way to a clearing just beyond the line of trees.

"Why did you let them kill me, Debbie? I asked you to stay."

The voice seemed amplified. It was coming from all around. I glanced in every direction, hoping for a glimpse of my tormentor.

"Come play. Stay forever."

I settled on a direction. Running further, I saw the glistening waters of our little stream and the river it flowed into just beyond.

"Dinah!" I called, pausing and panting. "Dinah, why are you doing this?"

My senses flared as I heard a twig crack behind me. Before I could turn my head, something blunt and hard struck me from behind. I tumbled. Everything went black.

Reality slowly seeped in. I realized that I was on my back. Rough hands were doing something at my feet. I tried to focus, but my vision was swimming.

"Dinah, is that you?"

I felt the person scramble from my feet to my head. Those same rough hands pushed under my back and rolled me. As I rolled, I realized too late that there was no ground beside me, only empty air. I awoke fully when I hit the cold waters below.

Immediately, I knew that my attacker had brought me to the river. I looked up at the bank as I kicked to the surface. My flashlight lay on the edge of the bank above, the only sign of my presence. As I kicked, I was horrified to discover that some weight was attached to my right foot. It felt heavy like a cinder block, but I told myself it couldn't be. Every muscle was straining just to keep my head above water. I excelled at swimming and visited the campus pool at least once a week to swim laps. But trying to stay up with a weight that heavy was a totally different experience.

I submerged, bending to grasp the rope tied around my leg. It was knotted tight, purposefully kinked to make it harder to undo. I struggled with it for a minute and then pushed upward to get a breath. I almost didn't break the surface. The speed with which I sank again told me that I probably wouldn't be able to get back up. My furious struggles to get the rope loose were just exhausting my air supply faster. I tried to keep my mouth closed and my nose plugged, but my lungs were screaming. I finally gave way and felt the rush of water into my nose and mouth. Bubbles billowed to the surface as I cried out in frustration and despair. A silent cry that no one could hear.

My vision started to swim.

"Come with me, Debbie. Stay with me."

I heard Dinah's voice in my head. *Maybe it's time. Time to be done with pain, doubt, and regret. I've lived enough for both of us. I'm ready, Di.*

Numbness began to creep throughout my body, and I started to relax. My sister was waiting.

CHAPTER SEVEN

NOVEMBER 23, 1995

"You have any idea how long I've been waiting for you two?" Dinah asked.

Trey and I slipped into the back seat of the station wagon.

"But we come victorious, Fair Maiden," Trey proclaimed, holding aloft a package of cranberries.

"The finest in the land," I proclaimed. "Mainly because they're the last left in the land. Or in the aisles."

"Well done, Noble Knights," Dinah said, starting the engine.

"Noble knights usually receive a grateful kiss from the beautiful ladies after rescuing cranberries."

I shook my head in mock disgust while Dinah said, "The Noble Knight may find he's bitten off more than he can chew."

I laughed at his pained expression, and Dinah joined me when she saw him through the rearview. Trey roamed the halls of Picardy Junior High flirting with every girl he laid eyes on, but never quite closing the deal. Delilah had nicknamed him "Captain Friend Zone" behind his back.

It was Thanksgiving. Trey had feasted at his own home and then wrangled an invitation to the Hebert table as well. Momma discovered that she forgot to buy cranberries on her shopping trip, so we had proceeded into town on our noble quest.

We reached the corner of Barton Street where Dinah pulled up to the sidewalk. I noticed a red Honda Accord parked in front of Johnson's Feed and Seed.

"Sit here. I'll be back in just a minute."

To my surprise, the door opened when she pulled it.

"Why are they open on Thanksgiving?" I asked Trey. He shrugged.

We waited for what seemed like hours. It was probably about twenty minutes. Dinah returned flushed and smiling.

"Sorry. Just needed to make a quick stop." She rolled forward without any further explanation.

We pulled into our yard where Daddy was working on his old brown pickup truck. I loved seeing him out in the yard. It meant he was home, something far too rare these days. He wiped his brow and smiled as we pulled up. I emerged from the car holding up the cranberries for his inspection.

"Good job!" he said. "Even you, Trey."

Daddy liked to tease Trey. He loved his girls, but I think he sometimes wondered what it would be like to have a boy too. Trey served as a nice substitute, though Daddy would say he didn't get any financial break out of the deal because he fed Trey as often as his own family did.

"These women wouldn't have made it back without me, Mr. Denny."

"I'm sure they're grateful," he laughed as I made faces behind Trey's back.

"Daddy! Daddy!"

We all stiffened as Dorcas' primal scream ripped across the yard. Daddy started running with the rest of us following as fast as we could. Dorcas was standing at the top of the hill overlooking our house, pointing and shouting.

"Delilah's drownded! Delilah's drownded!"

Dorcas scared me enough, but even scarier was the sight of Delilah's friend, Tianna Grayson, running up behind her. Tianna looked terrified and completely out of breath. Her curly hair was drenched. Her brown skin was cut and bleeding from the briars that grabbed her as she plunged through the underbrush.

"Mr. Hebert, Delilah fell into the river! I think she's hurt and can't swim!"

Daddy raced past her as Tianna fell into line with the rest of us. We reached the riverbank to see Delilah thrashing furiously against a swift current. The flood waters had swollen the river unnaturally, and it was raging. One look told the story. The big oak tree that fell during the storms this summer had collapsed completely into the river and rested near Delilah. She was trying to reach its branches, but the current kept pushing her away.

"It's my fault," Tianna moaned. "I dared her to walk out there. I didn't know it would collapse."

"Delilah!" Daddy called.

"Daddy!" she screamed, her cry broken by water gushing into her mouth.

"Swim to the tree, Angel!"

"I can't. My leg's hurt."

Daddy dived in the water, pausing only long enough to take off his shoes. He cut swift strokes through the water as we watched breathlessly from the shore. Delilah's head continued to bob up and down.

"Delilah!" Daddy yelled. "Relax. Stop fighting and float."

Delilah continued to thrash and bob.

"Delilah!" Dinah screamed. "Listen to Daddy!"

"Relax, Delilah!" Daddy said again.

Delilah finally listened. She stopped kicking and thrashing. Daddy reached her and threw his arm around her.

"Daddy, please get us out of here."

"Shhh ..." He reached up with his other hand to lightly stroke her hair. "Hold on. We're just going to let the current move us for a minute."

As the water pushed them, Daddy gradually worked his way toward the bank. Finally, they reached a spot where he could touch. He rose from the water with Delilah clutched in his arms, limp with her head buried in his massive chest.

We ran down the bank to join them. Delilah retched and spewed water for several minutes, but she appeared fine. I had never seen her that scared. We sat there for a while as she recovered her bearings.

Daddy grinned at her and reached down to cup her chin. "You are without a doubt my little fighter. Could go ten rounds with an alligator in the dead of night."

Delilah nodded and smiled weakly.

"Just remember, Angel, sometimes you only win the fight by knowing when not to fight. You would have drowned if you kept fighting those waters. Sometimes you've got to just let the current carry you for a while. Understand?"

"I think so, Daddy," Delilah's voice was trembling, and her body was shaking from both chills and shock.

"Come on. Let's get you back to the house."

Dorcas arrived with a towel; Trey took it from her and gently wrapped it around Delilah's shoulders as she stood. He steadied her as she rocked for a moment.

"Thanks, Trey," she said, giving him a slight and uncharacteristically warm smile.

We guided her back to the house where she was able to remove her drenched shorts and shirt in the safety of our bedroom. Tianna perched on her bed, apologizing profusely.

"Could you go downstairs and get my other t-shirt from the laundry?" Delilah said to Tianna.

"Sure." She bounded down the stairs, eager to make amends.

"I don't have another t-shirt in the laundry," Delilah said. "I just wanted to shut her up."

I grinned, glad to see some of Delilah's usual snark creeping back. I watched as she pulled a brush through her damp hair.

"What are you looking at?" Delilah asked as I continued to stare.

"Just thinking I'm sort of glad you didn't die."

"It's a good thing. No one would have any fun around here if it were just left to you, De-Bore-A."

"I take it back."

"Too late," she said. And then, a moment later, "Thanks, Debbie." I thought I caught a brief glimpse of moisture around her eyes, but it was gone before I was sure.

The kitchen was bustling with activity when we entered a few minutes later. Dorcas was darting around the room checking every dish out while Momma tried to navigate around her. Dinah was setting the table, and Daddy was finishing up his work on the truck with Trey's help. Everything was normal and nice that night. We sat around the table for a long time after we finished our food, chattering and laughing. It was rare, and it was good. I caught Dinah's eye at one point and smiled. She smiled back and seemed to be thinking the same thing.

We went to the living room and started playing games. UNO came first and then a round of Pictionary. I was playing on a team with Trey, Daddy, and Dinah with Dorcas serving as team cheerleader. Momma, Delilah, and Tianna were opposing us and winning despite their numerical disadvantage. Dinah commented more than once on how we would be "wiping the floor" with them if "we were playing a proper trivia game." My oldest sister, always prepped for tea with the Queen.

I was drawing a "Thing" for everyone to identify when a hard knock sounded at the door. Daddy opened it to reveal Glenn Roth and his son Tyler. Tyler's eyes were bloodshot, and he swayed unsteadily. Tyler blazed an erratic trail halfway through Picardy High School before he dropped out junior year. He was known as the town druggie, both buying and selling.

"Denny, we need your help." Glenn pleaded. He and his wife, Grace, were faithful members of Trinity Assembly of God and long-time friends of my parents.

"What's wrong, Glenn?"

"He's back off the wagon again, Denny. The devil's got him hard. Please help."

Denny placed his hands on Tyler's shoulders and tried to make eye contact.

"Tyler? Son? Can you hear me?"

Tyler raised his head slightly and nodded.

"Do you want Jesus to set you free from this bondage?"

"More'n anythin', Mr. Denny," he mumbled.

"That jackass can't even remember his name right now. He doesn't know what he wants," Trey whispered to me.

Dinah frowned and shook her head at Trey.

"Let's get him to the office, Glenn. Lucille."

Momma rose and led them away.

"Sorry, kids," Daddy said. "It was fun. Keep going."

They disappeared into the office. We sat for a few moments, most of us looking at the floor. I raised my black marker to finish my drawing on our little whiteboard. A loud crash from the office startled me. A stray line ran from my otherwise perfect drawing. Dorcas whimpered and climbed on the couch to bury her face in Dinah's side. Tyler's screams and Daddy's shouts issued from the office. Something slammed into the wall and then hit the door. It wobbled on its hinges but held fast.

I don't remember anyone suggesting that we end the game. People just started melting away, one by one. Soon Trey and I were the only ones left besides Dinah. We exchanged a look, and he rose.

"It's probably time for me to head back home."

"Sure." Dinah said. "Grab your stuff, and we'll run you back."

As I started to follow Trey to my room, Dinah called me back. Her hand disappeared into her pocket and reappeared holding her keys.

I gasped. "Really? But I've only been out of the yard twice."

She pressed them into my hands. "I'll have shotgun and can take over if you need me to."

"Wow! Thanks, Dinah! You're amazing! Trey! Guess what!" I caught Dinah smiling at me as I bounded up the stairs.

As I came back down the stairs, my mood was broken when I saw Dinah sitting on the couch, cradling Dorcas, with a look of deep sadness etched on her face and the sound of chaos behind the office door echoing in her ears.

CHAPTER EIGHT

An Excerpt from

DEVIL'S CIRCLE (1996)

by Lucille B. Hebert

Denny banged his wrench against the truck in frustration. Mechanical projects usually took his mind off his troubles for a while. Today, it was proving harder than usual.

The Picardy City Council refused to believe that Satanists were meeting in the area. They chalked up the ashes left over from ritual circles and the slaughtered cattle to teenagers trying to "spook folks." The police department did little to help. Only Jimmy Gorman believed Denny, and he was just a lowly deputy. He pushed back hard, but Sheriff Bailey refused to devote any more resources to investigating the ritual circles.

Denny tried to focus on his work. His one comfort was the sound of Lucille and his girls inside preparing the table for Thanksgiving dinner that night. Most of the girls. Delilah was swimming down at the river with her friend Lana.

He had just finished twisting a bolt back into place on the engine block when he heard Lana screaming. Denny saw her standing on the crest of the hill and ran to her.

"Mr. Denny! Delilah, she's drowning in the river!"

Denny ran as fast as he could down to the riverbank with Lana following. He broke through the trees and saw Delilah bobbing up and down in the river.

"Why isn't she swimming?" Denny asked Lana.

"She said something's caught her leg."

"I'm coming, Delilah!" Denny yelled. He threw his shoes aside and plunged into the water, reaching her in seconds.

"Daddy!" she screamed. Delilah threw her arms around Denny's neck. He grabbed ahold of her and started swimming toward the bank. They were jerked back as if Delilah were stuck in some vise below.

"Keep treading water, Angel." Denny dropped below the surface to examine Delilah's kicking feet. There was nothing there. He broke the surface again and took her in his arms a second time.

"Okay, let's go."

Again, their progress was stopped by an invisible force.

Denny released Delilah and backed up to see if he could spot what was causing the resistance. Delilah immediately plunged under the water. Before Denny could react, she shot back up again.

"Daddy! What's happening?"

Denny looked over Delilah's shoulder and saw a black-clad figure on the opposite bank. He wore a long black cloak with an amulet in the shape of a pentagram hanging around his neck. His black hair lay plastered across his head, and a black goatee adorned his chin. His eyes met Denny's, and he grinned. His hand was clasped around the golden chain of his amulet. Still staring at Denny, he held it up as if offering it for Denny's inspection. When he was sure that Denny saw him, the man dropped the amulet. It fell to his waist. Delilah plunged violently below the water.

"Delilah!"

Denny watched as the man raised the amulet again. Delilah broke the surface, sputtering and crying.

"Daddy! It's pulling me down."

She disappeared again. Denny looked back at the man, expecting him to raise the amulet in another display of his power over Delilah.

Instead, he just stood there glaring at Denny. Then a wicked smile stretched the corners of his mouth. Denny realized he had no intention of bringing Delilah back up.

Denny pushed himself down until he reached Delilah. She was starting to lose consciousness. He pulled his cross out of his pocket, praying that divine power could negate whatever dark forces were issuing from the amulet. He wrapped the cross' chain around Delilah's ankle and prayed. Then he wrapped his arms around her and pushed hard for the surface. This time no resistance blocked his efforts.

They broke the surface, both gasping for breath. Denny pulled Delilah with him as he made for the bank. Lana was waiting in near hysteria for them on the shore. Denny pulled Delilah up on the grass and applied CPR. She retched and spit up water, but appeared otherwise okay.

"Lana, run back to the house and get some towels."

Lana obeyed.

Denny heard her steps receding through the woods. He leaned against a tree and looked across the river. The man was watching. He bowed in Denny's direction like a gladiator acknowledging the merits of a worthy adversary. Then he pointed at Delilah. He made a slashing motion across his throat and pretended to wipe tears from his eyes. Denny's hands balled into fists and shook. He wanted to yell across the river, but he also didn't want to scare his daughter. The man waved and turned. Not wanting to leave Delilah alone, Denny was forced to watch helplessly as the man's dark profile melted into the forest.

CHAPTER NINE

I WONDERED IF THERE WAS PEACE on the other side of death. There must be. Precious little of it was present in this world. It had to be reserved for the next one. If there were a next one. I expressed my doubts about that once to Daddy and he'd just said, "There are no atheists in foxholes, Angel." I declined to point out the statistical impossibility of no atheists having served in the armed forces. What he said did give me pause though. What would I really do if confronted with the end? Would I stick to my questions or reflexively return to the prayers I prayed with Lucille and then Dinah before bed each night? People came from miles around when word circulated that the celebrated philosopher and atheist David Hume was dying at Edinburgh in 1776. Some were friends, and many were fans, but a few were curious souls who wanted to know if the noted skeptic would cry out for mercy in his final moments. He did not, choosing instead to meet what lay beyond on the same terms he had lived his life. That didn't stop a few people from circulating false stories of a deathbed recantation as they also did with Charles Darwin a century later.

The surprising thing about the end reaching out for me was all the things I didn't think about. None of the big questions I'd wrestled with haunted my mind. Instead, images played on loop. Trey and I laughing in his living room, Dinah tossing me the keys for the first time, Dorcas dragging me over to see her latest creation, and Pedro kissing me for the first time as the sun set like a fiery ball over the Cumberland River. I saw classes full of students and me relishing every moment with them. I heard Trey doing his Humphrey Bogart impersonation, "You had a nice run, Sweetheart."

"It wasn't all bad, was it?" I asked. Out loud or in my head, I'm not sure. There was peace and quiet as the light slowly faded.

Then the quiet shattered as an explosive force ripped through the water beside me. I snapped back for a second, my senses still fading back and forth between darkness and light. Someone grabbed my leg. *Did Ghost Dinah come back to finish the job?* I sensed a flurry of motion, and then my visitor was gone. For a moment, I started to fade back into the darkness. Suddenly they were back. I felt my leg moving back and forth as if someone was sawing just below it. My body was too numb to tell for sure, but it seemed as if my right leg was suddenly lighter.

Something painful hit my face, and my chest felt like it was going to burst. I realized the painful force was wind and that presence pushing its way into my chest was air. My sudden return to the surface kicked me into panic mode. I started to struggle.

"Hold still. Remember, some battles you can only win if you know when to fight and when to wait."

"Daddy?" I asked.

The words were coming to me in his voice. But I couldn't stop in my delirious state. I had to keep struggling for reasons known only to my subconscious. I pushed, struggled, and bucked against the current. My rescuer released me for a second. Maybe now I could stop fighting and sink back down to that quiet sanctuary. Instead, my world rocked as a firm slap rattled my teeth, shocking me into submission and reason.

"Now, lay back and let me guide you. Let the current carry us."

I sank back into the water and felt an arm encircling my chest. It felt small but muscular. Only the night sky filled my limited vision as we moved toward the bank. I experienced the sensation of being pulled from above and a hardness beneath me. *Land!* I lay on my back, absolutely spent.

Some ancient Asian philosophers said the first thing you encounter in death is yourself. A few Native American elders agreed over the centuries. I decided that must be true when I looked up and saw my own face peering down at me with anxious blue eyes. *Maybe I am dead after all, and I came to ferry myself across to the next life?*

I coughed and sputtered, rolling onto my stomach and letting go of everything that would come forth. It seemed to take hours. Exhausted, I rolled back and looked up at myself again. It was then that I finally noticed the forehead was a little too high and the nose too small to be me. The glint of a stud flashed from one nostril of the nose.

"I'm kind of glad you didn't die."

"Where am I?"

"Hell. I'm the welcoming party. You're going to love it. We torture Hitler at five and then prepare the furnace for Richard Ramirez at seven."

"Delilah! Delilah!"

I was confused again, hearing Dorcas but not seeing her.

Delilah raised her phone and said, "Sorry. I pushed your number and then she started puking again."

"Is she okay?"

"She will be."

"Thank God! Thank God! Thank God!" Dorcas moaned through the phone.

"Feel free to get around to thanking me whenever you get the urge, Dor."

"Shut up and get her home."

"Love you too, Shrimp. How is Dad?"

"He's stable. They still don't know what happened. They're running an EKG."

"Okay. Call me if anything changes. It may take a little while before we make it back to the house."

"Delilah ... thank you."

"See you soon, Kiddo."

"You're really here," I said in wonder as she hung up the phone.

"Lucky me," Delilah said. "Can you stand up?"

"I don't know. I'll try." I slowly rose. Delilah jumped forward to catch me when I started to fall.

"This could take a while," she said.

It took two more hours to be exact. We sank onto the living room couch just as the first rays of dawn started to pierce the sky above our home. Even Delilah was spent by the time we got there. She continued to stay in amazing shape due to the heavy demands touring placed on her. Dancing almost nonstop for three hours every night called for a strong heart and stronger body. I considered myself reasonably fit, but Delilah, whose frame was built like mine, rippled with sheer muscle from head to toe. We might not have made it out of the woods without help if she had a weaker constitution.

"Happy Black Friday. For once it truly lives up to its name," Delilah said.

"No doubt."

"Give me a minute to catch my breath, and then I'll see what there is to eat and drink. And I'll get something to wrap your ankle with to keep it from swelling."

"Well, you're quite the doctor these days."

"We do it for our backup dancers all the time. Can't afford to lose too many on a tour."

I still couldn't believe that Delilah was actually sitting beside me. We last saw each other just before the pandemic when she made a quick stop at Vanderbilt before her concert that night at Nissan Stadium. Pedro and I took her to a quiet café near campus for lunch. A couple of students did a double-take and came back for autographs despite her heavy shades and wig. My students gushed, "How do you know freaking Delilah, Dr. Chambers?"

"So ... blue?"

Delilah rolled her face toward me and grinned. She painted her hair with all the colors of the wind. You never knew what tint it would take next.

"For now. I'm going to really freak Momma out and become the thing she fears most."

"Not a rock star!" I gasped, pretending to cup my face with my hands like Macaulay Culkin in *Home Alone.*

"Worse," Delilah leaned forward and raised her hands with the fingers twisted like a gnarled oak tree. "A Smurf!"

"Not a Smurf!"

"I'm afraid so. Although I'm not sure I could do a Smurfette. Blonde's never been my color. Maybe Hefty."

"Or Grouchy."

"I'd knock the shit out of you if you were not a recovering victim."

"Sure didn't stop you on the river."

"You remember that?" Delilah smiled. "It's not every day you get to save a life and fulfill a lifelong dream at the same time."

"Just kick me when I'm down, why don't you." I could take Delilah when we were kids and did a time or two. But I was pretty sure those days were over given the time she spent on stage versus the time I spent in the library.

"Speaking of saving a life, how did you know? Where did you come from?"

"Hang on," Delilah left, returning ten minutes later with two cups of water and an ice pack that she applied to my ankle. She disappeared again and came back bearing a plate of cold sliced turkey leftover from the night before.

"Lucille lets no turkey go to waste," I said as we devoured the pieces.

"You're still playing the name game? I thought you would have gotten tired of that years ago."

"Don't start."

"Don't get me wrong. She annoys me like no one else in this world. But don't you think this name thing is a little silly?"

"It's important to me. You weren't there to hear what she said or see how hard she hit me."

"Fair enough. But I wonder. How would Dinah feel about you honoring her like that? Denying Mom her place in your life?"

I was frustrated because I knew she had a point.

"It doesn't matter. Why did you come?"

"I can't just have a sister radar that alerts me when you're in danger?"

"Really?"

"Okay. I decided there was no way I was coming back to this swamp-ridden hell hole when Dorky called last week."

"Please tell us how you really feel. Don't hold back."

"Never do. A couple of nights ago we were in Dallas for a show. I came back to my dressing room after the last set. There was a message scrawled on my mirror in red ink."

"What did it say?" I already knew the answer.

"WHY DID YOU LET THEM KILL ME? HELP ME DELILAH!"

"We rolled on to Houston Wednesday. I started thinking that since I was so close maybe I could hop over here for a day or so. We finished the concert that night, and the crew started packing up. I had just changed into my street clothes and was walking toward the bus. It was parked behind the arena. My manager was with me. Misty, the new one. Not Karen, the old one."

"Why did you let Karen go?"

"I don't know. She's just such a ... Karen."

"Why am I getting a rundown of your nocturnal walks with your new Karen?"

"We had just reached the bus when Misty said, 'That girl must want an autograph.'"

Delilah stopped and took a deep swig of water. I could tell she wished it were something stronger.

"I looked up the ramp leading to the arena, and she was there."

"Dinah?"

"I guess so. I mean, it looked and sounded like her. I couldn't see her face that well. She was going on about how we let her die. Then, blood started pouring from every orifice on her body. It was crazy! Puts the best special effects artists to shame! Misty screamed and jumped inside the bus."

"What did you do?"

"I asked why she was there and what I could do. She just moaned. Then she was gone. Like she had never been there at all. I ran up the ramp and searched. When our road crew came over, I asked them to help me. It was weird because I didn't really know what to tell them to look for. We combed the arena for a while and never saw anyone.

"I tried to sleep for a few hours. Just kept waking up wondering what the hell all of this was about. At daybreak, I rented a car and told Misty to cancel the shows for this weekend. I'm not her favorite person right now. I drove all afternoon and got here just in time to see the ambulance swing into our driveway."

"You walked into quite the circus."

"I'm used to it. You should have seen the look on those cops' faces when the cameras turned my way instead of theirs."

"I'm sure."

"They loaded Dad into the ambulance, and the cops managed to push the reporters back again. Mom was losing it, and Dorcas was almost as hysterical worrying about both Daddy and you. Her leg was a mess, so I told her to go to the hospital with Mom and Dad while I looked for you. And, well, you know the rest."

Delilah's phone buzzed.

"Yeah," Delilah said as she pushed the speaker.

"Is Diana there?" Dorcas asked.

"Yes, I'm here, Dor."

"I'm so thankful to hear your voice. Don't you dare ever run off and do something stupid like that again!"

Delilah chuckled at my chastened look. I couldn't argue with her. Once again, the kid had a point.

"Sorry, Dor. How is Dad?"

"He's conscious and talking a little bit. The EKG came back. He had another heart attack."

Delilah raised her eyebrows and mouthed, "Another?" to me.

"What do you mean by 'another,' Dor?" I asked.

Dorcas was quiet for a second. "He doesn't like to worry you."

"How many has he had, Dor?"

"Two over the last five years. Three if you count this one."

"I think we damn well will count this one!" Delilah said.

"Dor, you should have told us."

"Look, neither of you is ever around. We have to take care of things as they come." Dorcas's tone sounded wounded. That was the last thing I intended or wanted.

"I'm sorry, Dor. We're just worried. What did the doctors say?"

"They need to keep him for observation for a couple of days. Limited visitors and no interactions that may cause him stress."

"No stress. Well, that'll be easy," Delilah said.

CHAPTER TEN

DESCRIBING OUR LIVING ROOM AS A "WAR ROOM" might go a little over the top. Desperate times and all that. I found myself in the surreal circumstance of sitting in my old living room on a Saturday afternoon sandwiched between my two sisters for the first time in years. My two worlds were smashing together as Pedro spoke to us via Zoom about the progress or rather, lack of progress, the Nashville police were making on my home invasion case.

The old whiteboard which had once served as a tool for family games now stood before us covered with pictures connected by red yarn in a clumsy attempt to mimic the boards created by special investigations units. *CSI: New Orleans* we were not, but I liked to think it wasn't half bad for amateur work.

"I'll keep calling, Diana, but they just don't have anything solid. And I don't think they are prioritizing it since no one was harmed."

"Yet," I said.

"And that's only if you don't count Daddy," Dorcas said. "And the fact that Diana was almost murdered down here."

"Sure. I understand. But you have to see it from their perspective. Nashville's a big place, and they have a lot on their plate." The way Pedro talked to Dorcas and watched her while she talked was mildly amusing. For Pedro, she was like some rare species of bird to an avid birdwatcher.

I remembered him giving the same focused attention to Delilah when we met for lunch. I would have found it more amusing if it weren't for my suspicion that he was not just looking for clues to what made them tick. He was also trying to understand what made me tick.

"Thank you for your help, Pedro. I know you're busy and there's no reason you have to do all this."

"I have my reasons, Diana. Please take care of yourself."

"Will do. See you soon."

As soon as I closed the Zoom window, Delilah leaned over and threw her arms around me, saying in a husky seductive voice, "I have my reasons, Diana."

"Get off," I said, hoping my cheeks were not as red as they felt.

"I bet he's got some good reasons," Delilah said. She showed no mercy.

Daddy was settled in the hospital, and the doctors were saying they didn't see a need to operate. They couldn't find any new blockages, and the ones they had been watching were not closed further. Their prescription was rest and further monitoring. That decision earned Daddy a couple more days at the hospital before he was turned out by insurance. It also meant a suspension of any court proceedings or further progress on the Jordan manslaughter case for now.

We'd gathered at home to process everything and decide on a plan of action. Dorcas slept for about three hours when she returned that morning. She was exhausted and really needed several days of rest, but I didn't see that coming anytime soon. Her ankle was healing nicely enough that she could move around the house with only a little limp.

"I'll have to go back and do next week's shows. We were planning to take a break for the holidays around December 10. I can come back after that."

"You mean Delilah is not the soundtrack of the holiday season?"

"Only in a perfect world."

"I can stay through Christmas," I said. "Pedro arranged for me to finish my classes online. I'll have to go back by January if things are still up in the air."

Dorcas shuddered. "Surely this will be over by then. I can't imagine we could stand it much longer. I'm afraid Daddy will have a fatal heart attack if he sees Dinah again."

"How are we seeing Dinah?" I asked.

"Demonic manifestation," Dorcas said.

"Impersonator," I said.

"Mushrooms," Delilah said.

"What?"

"Maybe somebody's putting exotic mushrooms in everyone's drinks."

"Did you have any exotic mushrooms in Houston before you saw Dinah?"

"You really want to know?"

"Be serious."

"You're joking, but the same Satanists who killed Dinah are trying to finish us all off," Dorcas insisted.

We got quiet. Delilah gave me a look that asked, *you or me?*

"Honey," I began, "there were no satanists."

"What about the circle we saw?"

"They were Hoodoo practitioners who probably also attended mass once a week at their local Catholic Church. Voodoo and Hoodoo can be very syncretistic practices." At Dorcas' confused look, I added, "People who mix a variety of religious views to create their own blends. Remember when the New Orleans Saints brought Ava Kay Jones in to remove the playoff curse from them in 2000?"

"Yeah. Daddy went ballistic. He threw out a lot of good Saints merchandise."

"Jones herself blends Voodoo, Yoruba, and Catholic elements in her practices. She used a boa constrictor midfield in the Superdome just like in the rite we witnessed as kids. Those people that night were doing a ritual to commemorate those who suffered and died as slaves on this land and invoke their strength to help the living."

"Still sounds satanic to me," Dorcas said.

"I know. And I understand why it does to you. What you need to understand now is that those people had nothing to do with Dinah's death."

"How can you be so sure? And, if they didn't, who did?"

"That's a question we should have pressed a long time ago," Delilah said. "Mom and Dad know more than they've said. Definitely to us and maybe to the authorities as well. Mia's death may be unrelated, but I have a feeling if we get to the bottom of one, we may know more about the other. Anyone really think the coroner, Dad's good buddy, would remove that death certificate without Dad's permission?"

"Why were we all banished upstairs while our sister was dying in the kitchen below?" I continued.

"She didn't die in the kitchen," Delilah whispered.

"What?" Dorcas and I said, almost in unison.

"She didn't die in the kitchen. That was just the last place you saw her. I sneaked back downstairs after Momma chased us upstairs. You were comforting Dorcas and didn't notice."

"Why have you never talked about it before?"

"Why would you even have to ask me that, Diana? Who wants to talk about that night ever? Besides, I didn't see much. Just heard Dinah in Daddy's bedroom. She was just moaning by then. I think she was too weak to scream anymore, or maybe they had given her something to ease the pain. I was there a minute or two before Momma came out with blood-soaked sheets. She ran me back up the stairs. I could tell she was terrified. I've never seen her so scared."

It brought me some comfort to know that my sister at least expired on a soft surface. That she received some kind of medical attention, even if only the homegrown variety.

"I can't believe you've never shared that with me," I said. I tried not to sound hurt.

"I told Trey not long after. I thought he would have told you." Delilah realized too late how casually she'd said it.

"We weren't talking much then. It was a rocky year for us if you remember," I said.

"Yeah. I remember." The weight hovered in the air for a moment. Dorcas noticed. Her eyes were full of curiosity, but she knew better than to ask.

"Anyway," I said a little too fast. "That doesn't add much to what we already know."

"It's what Daddy was saying to Dinah that stuck with me," Delilah said. She sat eerily and uncharacteristically subdued.

"What did he say?"

"I'm sorry, Angel. We should have listened to you. I should have believed you. Please don't leave us." Dinah said the words in a flat monotone, but my mind conjured up images of my Daddy screaming it as his oldest daughter was ripped from him.

"What should they have believed?"

"I don't know. He never said."

"You can't think that Momma and Daddy would ever hurt Dinah," Dorcas said.

"I'm not convinced they would hurt Dinah," I said. "Not yet. But I do agree with Delilah that they covered something up about her death."

Dorcas slammed her hand on the armrest of the couch when I said, "Not yet." She was holding herself back. I felt sorry for her. For Delilah and me, finding the answers to the mystery of Dinah's death could be liberating, even if personally painful. In Dorcas' case, it represented a possible existential threat to everything she believed and had devoted her life to serving. Part of me didn't understand how she could not see that our parents were willing to stretch, if not trample, the truth all the time. How was she capable of being shocked by the possibility that they had been lying to us about Dinah?

"I'm sorry, Dor," I whispered. "Wherever it leads. Remember?"

She inhaled sharply and nodded, "Wherever."

"Where do we start?" Delilah asked.

"I've been thinking about that," I said. "Our parents ignited a full-fledged satanic panic with their version of events. *Devil's Circle* just widened it when it came out. Why did they do that?"

"I always chalked it up to grief gone wild," Delilah said. "A coping mechanism arising from their need to name their pain and deal with it."

"And I think you might be right. But what if there's more to that than we think? Why direct their ire at groups of people rather than a single person?"

"What do you mean?"

"It's like duck hunting," Dorcas said. "Or any kind of bird hunting. You don't use regular shells like you do with a deer or other large animal. It's too hard to hit them in the air like that and can cause too much damage to your game."

"You use birdshot," I said. Dorcas had a talent for illustration.

"Well, I don't. What are you two getting at?"

"Birdshot scatters slightly in the sky to hit the bird in motion," I said. "What if Lucille and Daddy had their suspicions about who hurt Dinah, but they weren't sure. Maybe even suspected multiple people."

"Maybe some of their suspects became targets in the panic that swept our school and the town," Delilah finished.

"Exactly. In this case, our birdshot analogy breaks down. Let's say instead you fire scattershot because you're not sure of your target. You reason you have to hit the right one if you take them all down. That's pretty much the idea behind every witch-hunt and satanic panic in history when you boil it down to its core. You're willing to sacrifice the innocent if it means stopping the perceived threat."

"I guess it was just a matter of time before we started talking guns down here," Delilah observed.

"So, who do we have?"

"Mr. Francis," Delilah said. "He was the main one they called in for questioning."

"Who was he?" Dorcas asked.

"Dinah's English and theater teacher," I said. "He was really good. People loved him. Even before Dinah died, there were some rumors going around about them." I pictured Crissy Hine's prissy face.

"That's terrible," Dorcas said. "Why were they spending time together?"

"He never really said. But while proving to the police that he didn't do it, Mr. Francis had to reveal his own secrets. They accepted that he wouldn't have had an inappropriate relationship with Dinah, but it cost him his job anyway."

"How could they be sure he wouldn't have had an inappropriate relationship with her?"

"He wasn't into people like Dinah," I said, always the diplomat.

"What was his problem with Dinah?"

Delilah groaned. "Just when I forget where I am, they remind me. He didn't like girls, Einstein!"

"Oh," Dorcas said. It still took a minute to sink in. "Ohhhh."

"And there it is," Delilah said. "You should drive on the same side of the street a time or two, Dorcas. You might like it."

Dorcas shifted uncomfortably in her seat. Delilah was like a cat playing with a mouse.

"We don't need any stories about ménage à trois with backup singers or dancers," I said. "We have Mr. Francis."

"And Terence Dearman," Delilah said.

"Sam Dearman's son?" Dorcas asked.

"Yeah. He was a suspect for a little bit before Momma and Daddy vouched for him. I'm not sure why. The police took him in for questioning. They never released the reason because it might hinder their case. Left the rumor mill to run wild. Terence didn't even finish high school here. He moved to Houston with his mom, Sam's first wife, and finished school there. Sam's had a rough time in Picardy here when you combine all the hostility when he started attending a white school and then all the garbage about his son too."

"Why would they suspect him?" I asked.

"Not sure. There was a lot they weren't telling."

Sarah Kelly, Bryce Collins, Hakeem Ariel, and several others were added. All people who in one way or another had suffered in the onslaught unleashed by our parents' paranoia. We also added the Jordans and a follow-up conversation with Pastor Dixon to the list.

"I see one big problem with me going around talking to these people," Delilah said.

"People will freak out, and the crowds will never leave you alone."

I said this fully aware that three teenage girls were standing at the edge of our driveway holding up a large sign that proclaimed: WE LOVE YOU DELILAH! Thank God for trespassing laws. Though they had their limits. Two men had sneaked into the driveway and removed one of Delilah's hub caps. She didn't have the heart to post on social media that it was a rental.

"I can do it," Dorcas said.

"Some of these people may not react well to being questioned. Even after all these years. I would feel better if someone would go with you," I said.

"Trey can go, Diana. He would do it for you."

I avoided Delilah's glance and said, "Sure. That could work."

It struck me how sad it was that Trey's name was the first one Dorcas mentioned. I guessed they never saw each other most of the time. My sister's life revolved around my parents and the "ministry." She cultivated many casual relationships, mostly people at church, but she didn't have anyone close enough to trust with something like this. She had to borrow my special friend, a friend I hadn't been close to for years. I didn't want to think about how sad that was for both of us.

"One last thing," I said. "Pay attention and see if anyone mentions a red Honda Civic."

"A red Honda Civic," Dorcas repeated. "Why?"

"One dropped Dinah off at the house twice in the weeks before she died. I've always wondered who it was. I don't think it was one of her friends. Cheryl picked her up usually. But it wasn't Cheryl's car that dropped her off those nights."

"You never saw the driver?" Delilah asked.

"No. I only saw the car because Trey and I were watching Dorcas, and I was waiting up for Dinah."

"I'll listen for that," Dorcas said. She glanced at her watch and said, "Daddy should be ready for us now."

"Okay. Let me grab my keys and purse," I said.

As I gathered my things in our shared room, I heard a soft knock behind me. Delilah stood at the door.

"Hey," she said.

"Hey yourself. You need something?"

"No ... I'm good," she started to go and then stopped. Turning back, she fidgeted with the multiple rings on her fingers. I looked up again expectantly. "Should we talk about this Trey thing?" she finally said.

"What Trey thing?"

"Come on, Diana. You say you let it go a long time ago, but there's still ice in the air every time it comes up."

"It's not a problem. I love you both. It was a long time ago."

"For what it's worth, I'm sorry."

"You've said that before. You don't have to keep saying it."

"Why do I feel like I do?" she asked.

"That's your issue," I said, too bluntly. She shrugged and headed downstairs. "Can't say I didn't try," she called over her shoulder.

We fought our way to the car and then fought our way again into the hospital.

"Dr. Chambers! Dr. Chambers!"

"Delilah! We're your biggest fans, Delilah!"

"Ms. Hebert, can you comment on how your father is doing?"

I noticed at the hospital that the elite media had been joined by internet fan clubs and podcasters. These internet hounds were the ones I feared and respected the most. If you want to find a random fact about true crime, go straight to the hardcore fans who run the websites and post on the message boards.

We made it to the second floor where we were greeted by Daddy sitting up in bed with a pillow behind his back and a container of half-eaten Jello on his lap. Lucille hovered beside him to adjust his pillow and raise a thermos of water to his lips every few minutes.

"He's doing well," she said. "He should be ready to come home in a day or two. But no noise or excitement."

"Yeah, about that," I said. "We were thinking it might be good to put the two of you up in a hotel or maybe with friends for a few days."

"A hotel," Lucille said. "Why?" I tried to give her a subtle signal that maybe we should talk about it outside. Daddy caught it and said, "She's worried because we can't guarantee home will be free of stress."

"I know," Lucille said. "I just don't want to give in to intimidation."

"We have to," Dorcas said. "Until we sort all this out, maybe you and Daddy should stay somewhere else."

"If it really is Dinah, there's nowhere I can go, Angels," Daddy said. "She can find me wherever I am. And maybe she should."

Lucille bit her lip and shook her head. "I don't like it. But whatever we need to do I'm willing to do."

"I'll call around and make some arrangements," Dorcas said. "Maybe we can keep it quiet for at least a little while."

She walked out to make her calls.

"Can we talk to you outside for a few minutes?" I asked Lucille.

"Of course," she said. "Denny, I'll be right outside."

We walked down the hall and settled into some seats in the visitor's lounge.

"I want to say how much we appreciate you both being here," Lucille said. Delilah's expression read, "Who are you and where's my mother?"

"Thank you," I said, not knowing what else to say.

"Sure," Delilah responded.

"So, what did you want to talk about?"

Delilah and I exchanged an uneasy look.

"It's about Dinah, Mom," Delilah said.

"What about her?"

"We need to know how she died, Lucille. Not just the sanitized version or the official story. We think finding out who killed her holds the key to discovering who's after us now."

"You know what happened. I wrote the book. You were there."

"Cut the crap, Mom!" *Oh boy, here we go. We said we'd take it slow, Delilah.*

"Excuse me," Lucille said. She wasn't quite in battle posture yet, but I could see her guns locking and loading behind her frustrated expression. "Don't speak to me that way, Delilah."

"Diana almost died, Mom! Some sick bastard tied a weight to her ankle and threw her in the river to drown. If I hadn't come when I did or if the freak hadn't left Diana's flashlight on the bank where they dropped her in, we might not have gotten to her in time. How many daughters do you need to lose before you stop all your bullshit?!"

Lucille turned a pale face to me. "Is that true?"

"Yes. We didn't want to tell you yesterday because you had enough on your plate with Daddy."

"Praise God that He protected you," Lucille said. She meant it. I could at least rest easy in the knowledge that she cared if I lived or died. Baby steps.

"He was doing a shitty job when I showed up to do his job for him," Delilah said.

"God uses all kinds of people, even the most unlikely."

"Why, you ..." I grabbed Delilah's arm before things escalated further. We needed to get back to Dinah. People across the waiting room and down the hall were starting to stare.

"I checked for Dinah's death certificate and also for an autopsy report. I came up empty on both counts."

"That's terrible, Deborah. The Public Records Office here has always been such an embarrassment."

"What the freaking hell!"

"Delilah, your language is appalling!"

"That's why I said freaking. Cleaned it up for you, Mom."

"You've got to help us," I pleaded. "For God's sake, this is your daughter we're talking about."

"Don't you think I know that?!" Lucille barked. "Don't you think I spend every single day wishing she were here with us? Wanting to turn back time and ..." She dabbed her eyes.

I was never sure when Lucille cried if they were genuine tears or crocodile tears. She could shame any shady eighties televangelist with her capacity to fake tears.

"I'm done with this! Good luck!" Delilah said to me as she stomped out of the waiting area.

Lucille and I sat in silence for a while after she left.

"Two days until the first fight is a record," I said.

She nodded. "We've always seemed to have that effect on each other. I'm not sure why."

"At least you never hit her."

"Deborah. I ..." She reached up and touched the edge of my blonde hair with the back of her hand just above my forehead. I felt an impulse to pull away and forced myself to remain still. *Let's see where this goes.*

"You what?"

"I ... There are things I should have never done." Lucille proclaimed a faith built on forgiveness and grace, yet she had the hardest time apologizing.

"I know. I just wish it were easier for you to say it."

She was still stroking my hair. It was the most physical contact we'd had in twenty years.

"Remember that there are black roots under those blonde tresses."

"Is that supposed to be a heavy-handed spiritual metaphor?" I asked. I didn't need reminding about my black roots, physical or spiritual.

"It means remember who you are. We've never been perfect. Far from it. But we're your parents. Give us a little grace and trust us. We did what was best. Leave it be."

"I want to, Lucille. Finding out about Dinah is about more than just closure now. We're dueling with someone dangerous, and the more we know, the better."

"Leave it alone," Lucille said. "Leave it all buried where it belongs."

"Why?"

"Because you may not like what you find."

"I'm willing to take that risk."

"Are you? Foolish girl. You have no idea. Your daddy wants to keep picking at it too and look where he is. Leave it alone." Lucile didn't sound threatening; she was resigned and sad. "If you honor your sister, leave it alone."

"I can't. Because I honor my sisters who are still here. They deserve to live without this shadow hanging over them. I deserve to live free of it. We're going to find out. We'll talk to people. Get to the truth."

Lucille patted my hand. "I wish I could do what you want. I really do. But the best thing I can do for you all is keep you safe."

Delilah returned, still sulking, and beckoned me to go. I rose and said to Lucille, "This is not over. We will get to the truth with or without your help."

CHAPTER ELEVEN

DECEMBER 1, 1995

The last bell rang. I slammed my locker harder than usual, energized by the prospect of another weekend. Just three weeks until Christmas break. I was ready. When I shut my locker, Crissy Hines stood there waiting.

"What's up, Freak?" she said.

"Nothing, Crissy. Getting out of here for the weekend."

"Really. How're you getting out of here?"

"Same way I do every day. My sister's picking me up," I said. "I drove last week. Pretty soon I'll be driving myself."

Crissy snorted. "You think your family can afford something besides that broken down station wagon? Or that crap-colored pickup your daddy drives?"

My hands balled into fists. Momma's voice came to me, saying something about turning the other cheek. Last time she said that Delilah brought up somebody named Malcolm X saying we should turn other peoples' cheeks. Momma didn't take that well. There was no need to do anything to Crissy's cheek. Her butt, though, I would gladly kick.

"Screw you, Crissy."

"Ohhhh, she's temperamental today. You PMSing, Hebert? You know your sister's here early?"

That I didn't know. "Early? She's sitting in the parking lot?"

"No," she said slyly. "She was sitting in Mr. Francis' office talking. He's got free period now, you know."

"So."

"I thought she graduated last year."

"She did."

"Cheryl Hall told me she used to hang out with him after school last year too. A lot. Seems a little improper to me. Why's she still coming around, Hebert?"

I could feel my cheeks burning. Cheryl Hall was standing with a cluster of girls at the end of the hallway, looking our way every few minutes.

"I don't know. That's her business. Not mine or yours." I brushed past Crissy and headed for the parking lot.

"I'd want to find out, Hebert," Crissy called after me. "People talk."

Dinah, Delilah, and Dorcas were waiting for me in the station wagon.

Trey bounded up beside me and saluted. "Reporting for childcare duty, Ma'am!"

I normally would have laughed. Today I was too distracted.

"What's wrong?"

"Tell you later," I said.

We climbed into the station wagon and rolled to the house. Once everyone was settled inside, Dinah disappeared into her room. She returned wearing a nice blue jean skirt and white blouse. Her black hair was combed back neatly and pinned with a fancy hairpin that Momma bought her freshman year for her one foray into theatrical performance. She played Lisle in the *Sound of Music.* Everyone praised her performance and said she was a natural.

Unfortunately, Momma took a dim view of theater and fiction overall. She said pretending to be someone else or losing yourself in someone else's life was despising what the Lord had given you in the real world. Ironic, given the pure fiction she churned out in the

Demonologists' series. I think the part that scared Momma the most about the whole episode was how well Dinah did and how much she enjoyed it. As Delilah liked to say, Momma shut that down quick. Mr. Francis had directed the play and encouraged Dinah to pursue theater.

"Will you and Trey be okay with Dorcas?"

"I think we can take her."

"Funny. There's leftover spaghetti in the fridge."

She started for the door. I noticed her car keys lying on the table.

"Hey! You need these?"

Dinah paused. "I'm getting a ride from Cheryl. But I'll take them just in case. Thanks again!"

She scooped up her keys and hurried out the door. I watched her walk down the driveway from our front window. A few minutes later, Cheryl's blue mustang pulled up beside our mailbox. Dinah jumped in, and the car sped away. We'd repeated this ritual three times this week. Trey and I watching Dorcas until about eight, Dinah leaving the house dressed up, and me watching Cheryl wheel into our driveway to spirit her away. The first time, Cheryl brought her home too. The next two times, Dinah returned a little later and was dropped off by a red Honda Civic. I never saw the driver. Dinah's exit from the Civic was quick and abrupt, almost as if she found it awkward and was eager to get out. When I asked who had dropped her off, she said, "A friend." She clearly wanted to let it drop. I wondered if any of this was connected to the rumors Crissy Hines was spreading.

"Crissy Hines is an empty-headed bimbo," Trey said when I told him. "The only way she remembers her cheers is to write them on her palm."

He jumped to his feet and imitated a cheerleader. "Two bits, four bits, six bits ..." With each "bit," he examined a different body part looking for Crissy's imaginary cheat sheet. I collapsed onto the couch laughing.

"What's a blimbo, Debbie?"

"Nothing, Sweetie. Trey's being bad again."

"Stop being bad, Trey," Dorcas said, taking the opportunity to jump from the couch to his back.

Trey grunted as he absorbed the impact. "Now you're stuck on the bucking bronco of Picardy!"

Dorcas screamed with delight as Trey bounced her around the room.

Later that night, Dorcas settled into bed beside me, and we read three children's books. After *The Cat in the Hat*, I brushed her hair and tucked her into bed.

"Goodnight, Dor."

"Night, Debbie. Debbie?"

"Yeah."

"Where's Dinah?"

"I'm not sure. She's busy tonight. You can see her in the morning."

"I hope she doesn't start leaving like Momma and Daddy."

My heart shattered into a million pieces. Momma and Daddy left last Sunday afternoon, and there was no word yet on when they would return.

I went back into the room and hugged her tight. "Don't worry, Sweetie. They'll all be back soon."

"You won't leave; will you, Debbie?"

"Are you kidding? No way. Now get some sleep."

She rolled over and pulled her favorite teddy bear close.

I walked down the stairs, struck by the silence of our usually bustling home. Delilah was staying with Tianna for the weekend. Dinah was gone wherever. And Trey ...Where was Trey?

I noticed that the white door to the storage room at the back of the house was open. *Great!* Daddy had been promising for years to move the "artifacts" out of the house and into the barn. He said the only thing stopping him was the need to design some weather-proof cases to hold the more fragile items. I was hoping he'd get to it soon. That stuff gave me the creeps.

"Trey!" I called.

Nothing.

I approached the open door and slipped inside. Tarot cards littered a coffee table by the door. A crystal ball secured from Madam Jewel's Mystical Arts in the French Quarter reflected the moonlight. Voodoo dolls hung from a plastic display turntable that Daddy bought when the local Schwegmanns closed. Their wooden faces and straw hair cast frightening shadows around the room. Their jagged teeth seemed poised to devour me. I started feeling for the light switch, but I couldn't find it. None of the kids were allowed in here often enough to get familiar with the room.

No luck with the lights. I turned to look at the opposite wall for a backup switch when I saw the infamous queen of the collection staring at me. Christine sat gazing out of the box where she had remained since my parents recovered her in the early 80s. It was ironic that Crissy Hines, actually Christine Aurora Hines, shared a name with our little hellspawn. Someone had a sick sense of humor. I approached Christine with caution.

"Hey, Christine. What's new?"

Christine sat with her weird smile frozen in place.

"Guess you don't get out much. Too bad."

I heard a bump behind me.

"Trey?"

I turned to look behind me and saw no one. As I backed up, I felt Christine's display case against my back. A second bump caused me to jump. Suddenly, another louder bump sounded right beside me. I whirled and found myself staring straight into Christine's demonic face. I unleashed a scream loud enough to wake the dead. My feet slipped as I scurried away from Christine.

I stumbled and knocked the coffee table over, scattering the tarot cards across the floor. With some distance between me and the display case, I saw that Christine had tipped forward and her head was now resting against the glass of the display case. I must have bumped the case when I jumped at the other sounds. I took another step back and collided with flesh and bone. My second scream split the night.

"Hey! It's just me." Trey said.

"What are you doing?" I yelled.

"Thought I would give you a little scare. Checking out this crazy stuff! How come we never go in here?"

"Because it freaks me out. And because my parents say we can't. It's dangerous."

"All the fun stuff is." He reached back and flipped the light switch.

The glow revealed my face, white as a sheet, and my body shaking uncontrollably.

"Hey, what's wrong? I didn't mean to scare you that bad."

"You can't ... You just ... This stuff's no joke!" Tears welled up in my eyes as I fought to control the shock tremors still coursing through my body.

"I'm sorry, Debbie."

Trey realized how terrified I'd been. He stepped forward and pulled me to him. I settled into his embrace with my head on his shoulder. It took a few minutes for the trembling to subside.

When it did, I raised my head and said, "Thanks. I'm better now."

Trey didn't speak. He was looking straight into my eyes. I tried to speak but couldn't find any words. He leaned forward. Warmth cascaded through me as his lips touched mine. For a moment, I melted into the powerful sensations and the comforting nearness of him. Then confusion ripped through me. I pulled back, disoriented and unsure.

"Debbie, I ..."

"What are we doing, Trey?"

"I think it's called kissing, Debbie."

"You know what I mean. I've never done this before."

"Me either. It was nice."

"It was." I noticed he was looking unsure. He could see my own confusion. "Really, it was. I've always loved you."

"I love you, too."

"I love you as my friend. I don't want to lose that. Every other boy I meet just has one thing on their mind. What we have is different." I desperately wanted to find the right words, but my brain was failing me. He looked cut to the core.

"You're not into me?"

"It's not that. I promise it's not. You caught me by surprise. I'm just not sure how I feel."

"Really." He swallowed and walked out of the room.

"Trey! Please wait!"

I followed him out, still calling his name. He stopped in the living room.

"Look, I'm sorry I surprised you. Maybe I should have asked. But it just felt right. Good."

"It was good."

"Then why are you acting like it was wrong?"

"I'm not sure I'm ready for things to change."

He shook his head and picked up the phone.

"I'm calling my mom to come get me. We can talk more tomorrow."

"That's probably a good idea," I said. "Give us time to think."

We tried to act normal, but our kiss and the fallout lingered in the air until his mom arrived. He said goodnight and left without looking at me. I sat on the stairs afterwards thinking. There were no tears. What I told Trey was true. I was in shock. Part of me wanted that kiss to go on forever and another part of me feared what it would mean if it did.

I went up to my room and fell into bed. I gazed over at Delilah's empty bed. It was the last thing I remembered before I drifted off to an uneasy sleep.

I snapped awake around midnight. Moonlight spilled through our window. I wasn't sure what had woken me up. The sound of running water came from our bathroom. *Who's taking a shower at this hour?* I stumbled to my feet and stepped out into the hallway. Dorcas was nestled under her covers. Dinah's bed was empty. It had to be Dinah in the shower. The door opened a moment later, and steam billowed out like a sauna. Through the steam, I could see Dinah's slender form walking out wrapped in a towel.

I stepped forward to tell her I was there and gasped in surprise. Her porcelain skin was beet red. She looked like one of the million crawfish we condemned to the vat each spring as they writhed in the boiling water, destined to satisfy the cravings of our family. There was something in the way she walked as well. She moved stiffly like she was nursing bruises all over.

"Dinah?"

Her head snapped in my direction. She looked startled.

"Debbie! Hey ... Dorcas do okay tonight?"

"Yeah. Are you okay?" I was scared. It had taken Dinah a moment to say my name. She looked at me in that moment as if she didn't recognize me. Like she was struggling to identify me.

"Me? Sure, I'm fine. Just tired."

"You ran your shower a little hot."

"Guess I did," Dinah had her arms folded across her chest now. I noticed that she was rubbing her hands along the skin of her flushed elbows in a frantic pattern. My sister radiated calm all the time. No one would ever describe her as fidgety. "Look, I'm really tired. Can we catch up tomorrow?"

"Sure, goodnight."

"Goodnight, Debbie." She slipped into her room and closed the door.

I stood in the hall a little longer, wondering if I should do anything else. Five minutes passed and Dinah didn't return. I went back to bed. My dreams were troubled by visions of Trey leaning in to kiss me. Just as our lips started to touch, Christine pulled him away and clapped her porcelain hands around his throat. I screamed as his face turned red and Christine cackled with devilish delight. Several times I heard uncontrollable sobbing in my dreams.

At one point I pierced through the veil of sleep and looked at my alarm clock. Almost morning. Just before I drifted back to sleep, I had the vague sense that the sobbing sound had followed me out of my dreams. Or into them.

CHAPTER TWELVE

An Excerpt from

DEVIL'S CIRCLE (1996)

by Lucille B. Hebert

Dinah brushed Dorcas' hair and pulled her covers up to her neck.

"Goodnight, Dor."

"Goodnight, Dinah. Will Momma and Daddy be back tomorrow?"

"Maybe. They're doing the Lord's work. Remember what we have to be?"

"Good little soldiers for Jesus!"

"That's right. Sleep tight."

Dinah closed the door and went down to the living room. Deborah and Trey had been sitting on the couch when she went upstairs. Now they were nowhere to be found.

"Debbie! Trey!"

Silence answered her calls.

Dinah looked in the kitchen. No one there. When she emerged from the kitchen, Dinah noticed that the door to the artifacts room was ajar.

"Debbie? Trey?"

She stepped toward the door.

"Debbie and Trey just want to play."

The singsong little voice sent a chill down Dinah's spine. She'd heard it before. Dinah whipped around and searched for anything she could use as a weapon.

"Dinah! Dinah!"

Dinah looked toward the couch and saw her. Christine was peeking out from the edge of the couch, her one visible eye winking at Dinah.

"Christine. How did you get out of your case?"

Mocking childish laughter rippled from the couch.

Dinah wrapped her arm around the living room lamp. She prepared to throw it if Christine made any sudden moves.

"What have you done with them, Christine?"

Christine's only answer was another chilling laugh.

"Debbie!"

"Dinah!'

Deborah's cry sounded muffled. Dinah backed toward the artifacts room and peered through the door. She almost screamed. Deborah was pinned to the wall about three feet from the ground. She struggled in vain to escape. Trey was below her, his hand caught in the viselike grip of the iron maiden.

"Dinah, Christine did this! We bumped the case and it opened!"

Dinah hurried to the case. The key was hanging out of the lock. Someone had opened it and left it closed just enough that no one would notice it was open. She reached for a bottle of holy water. The shelves on the left side of the room were full of it, blessed by both a priest and a Pentecostal preacher. Clutching the vial, Dinah started to reenter the hallway.

There was no need. Christine had followed her in. Her ghostly porcelain face was distorted through the prism of Madame Jewel's crystal ball.

"Time to go back in your case, Christine."

Christine cackled again. "Are you a fool? Let's ask Madame Jewel!"

The crystal ball clouded, and then vibrant colors began to sweep around its edges.

The image of a man dressed all in black appeared.

"He's my friend. He'll be your end."

As Christine spoke, the image shifted to a circle of people lit by blazing torches. They wore robes and masks. The masks were shaped like goats, horses, and mythical beasts Dinah didn't recognize. Then the image shifted again. Dinah froze and fought to keep from vomiting. She saw herself in the crystal ball. Her body was lying on a bed. Blood covered her clothes and the sheets. The icy blue complexion of her face carried the obvious pallor of death.

"Rest your little head. You'll soon rest it dead."

Dinah yelled and jumped forward. She tossed the holy water on Christine's head. The vicious doll let out a screech and leaped for Dinah. The momentary distraction had broken Christine's spell.

Deborah dropped to the floor and Trey was able to pull his hand free of the iron maiden. Trey grabbed Christine. Deborah joined him, and they managed to pull her off Dinah. Dinah rose, holding her throat and gasping. Christine was screaming and shouting. None of it was coherent. A steady stream of blasphemies and curses issued from her.

It took all three of them to force the doll back into her case. She bumped against the glass for a few minutes and then went inert. A casual observer would think she was an ordinary doll.

The three of them stood gasping for breath.

"Thanks, Dinah," Deborah finally managed.

"You're welcome. Someone opened Christine's case."

"It wasn't us," Trey said.

"I know," Dinah answered. She was lost in thought as the frightening images from the crystal ball ran before her again.

Dinah glanced at it. The crystal ball, like Christine, sat inert and clear as if it had never displayed anything.

Deborah followed Dinah's gaze and noted her haunted look.

"What did you see, Dinah?"

"Nothing, Debbie. Maybe the people Daddy and Momma are looking for. I'm not sure."

Trey and Deborah exchanged a troubled glance. It was not like Dinah to be spooked.

"Hey, let's go get some hot chocolate. Calm our nerves a little."

Trey and Deborah nodded.

As she stopped to turn out the lights and lock the door, Dinah took one last look at Christine. Was it her imagination or did the porcelain eye wink again?

CHAPTER THIRTEEN

WE RETURNED TO THE HOUSE AFTER DUSK driving five miles an hour the last few yards to avoid running over the reporters who formed a wall all the way up to our property line. Sunday night we decided that I would drive Delilah to New Orleans to catch her flight. She planned to join her crew in Miami, complete her tour, and return on December 11.

"Mr. Francis lives in New Orleans now," I said. "I might stay over Monday if he can see me. He's retired, so he might be around during the day. Dor, you can stay here to get Daddy and Lucille settled. You might even be able to knock out some of the safer names on our list. Just don't tackle any of the potentially aggressive ones until I get back."

"Only if you agree to let me call Trey and see if he can meet you there," Dorcas said.

"He can't. He'll have to teach on Monday."

"At least let me check."

"Why? There's no reason to bother him."

"I'll feel better if I know you have someone watching your back," Dorcas said. "You did almost drown. Remember?"

"Fine."

I went upstairs and checked my phone before bed.

Pedro had left a voicemail.

"Hope you're okay. Call me when you can."

I sent a quick text to thank him and promised to call soon. I heard Dorcas come in soon afterward. Delilah took a shower, and then her shuffling feet announced that she was getting into Dinah's old bed. The Hebert girls were sleeping under the same roof again.

Delilah and I drove in silence most of the way to New Orleans. She glanced at me several times. I could tell she wanted to say something.

"What?"

"Nothing," Delilah said.

"Something."

"I was just thinking how hard it is to expose the hidden parts of yourself."

"You've never seemed to have a problem with that."

"It's harder for me than it may look. All I've ever wanted is for people to love me. That's what it's all about."

That admission was huge for her. Delilah's brand seldom allowed introspection and self-awareness.

"What are you talking about? Everybody always loved you. You were and are the cool sister. Tianna, Kevin ... Trey."

Delilah looked over at me and shook her head.

"You still don't get it, do you? After all these years."

"Get what?"

"Trey."

"I get that I walked into our bedroom on one of the worst days of the worst year of my life and you were kissing my best friend. My sister was dead, and my other sister was stealing the only person who understood me."

That day ranked as the second worst of my life. We buried Dinah just two days before. Things between Trey and I had been awkward at best since our kiss. He had arrived to talk, and I was gone to the store. When I returned and opened the door, they were sitting on Delilah's bed kissing passionately. They separated immediately and tried to talk to me.

I ran out the door, down the stairs, and into the woods. What was left of my world seemed to crumble at that sight. As I sobbed against a tree, the thing that surprised me the most was how heartbroken I was. *At least I know how I feel now.* Cold comfort.

"No need to say sorry, huh?"

I bit my lip. She was right. I acted like it didn't bother me, but every time that scab got poked, venom poured out.

"I'm sorry. It shouldn't bother me."

"That's just it. It should. And I get that. I was hurting too and needed someone. He was too, Diana. You were fighting weeks before we happened."

"Are you saying it's my fault that you borrowed my best friend for almost half a year?"

"It's not anyone's fault. We only dated for four months. And it was good in so many ways."

"I'm happy for you."

"But the whole time, it felt like I was standing in for someone else. Every time we kissed, I felt like there were three of us there."

"I would have thought you would appreciate a good ménage à trois," I said, allowing myself a smile.

Delilah smiled back, and then she turned serious again. "I missed you the whole time. He never said it, but I knew Trey missed you too."

"What do you mean? I was around. It was hell seeing the two of you together. I cried myself to sleep more nights than I care to admit. But I tried."

"You were amazing. But it was never the same again. With me and you or you and him."

"Things change. People change."

"Diana, do you understand what I'm trying to say?"

"That you want us to be okay? We are. I promise. I still get testy about it, but it worked out fine. Trey and I made up. You two eventually broke up. Probably better for you both. We were still friends all through high school."

"Yes, we were. But it was never quite the same. You were never quite the same."

"What do you mean?"

Delilah hesitated. "There were times when I felt like I lost two sisters that night. And I wasn't sure which one."

"What?" I asked, truly confused.

"It was almost like you wanted to live for Dinah the life she didn't get to live. I had a hard time telling where Debbie ended and Dinah began. And which one had actually left us."

"Wow! Pedro would have a field day with that."

The Louis Armstrong New Orleans International Airport appeared in the distance. Ahead planes ascended and descended with regularity as ground traffic streamed into the complex.

"I've got one question for you before I leave. Think hard about it when you're with Trey tomorrow."

"What's that?"

"Do you think Trey would have ever walked into our room and kissed me if you had kissed him back that night in the artifacts room?"

"What? I don't know. It doesn't matter now."

"Yes, it does. You should find out."

I pulled up to the "Departures" lane.

Delilah stepped out and slipped her duffle bag over her shoulder.

"Promise me you will."

"Maybe. I love you."

"Love you too. Stay dull."

"Stay crazy."

I watched her disappear through the sliding doors.

Three hours later I'd settled into my hotel room. I looked up Aaron Francis' address in preparation for our visit. He lived with his husband in the Garden District. A step up from his teacher's salary. I remembered hearing he became a principal after he left Picardy. I pulled my shoes off and was contemplating a shower when I got a text:

Fancy a sugar high?

I smiled and texted back:

Sure. You raid the Mars factory?

Trey replied:

I was thinking something a little nicer.

An hour later we were sitting outside eating beignets at the Café du Monde. Dusk was creeping over the waterfront, and the Crescent City lights were beginning to twinkle. Brilliant Christmas lights added their special shine to the usual luster of Jackson Square. Couples in carriages pulled by dappled horses rattled past. Tourists paused to gawk at the river, listen to the saxophonists, or take pictures of St. Louis Cathedral.

"This is nice. Thank you for suggesting it. And thank you for coming. I know it wasn't convenient."

Trey nodded. "I can spare a personal day or two for an old friend."

"How was your family?"

"Good. My mom says hello. The kids are doing okay. The divorce was hard on them, but kids can be tough when they need to be."

Didn't I know it!

"And your ex?"

"Erin? She's fine. We do pretty well working together for the kids. There was never really an explosion in our marriage. I don't think we ever fought that hard. Things just sort of fizzled after a while. There just came a point where we realized we were holding each other back instead of helping each other forward."

"That's good," I said. "Good that you can still get along, I mean."

My thoughts were circling back to endless conversations Pedro and I had about where things were going. How I was not ready to "define" what we were. Pedro told me at one point it was like I was holding out for a better offer, a comment that set me off and led to one of our worst fights ever. Now all I heard was Delilah. "*It was like there were three of us there the whole time.*" Delilah, why can't you just leave well enough alone? And I could imagine her saying, "*Then I wouldn't be Delilah, would I?*"

We finished our beignets and strolled through Jackson Square, savoring the sights, sounds, and smells of the waterfront. Salty air, glittering lights, and the occasional whiff of bourbon teased my senses.

"There's a bar around the corner with some great live music," Trey said.

"I think I just want to walk for a while if that's okay. This just feels so normal. I need to be normal for a little while."

"Whatever you say, Ms ... What do I call you now?"

"Chambers. Diana Chambers."

"So, you're sticking with it?"

I'd given that question a lot of thought over the weekend.

"Yes. Deborah Hebert is who I was, and she will always be a part of me. I realize I can't escape that now and maybe I shouldn't. But I'm more than who I was. I can also choose who and what I will be. There's no harm or shame in that if you can own who you've been at the same time. That sounds like the worst fortune cookie in the world."

He laughed. I relished the sound and remembered how much I loved it.

"I think I follow you. I'm glad to have known Debbie and look forward to knowing Diana better. I don't care what you call yourself. You'll always be my best friend."

We were standing on the riverfront boardwalk with the glistening waters of the river reflecting the moonlight. The majestic skyline of the city glowed all around us. The rich tones of distant saxophone music gently massaged our ears.

"Always?"

"Yeah. We've had our bumps, for sure. Definitely some regrets. I don't want to ever say dating your sister was a mistake. She's great in her own crazy, edgy way. But I think we both knew from the start it would never last."

"I know you didn't mean to hurt me."

"That's just it. I think I did. Subconsciously. Because I felt like you rejected me. It wasn't fair to either you or Delilah. Especially not when you had just lost your sister. I'm sorry."

I nodded sadly and gestured to the river.

"Water under the bridge?"

Trey laughed and gazed at me.

"I was too young and immature to understand that you needed some space to figure out what you wanted. Sorry for that too."

"I think we spend most of our lives trying to figure out what we want and who we are. Time we should be spending enjoying who we are and savoring what we have."

"Now that's a winning fortune cookie! So, we know we want normalcy and a walk on the river. Anything else you want tonight?"

I smiled at him as a ship's horn blew in the distance and a slight wind started to ruffle our hair. *Only to go back and change so many things.* But I couldn't go back. Pedro said that all the time. We can't go back, but we can move forward.

"I would love to change so many things over the years," I said. "But I can't do that, can I?"

"No," Trey said. "Time moves on. We can't get it back."

I could never go back to any of those days before my sister died. Never knock on her door and ask why she acted so strange that night I saw her leaving the shower. Nor could I go back a few hours before to the artifacts room. Nor should I. I did what was right for me then even if it led to some painful consequences.

"A friend of mine says we can't go back, but we can move forward."

"That's a nice thought," Trey said.

"It is. And I think he's right. Though not in the way he thinks."

"How so?"

I took a step forward and touched his shoulder. His gaze locked with mine.

"What are we doing, Diana?"

I cupped his face in my hands and pulled him toward me. Our lips met, and I was thrown back in time to that moment when they touched for the first time. This time, though, our kiss was prolonged and passionate, both of us leaning into each other. It seemed like a blissful eternity before we pulled back with his arms still wrapped around me.

"I think it's called kissing, Trey." He smiled at the memory. I leaned in and kissed his cheek, whispering in his ear, "I like to call it moving forward."

"What does that mean?" he asked.

"I don't know yet," I admitted. "But I know it's what I want to do."

Trey linked his fingers through mine.

"Then we'll figure it out. Together."

I lay in bed that night unable to sleep; sheer euphoria flooding through me. Trey had gotten a room a few doors down. We agreed that sharing a room was not the best catalyst for sorting things out at this point. I was surprised how reluctant I was to make that choice and how much I ached when he left to go to his room. Finally acting on my feelings for Trey unleashed a river within me. A river I didn't even know was there. *Delilah, you are such a troublemaker!* My sister carried her own regrets, and I suspected that she was trying to make things right in her own way.

The next morning, we ate breakfast at the hotel and set out for Mr. Francis' home, which turned out to be a nice two story antebellum. Aaron Francis welcomed us warmly. He had aged well. He wore short gray hair and his wrinkled face bore the marks of care, but he seemed active and healthy still. Mr. Francis ushered us into his living room and brought glasses of lemonade for us.

"Excuse the mess. Richard's still going into the office some, but a lot of the overflow ends up here."

I was thinking the house looked immaculate compared to my apartment.

"I remember both of you," he said. "I'm sorry I never got to have you in my classes."

"That's what we wanted to talk to you about, Mr. Francis," I began. "About my sister."

He nodded. "When I saw what happened with Mia Jordan, I knew it was only a matter of time."

"We don't want to bring up painful memories," Trey said. "But we need your help to understand what happened to Dinah."

"I wish I could tell you. I believed Dinah was a very special young lady with so much potential. She glowed on that stage in *The Sound of Music.* I begged your mother to let her do other performances. She refused. Your parents felt threatened by her love for the stage and the life of the mind in general. I sensed that they were looking to her to carry on the family legacy, so to speak."

"I think they had that hope for all of us at one time or another," I said.

"It broke my heart to see it," Mr. Francis said. "When you live your life in secret, not able to share all of who you are, it does something to you after a while. It eats away at who you are."

I knew better than he might think.

"I tried to forget about it and focus on the other students, but I couldn't just let it go. I started to lend Dinah books and connect her with people who had common interests. The internet was still new then, but there were chat rooms where she could get some encouragement and community. She was phenomenal. Loved to learn."

"Why were you meeting with her after school?" I asked.

A shadow passed over his face. "That's where I was not as careful as I should have been. We started meeting off and on her junior year to work on college applications and standardized test prep. She wasn't getting any help from your parents for sure, and our guidance counselor spent most of his time taking naps in his office."

Good old Louisiana education. Gotta love it.

"I know Dinah got into Princeton."

"And Harvard. And Yale." Mr. Francis smiled at my stunned expression. "Those first two were her senior year. She talked to your parents. They were adamant that she wasn't going. She was seventeen with no independent source of income. What could she do? And she was worried about the rest of you. She talked a lot about her concerns for all of you if she left. Who would take care of you? She couldn't let that go no matter how much I told her it wasn't her problem."

My heart was heavy at the thought of Dinah poised on the edge of living her own life and delaying it for us.

"The next year she made it into Princeton. This time with a full ride. And she was eighteen. I told her she couldn't let the opportunity pass. We were meeting again just before she died to work on other sources of funding to cover her room and board. She was hoping to combine that with the money she was making from her job and head off to Princeton in the fall of 96."

"Her job?" Trey and I both said.

"Yes. At Johnson's Feed and Seed. Old Man Johnson excelled at selling and planting, but he was terrible with finances. Almost ran the place into the ground several times. Dinah got a part-time job keeping the books for him."

Trey and I looked at each other. Things were falling into place. That's where Dinah went those evenings we watched Dorcas.

"She went at night?"

"Yes. Johnson would close up in the afternoons and leave all the receipts, a couple of days' worth, for her. She'd make sure everything was tallied and take care of paying any outstanding bills. If she did it as well as she did everything else, Johnson got quite the bargain for what he was paying her."

My mind was reeling. New possibilities were opening before me. My sister lived a separate life unknown to all of us. Relationships and connections we had never considered could be linked to her death.

"What kind of man was Mr. Johnson?"

Trey looked at me curiously. I tried to give him a look that promised to catch him up later.

"There was no better man in Picardy than Arliss Johnson," Mr. Francis smiled at the memory. "When I came out and was forced to leave, he stopped me one day and said, 'Boy, I don't understand that stuff you're into, but you're okay in my book.' That's progress in Picardy, Louisiana."

"And you had to leave because of my sister?"

"Saying it was because of her may be a little strong. But my sexual orientation was outed during the investigation. People were saying that we'd had a sexual relationship and that's why I killed her. To cover it up. I had been seeing someone for several years in secret. He was my alibi for the night Dinah died. Once that came out, people realized that I wouldn't have preyed on Dinah like they were suggesting. Nor could I have physically done her any harm that night since I was out of town."

"But the damage was done," I said.

He nodded.

I gathered my courage and asked, "Mr. Francis, do you harbor any resentment toward or thoughts of revenge against my family?"

He smiled. "I'll be the first to tell you I'm not their biggest fan. Those *Demonologist* movies make them out to be spiritual superheroes of some sort. They're far sexier and sincere on the screen than I find them to be in real life. But I don't harbor any ill will. Even bad things happen for a reason. I needed the push to get out of Picardy and to bring all my life out in the open. I've had a good career, lived a great life, and enjoyed it all with a fantastic partner. What more could I ask?"

We rose and thanked him for his time.

"And thank you for helping my sister. It helps me to know that she had hopes and dreams. And that she knew someone believed in her."

"I'll always remember her as one of the best I ever taught," he said. "Both of you take care of yourselves."

I was quiet as we drove through the mossy tree-covered streets of the Garden District in Trey's green Kia Sport.

"Penny for your thoughts, Herr Doktor."

"That's where she was those nights we were watching Dor."

"Working. Yes, for a little bit. But it only lasted about two or three weeks if I remember. That's a short-lived job."

I nodded.

"Why did she get a ride to work?" Trey asked. "None of us had a license yet. Though I guess Delilah could have and would have driven us in a pinch?"

"She obviously didn't want anyone to know. People in Picardy would talk if they saw the station wagon sitting outside Johnson's Feed and Seed on a regular basis. It was a perfect job for her. She could work after we got home from school and without customers having to know she worked there."

"Why wouldn't she tell you?"

"I think Lucille and Dad were the main ones she wanted to keep in the dark. She probably thought it best not to tell us so we weren't complicit if she got caught. Maybe she thought she would present the completed financial package to them once she'd earned the money and they would agree to let her go."

"Do you think she would have defied them and gone anyway?"

"Once I wasn't so sure. The more I learn, the more I think she would have."

"How would they react to that?"

I knew what he was asking. The question troubled me more than I wanted to say. I was about to answer when a sharp bump threw me forward in my seat.

"What the hell?!" Trey shouted.

A black GMC Sierra had followed us for a while. I remembered seeing it several streets back. As we turned onto Washington Avenue, the truck surged forward and bumped us a second time.

"Once could be accidental," I said. "Twice is not."

Trey nodded and stepped on the accelerator. The truck matched our speed. We were approaching Lafayette Cemetery No. 1 when the truck slammed into us harder. Trey tried to control the Kia, but it swerved toward oncoming traffic. Trey overcorrected, and I felt the car lurch. My world tumbled end over end as the Kia flipped and came to rest on the driver's side. Shattered glass from Trey's window lay scattered all around us. I felt a little blood trickling from my forehead, but everything else seemed intact.

"Out the window!" Trey shouted.

I pressed the button and to my relief my window still descended. Ripping my seat belt off, I pushed myself upwards and wriggled through the open window. I dropped beside the car and wobbled a moment as I fought to get my balance. Trey followed. His face contorted with pain when he landed on the pavement.

"Are you okay, Trey?"

"Fine. Just a sore back and leg. You?"

"I hit my head on something, but I don't think it's too bad."

"What a mess," he said. "We need to call somebody."

The passenger's side mirror exploded just a few inches from my head. A second gunshot rang out, clipping the door. The black truck was coming back. A masked figure sat in the driver's seat, their left hand resting on the wheel. Their passenger, also masked, was leaning out his window. Sunlight glinted off the beretta in his hand.

CHAPTER FOURTEEN

TREY GRABBED MY HAND AND PULLED ME toward the cemetery gate. I didn't need further encouragement. We raced through the gate and entered the expanse of above-ground tombs. White silhouettes surrounded us on every side. We reached a section filled with stately looking mausoleums and crouched behind one of them.

"Let's see how determined they are to find us," Trey said.

We waited in breathless anticipation. Running footsteps caused us both to sink lower behind our cover. Two dark figures met at a cross section of the cemetery walk. They were conversing, but none of their words reached us. Both sported antiquated black ski masks and carried automatic pistols. They were big men, wearing flannel shirts and jeans.

"Bubba's merc brigade," I whispered.

"They won't be able to walk around here long without attracting unwanted attention," Trey said.

Sirens wailed in the distance. Someone had called in our accident. The men looked in the direction where Trey's car lay in the street. Both nodded and started to walk away.

We watched them hurry away. We waited a full twenty minutes before walking cautiously back to the car.

Trey explained the situation to the police. They took his information and gave him the number of a tow service for the car. One officer recorded our description of the two men and promised to get back to us with any updates. We called an uber and settled into the back seat, shaken and full of questions.

When we reached the hotel, Trey got a towel and gently cleaned the small cut on my forehead. I winced as he poured peroxide into the tender flesh.

"You okay?" His anxious eyes studied the cut.

"Fine. It just stings a little."

"That's what we want. No pain, no cleanse. Don't see any glass shavings in your cut. Maybe we should have taken the cops up on their offer to drive us to the hospital?"

"I'm fine. Really." I touched his arm. "Does your back still hurt?"

"It's a tiny bit sore, but nothing's broken. Especially considering the state of the car, we were lucky."

Trey leaned down and kissed my forehead where the cut sliced diagonally like an angry lightning bolt. "I should let you rest."

I watched him put the towel back in the bathroom and walk toward the door. The throbbing from my cut was ebbing, and the shock was wearing off. In its place a profound sense of gratitude settled. Gratitude for life, feeling, and hope accompanied by an intense hunger to live and feel to the fullest.

Trey was opening the door to leave when I stepped beside him and pushed it closed again.

"Stay."

He paused and looked at me with questioning eyes.

"Are you sure?"

"Yes. I've never been more sure of anything in my life."

"I thought we said we'd take our time and figure things out."

"We will. I've just had my second brush with death in a week. Received my third reminder that it could all be over in an instant. Until yesterday, I thought I had done everything I needed to do and, if I died, I could be at peace with that."

"Until yesterday?"

"Until yesterday."

I slipped my arms around his neck and pressed my lips to his.

"It may just be the trauma talking," he said when I pulled back.

"Then let it talk," I whispered.

I kissed him harder and pulled him further into the room. It was awkward at first as we fumbled out of our clothes. We laughed together at our uncoordinated undressing and clumsy journey to the bed. Trey asked what I wanted and was attentive to my responses as we explored each other fully for the first time. It went from awkward to comfortable to good. And then it became something else. We became something else. Something beyond any intimacy I had ever experienced.

An hour later I lay nestled in his arms while the evening shadows lengthened outside.

"And what was that?" he mumbled with a smile.

"Amazing," I whispered.

"It was pretty amazing," he agreed. "We're pretty amazing together."

"Well worth the wait," I said, kissing his shoulder.

"I love you, Debbie and Di. I always have."

"I've always loved you too. More than I ever knew I could love anyone."

"So, have we ruined our friendship?"

I stroked his cheek and looked into his eyes. Those eyes that saw something beautiful in my scraggly dark hair and tattered hand-me-down dress all those years ago.

"I like to think we've deepened our friendship."

"Me too." He propped himself up on his arm and gave me a teasing grin. "Is it safe to say now I've given you something better than M&Ms?"

"I think you underestimate the value of a good M&M," I said with a sly smile.

He playfully grabbed a side pillow and dropped it on my head. I deflected it and mercilessly tickled his chest. We wrestled for a minute before collapsing, panting, in each other's arms again.

"Speaking of M&Ms, are you hungry?"

I nodded. "But I don't really feel like getting back out."

"I'll call for some delivery. Pizza?"

"Sure." I stretched and watched him move across the room. As bizarre as it seemed given all the horrors of the day, I was the most content and relaxed I'd been in years. Everything felt as it should be. I'd only known Trey again for a matter of days, but being with him felt like coming home in a deeper sense than just time or place.

I rolled over and grabbed the remote. I turned the television on and got up to don a t-shirt. Sitting back on the bed, I flipped the channels as Trey ordered over his phone. I jumped past several news channels and a cooking show. Then the picture changed to something more familiar.

Four dark-haired girls stood shivering in a dark basement.

"Is Christine going to hurt us?" the smallest little girl said. It was "Dorcas" as portrayed by Jill Reitsma.

"No, Momma and Daddy will stop her first." Sharla Compton made the same face she always made for pretty much every reaction shot, whether the scene was scary or not.

"I never thought she looked anything like you," Trey said, noticing my dubious entertainment choice.

"Better or worse?"

"Well. I'm a little biased," he said while massaging my shoulders.

Christine suddenly erupted from nowhere. The girls screamed and scattered. The actress Selena Malone stepped in front of Christine. She played Dinah even though she was almost ten years older than Dinah was in real life.

"Now she they cast very well," Trey said. "She looks and sounds so much like Dinah it's scary."

"People say she's one of the hottest celebrity actresses today. I still think Dinah was prettier than her by far."

"Agreed," Trey said.

Dinah/Selena was trying to lure Christine away from the other girls. She stretched her arms out toward Christine. "Come this way, Christine. Come on." Something about the gesture triggered a memory.

I reached up to my shoulders and put my hand on Trey's.

"What's up?"

He leaned down.

"Diana, you look like you've seen a ghost."

"I have," I said.

The next morning, we drove to the offices of Bayou Productions. After a lot of arguing and a few threats, the secretary gave us Selena's local address. Fortunately for us, most of the actors starring in the *Demonologist* movies stayed in New Orleans for much of the year. We drove to her home and knocked for a while before a maid admitted us.

Her ornate living room was a testament to the utility of having a good decorator. Impressionist paintings and silk tapestries from China covered the walls.

"Exotic," Trey said. "What do you think all this stuff is worth?"

"Best money can buy," Selena appeared, wearing a pink halter top and black jogging pants. "Sorry; I'm kind of slumming it. You caught me around workout time."

With her hair up like it was now, she didn't really resemble Dinah all that much. But when she put on the right clothes and styled her hair, there was an eerie similarity.

Selena sat down and looked at me in wonder. "You're Debbie Hebert? Wow! It's great to meet you. I've talked to your parents and younger sister, but I think Delilah's response to my invite was something along the lines of 'Go to hell, Bitch.' Of course, something could be lost in the translation."

"That's my sister," I said.

"You wouldn't have gotten past the front door without that connection," she said. "I'm sorry about what your parents are going through. We've had a total blackout on production for the latest film until this thing gets resolved."

"Yeah, about that," I said. "What have you been up to since production shut down?"

"Oh, you know. Lots of stuff to get ready for. I'm leaving in January for a shoot in Sydney."

"Been to Houston lately?"

Selena paled noticeably.

"Maybe."

"What about Nashville? Picardy?"

"I can't be everywhere."

"Not everywhere," I said. "Just those particular places."

"Look, I thought this was about the films. Or some fan stuff. I don't need to go over my whole itinerary with you."

"It's probably best if you do," I said.

"Why?"

"Because it's either with us or the police," Trey said.

Selena's creamy white complexion, so much like my sister's, turned even paler. "Look. They said it was a promotional thing. A studio stunt to amp up for the next movie. I thought all of you were in on it. That it was being filmed the whole time by someone on a phone or small camera."

I was up and cleared the space between me and Selena before Trey realized what was happening. He barely managed to grab my hand before I delivered a vicious slap to Selena's face.

"No! Diana, don't!"

I allowed him to pull me away. Selena shrank against the plush chair she occupied.

"My dad almost died because of you!"

"I'm sorry," she said. "I didn't know until your dad had his heart attack. That's when I realized you guys weren't in on it. I thought he was faking all that too until I saw the news reports that night."

"That was you in the woods that night?"

"Yes."

"Did you push me into the river?"

"What?" She looked confused. "No! Of course not!"

"Who put you up to this?" Trey asked.

"I never saw him. Just spoke to him on the phone several times. He said he was an executive with the studio in California. Gave me the name Jim Larson. It checked out when I called the studio. He must have really done his homework. He would leave information about places where I could pick up all the stuff I needed for each ... performance."

"What did the 'stuff' include?" Trey asked.

"Special effects gear, instructions complete with place and script, a microphone for projecting my voice long distances and an earpiece he could use to give me instructions on the spot."

"Did he provide you with replicas of the purple top and white skirt that Dinah was wearing?" I was trying to hold in my fury.

"No. I already had those."

"Those?"

"I've got a bunch of those outfits."

"Why?"

"For the next movie. The projected title our publicists put out there is just a placeholder. We're actually adapting *Devil's Circle* next."

My knees buckled, and I found myself falling back onto the couch.

"*Devil's Circle!* Who greenlit that?"

"Your mom."

Trey placed a steadying hand on my shoulder. He was trying to calm me, but one look at his flushed face revealed how furious he was himself.

"She didn't have permission from anyone else to do that," I said.

Selena shrugged.

"That part's not my business. I just learn the lines, do a little research, and get into costume. I'm really sorry about messing with your family. Maybe I should have checked it out more."

"Maybe," I said sarcastically. "What about the blood?"

"Blood packets. Just syrup and dye. We've already been doing some pre-production special effects work. Whoever set this up didn't just fool me. There were two or three makeup artists and special effects people in the loop too."

I didn't want to ask why they needed the blood packets. Hearing her say it out loud was more than I could take at this moment. They were planning to film my sister's death scene. Not the real one. It was visceral and bloody enough. The horrible, extended version envisioned by Lucille in *Devil's Circle* was even worse. Tears were stinging my eyes.

Selena saw them. Tears sprang into her own eyes in response.

"I'm so sorry. Please forgive me. Playing your sister is an honor for me. I hate the idea that I've tarnished her in any way."

"There is nothing you could ever do to diminish my sister in any way," I said. The words came out harsher than I meant.

Selena started to cry harder. Trey took my arm and shook his head.

"She's guilty of being too gullible. Who of us hasn't made that mistake?" he said gently to me.

"I know. You're right. Selena, is there anything else you can tell us about this person? Anything about his voice that stands out?"

Selena wiped her eyes and tried to focus. "His accent is very southern. Unless he's faking it, he's from down here. He kind of rolls his r's in a funny way if you listen close."

Trey leaned closer to her. His eyes were afire with sudden inspiration.

"Selena, have you told him you know he's not connected to the studio yet?"

"No. I haven't talked to him since that awful night last week. That's how it goes with him. You won't hear from him for a few days, and then there he is."

I could see what Trey was thinking.

"Can you keep it to yourself for a little while longer?"

"Hell, yes," she shuddered. "I have plenty of security, but I still don't want anything to do with a psycho who would go to those lengths to hurt someone. Besides, who would I tell? As far as I can see he hasn't really hurt the studio aside from the harm he's done to your family."

"I'm going to air drop you my number," I said. Selena was already reaching for her phone. "When and if he calls again, can you let us know?"

"I will," she promised. "I helped make this mess; I want to help clean it up if I can."

"Thank you, Selena," Trey said.

She looked at me with such vulnerability that I was reminded how young she was to be navigating this very adult world. *Kind of like Dinah.*

"Thank you, Selena. I appreciate your being honest with us. And all your help."

She nodded. "I know you don't like what we do with your story in our movies. Delilah made that clear. I just hope maybe you'll take some comfort in the fact that you and your parents are heroes to people you will never meet. They tell me all the time how much you inspire them."

"I'm not comfortable being a living myth, Selena."

"Sometimes it takes a myth to help people be better."

Once we were seated back inside my car, Trey said, "Now she gets the prize for best fortune cookie saying this week."

"She gets honorable mention."

"You're just jealous, Dr. Chambers."

"You better learn your place, Mister. A man in desperate need of a ride home should learn to respect his driver."

"Great. You get my car smashed, and now you're threatening to take my ride away. The least you can do is give me a car ride."

"I already gave you something better than a car ride this week," I said seductively.

"You're going to place a car ride on the same level as M&Ms?"

"You're going to place M&Ms on the same level as our first time together?"

"I see this is descending into a conversation I can't possibly win."

I reached over and patted his knee. "It's not descending. It never was a conversation you could win."

He laughed and turned to view the dazzling cityscape as we sped past. We rode in comfortable silence as the expansive causeway gave way to forested swamp land. A green sign greeted us reading: PICARDY 55.

"I just realized the most challenging thing about our blossoming relationship," I said.

"What's that?" Trey asked.

"I'm going to have to tell Delilah she was right."

CHAPTER FIFTEEN

DECEMBER 24/25, 1995

"You think you're always right, Delilah!"

"Because I am!"

We were wrestling over the Christmas lights on the front porch. Delilah had insisted on putting them up with duct tape despite my suggestion that nails would be better. Louisiana humidity had done its worst by Christmas Eve and now our lights were lying across the porch. They fell even though we'd enjoyed a few days of colder weather. We'd even gotten a few snow flurries on the 23, the rarest of rarities for Picardy.

"We need Trey to help us. He might be here if you hadn't chased him off."

"I ... didn't ... chase ... him ... off," I said as I pounded a nail into the porch overhang. "I don't need Trey's help or yours to do this. Trey and I are fine. We're just taking some time to figure things out."

I claimed to be fine with things, but I noticed the nail I'd just pounded in would need to come out a little. It was buried all the way to the head. I'd also chipped the overhang in my fury.

"Let me tell you about the ways of men and women, Sweetheart." Delilah didn't realize she was using one of Trey's favorite words from his Bogart imitation. It drove another stake into my heart.

We'd tried to talk, and we just kept going around in circles. Then we'd opted for ignoring the problem, which led to its own complications. Trey still came around, but there was a definite change in our dynamic. I didn't know how to get back to where we were before that night in the artifacts room.

"Debbie! Delilah! Come inside and wash up. Momma and Daddy will be home soon!"

"Okay," I shouted back, removing two nails from my mouth.

Another problem added to the list. Dinah was back most of the time after that weird two and a half weeks of disappearing three nights a week. But she wasn't really back. Something was different about her. She continued to be uber competent and caring as always, but her vivacity and joy were diminished. Dinah seemed distracted and thoughtful more often. I caught her peering into the distance with a sad look on her face several times.

When Dinah saw me, she would force a reassuring smile. Reassuring smiles by their nature lose all power when forced. I was not reassured. I was afraid. It seemed like everything was going haywire. Trey, Dinah, and the damn Christmas lights were all upending my world. About the only thing I felt I could count on was Delilah being annoying. That came twenty-four seven with a side of irritation.

We tramped into the kitchen where Dinah and Dorcas were making cookies. Dorcas held a dough-covered finger up for me to lick.

"Hey, Debbie! Want some cookie dough?"

"Gross! I'm not gonna lick that off your hand."

"I will," she popped her finger into her mouth.

We had dinner that night. The chattering of little girls fills a room like few things do. Young women, I corrected myself. As I looked around the table, I realized only Dorcas could really claim that title anymore. We were growing up with all the pain and joy that involved. Dinah was looking off into the distance again like the cares of the world were on her shoulders. Then she noticed me. Once again, we performed our ritual of glance and reassuring smile. *What's bothering you, Dinah?*

As Momma and I scraped the plates after dinner, Dorcas bounded into the kitchen.

"Debbie, Trey's outside."

I walked to the front door. Trey was standing on the porch with a colorfully wrapped package in hand. His parents were sitting in the car with the engine running. I waved to them and accepted the package from Trey.

"Little gift for you, Sweetheart," Trey said as Bogart.

"Thanks," I said. "Dorcas! Can you bring Trey's gift?"

"Sure! I've been shakin' it, Trey. I don't think it's clothes. That's good."

We exchanged a smile at Dorcas' childlike wonder.

"How are you?"

"Good. We just finished dinner. About to open presents."

"No cases tonight? Any drug fiends busting up the fun?"

"Not yet."

"Hopefully not."

Dorcas shoved Trey's present into his chest so hard he grunted and exhaled.

"Thanks, Dor," he said.

"Welcome!" she shouted and skipped away, oblivious to anything but the pile of presents waiting under the glittering tree.

"Well," he said. "My parents are waiting in the car. We're on our way to Grandma's. Shouldn't keep them waiting."

"Cool," I said. *Cool?* Departures had gotten awkward for us.

"See you later. And Merry Christmas!"

"Merry Christmas!"

I heard Delilah inside saying, "Trey's leaving! Hurry!"

I heard a flurry of feet as I watched Trey walk back to his car.

"Come on, Dinah!" Delilah hissed. They all came out to stand beside me on the porch.

"One ... Two ... Three," Delilah counted.

"Bye, Trey!" We all shouted in unison.

Trey grinned and bowed. He took one last look back at me as he opened the car door and smiled. I could see in his eyes the same longing to bridge the distance I felt. *How can it be so hard when you both want it so badly?* I felt a strange sense of comfort wash over me. Somehow, we would get back to each other. I didn't know how, but I believed it with all my heart.

We opened presents that night. Dorcas scurried around us all. Once she tore the wrapping from her own gifts, she ran around "helping" us with ours too. I opened Trey's gift. A little gold locket embossed with the word: FOREVER. I wasn't quite sure what forever meant, but I decided to take it as the peace offering he meant it to be. My parents bought us assorted clothes and a "fun" present or two.

"What is this? It looks like it came from the Amish collection," Delilah complained, holding up a sweater that Carrie White's mother would have picked for her daughter.

"The Amish are a people of strong faith and humble modesty," Momma said. "You would be lucky to be mistaken for them."

Delilah moaned and fell into my lap. "She's killing me. One fashion disaster at a time."

I ruffled her hair, leading to further exclamations about how one couldn't maintain a good "do" in backwards Picardy.

Finally, my daddy winked at me and said, "Dor, you better get upstairs. Santa Claus is already on his way."

Dorcas screamed and bounded up the stairs, a flurry of wrapping paper and boxes flying in her wake.

Momma shook her head, trying to look disapproving. She failed as the ghost of a smile spread across her lips. The Santa Claus debate waged fast and furious in our house for a year or two when Dinah was a baby. Daddy was determined that his daughters would enjoy the same family Christmases he had, complete with Santa's gifts on Christmas morning. Momma questioned the idea of "filling kids minds with myths and fables." Daddy won by spreading a bounty of gifts across the living room for three-year-old Dinah that delighted her and convinced Momma to share the joy of Christmas morning.

We each said goodnight and went to brush our teeth. Delilah and I settled into bed. She drifted off to sleep, and soon the rhythmic sound of her breathing filled the room. I was wired for some reason. My tossing and turning produced no rest. I heard Momma and Daddy open the front door downstairs and head for the barn about midnight. They'd bought Dor a new bicycle and a dollhouse with "some assembly required." I sneaked to the window and watched them go into the barn, Daddy in his long johns and heavy jacket and Momma in her long blue robe with house shoes. Winter had arrived in Picardy. I could see Daddy's breath as he held the door for Momma. They went inside, and the door closed behind them.

I got a glass of water downstairs and returned to my bed. Sleep had started to pull me under when another sound snapped me awake. I heard Dinah's door open. She softly walked past our rooms and down the stairs. I heard her open the front door and go outside. Curiosity overcame my exhaustion. I scrambled to my feet and hurried back to the window. Dinah wore her robe open with a sweater and jogging pants beneath it. She walked across the yard to the barn door. She stopped and seemed to be collecting herself like she did that night I saw her go into the office with my parents. Dinah eased the barn door open and slipped inside.

I slipped back in bed and went to sleep. My slumbers were shattered by screams and shouts. I opened my sleepy eyes and looked into Delilah's wide ones across the room.

"What the hell?" she whispered.

I was too scared to note her breach of proper Hebert language. Multiple voices were shouting and screaming outside. The freak show had come to town, as Trey liked to say. I assumed there was a deliverance ministry session going on downstairs.

"They're casting a demon out of somebody," I mumbled.

"It must be pretty bad for them to take the person out to the barn," Delilah said.

I nodded and rolled over, trying to cover my ears with a pillow.

"Just once why don't you try giving a damn about me and what I need!"

My eyes snapped open again. That wasn't some random deliverance client. It was Dinah. Using very un-Dinah like language. I turned back to the window.

"I didn't think she had it in her," Delilah said.

"Come back here, and let's talk about this!" Momma screamed.

"It seems you're done talking," Dinah yelled. "Do you care about any of us?"

"Child, you don't have any idea what all we do for ..."

"You don't have any idea what I do!"

"Obviously not since you decide to hide things from us!"

"Lucille!" Daddy's voice was sharp.

"Come back here, Young Lady!" Momma screamed.

"I'm not a 'Young Lady.' I'm a woman. I'm eighteen years old, and if you won't believe me or help me, I'll help myself."

Delilah and I were frozen in place. We heard the door of the station wagon slam.

"Denny, stop her!"

"She needs some time to calm down, Lucille. We all do." The rest of what he said was inaudible to us.

The station wagon cranked, and we heard it drive off. The squeaky hinges of the barn door told us our parents had gone back inside. Delilah and I didn't speak. We had no idea what to say. I finally dropped asleep.

I woke the next morning to Dorcas' screams and shouts. She galloped down the stairs to see what Santa brought while the rest of us slowly followed in her wake. While Delilah started downstairs, I made my way to Dinah's room. I was terrified I would open the door and there would be no sign of my sister. Relief poured over me when I saw her standing in front of the bathroom sink in her nightgown.

"Merry Christmas, Dinah!" I didn't know what else to say.

"Merry Christmas, Debbie."

"You going downstairs for breakfast?"

"I think I may skip breakfast. Not feeling the best. But I'll be down for coffee in a few."

"Okay. Love you."

"Love you, Debbie."

I walked to the top of the stairs and looked back. Dinah's head was bowed over the sink. I continued down the stairs, feeling like my whole world was more unsettled than ever.

CHAPTER SIXTEEN

An Excerpt from

DEVIL'S CIRCLE (1996)

by Lucille B. Hebert

Denny wrestled the dollhouse from its box while Lucille rolled the pink bicycle to the front door of the barn.

"You'd think these things would be easier to put together than a car engine," Denny said.

"Isn't it?" Lucille asked.

"No," he said with a smile.

Lucille stepped over and held the two main sections of the house together while Denny tightened the screws binding them.

"Fits good," Denny said.

"Fits well," Lucille said.

"It fits." Denny said with a teasing smile.

Lucille shook her head and reached for the next piece. She paused when the barn door squeaked behind them.

"Dinah! What are you doing up?"

Dinah didn't respond to Denny's question. Her eyes were glazed and red. She stepped forward almost like she was sleepwalking.

"Dinah," Lucille said.

Dinah turned and fixed a hostile stare at Lucille. Lucille stood unmoving, startled to see Dinah act this way.

"You never cared about me. You don't care about any of us. We could all die for all you care!"

"Dinah! Don't speak to your momma that way."

"They're going to kill us all. Because of you," Dinah's tone was low and menacing.

Lucille had never heard her use it before. Her hand slowly rose from her side. A kitchen knife gleamed under the single light of the barn.

"What are you doing with that, Dinah?" Denny eased his screwdriver to the ground and crawled slowly toward Dinah.

Dinah raised the knife to her neck. "Goodbye, Daddy."

"No!" Lucille screamed. "By the power of Christ, we command you to let her go!"

Dinah's arm shook, but the knife remained in place.

"By the blood of Jesus and in his name! Release her!" Lucille's commands were having an effect. Dinah's face distorted as whatever was controlling her began to lose its grip.

"Momma, help me!" she pleaded.

"We're coming, Angel." Denny moved closer.

Dinah's face went hard again. "Your interference will cost you this one."

A trickle of blood started running down Dinah's throat as she applied slight pressure.

"The power of Christ compels you, Demon!" Lucille said.

For a split second, the hand holding the knife wavered. Denny jumped and grabbed Dinah, making sure to secure the hand holding the knife and pull it away. The knife clattered to the barn floor. Denny and Dinah collapsed together. Once they hit the ground, the enchantment was broken. Dinah sobbed into Denny's chest as he gripped her tightly.

"What was wrong with me, Daddy?"

"I'm not sure, Angel. But we're going to find out."

Lucile joined them and wrapped her arms around them both. They took Dinah upstairs and got her settled in her bed. Lucille tucked her in and closed the door once she was asleep.

Denny was shaken. "We can't lose her, Lucille. She's not possessed. She can't be with all the protections we have here."

"What about a curse? I know she's been sneaking off to hang out with other kids. What if someone placed a hex on her?"

"It's possible," Denny agreed.

"We need to find out where she's been and who she's been around before this gets worse. She could hurt herself or one of the other girls."

Denny nodded. "I'll talk to her some more tomorrow when she's more lucid. See if she can tell me anything that will help us figure it out."

"I'll try to use my abilities to see if I can see anything. Maybe pick up some items from her room and vision cast."

They started for the stairs, passing the rooms of their girls. Four little dark-haired girls sleeping soundly, dreaming dreams of Christmas morning. Innocent and content. Lucille prayed that God would protect them from the storms to come.

CHAPTER SEVENTEEN

WE PASSED THE MCMARTIN VULTURE CAMP as dusk settled over our little homestead. It had grown quite a bit in our absence. Even with the window up, I could hear several people say, "It's Deborah." I shook my head in disgust. *That will be fun for a while.* Several reporters blocked our way. I had to lay on the horn, and Trey had to shout at them to move before they finally cleared the way.

"You sure you want to take my car tomorrow? You'll probably be followed all day."

"I really don't have much choice. I hate to take Mom's, and I need to get to school early tomorrow. You sure you don't mind me taking it?"

"No. Dorcas and I will be going to all the same places anyway."

"Hopefully, the shop in New Orleans will have mine ready by the end of the week."

Dorcas was sitting in the living room when we entered, her foot propped on an ottoman and a steaming cup of tea in her hands. She looked overjoyed to see us. I imagined the house had to be unbearably quiet without our parents here.

"I got them settled at the Hightower's house. Tammy said they could stay for a week or two. So far nobody's traced them there. That probably won't last long."

"Thanks, Dor. We have a lot to catch you up on."

"I'm gonna go and let you handle that," Trey said. "Have to be up early tomorrow."

"Okay. Thanks, Trey. For everything."

"I'll see you tomorrow night. Be careful, Diana."

"I will."

Trey leaned in and kissed me. I responded without thinking. It was only when he smiled and headed for the door that I turned to see Dor staring at us with her teacup halfway to her mouth. Her surprised expression morphed into a Cheshire cat grin.

"I guess you do need to catch me up."

I smiled and walked to the door to watch Trey drive away.

"What's this?"

The eternal question, Dor.

"I'm not sure, Dor. We have a lot to talk about still. He has kids. He's here. I'm in Nashville. I still have unresolved issues with Pedro. We have this mess with Daddy and Lucille." Logical Diana was making an unwelcome appearance in the midst of our whirlwind two-day romance. "It probably doesn't make much sense."

Dorcas smiled at me. I never appreciated until the last few days how pure and unconditional her love for me, for all of us, had always been, even when I had not returned it well.

"There are so many things right now that don't make sense," she said. "There has never been anything that makes more sense than you and Trey. It's about time. The rest is just about details. You'll figure it out if it's meant to be."

"Meant to be? Is that even a thing, Dor?"

"How can I see the two of you together and not believe it?"

We moved to the hard part of the conversation. She was encouraged to hear Mr. Francis' stories about Dinah, horrified by the attack on us, and furious when I told her about Selena's portrayal of "Ghost Dinah." I talked her down from calling a lawyer and explained Selena's promise to call us if her mysterious employer contacted her again.

Dorcas' turn came next, and she didn't disappoint. She'd decided to handle things from the other direction by starting with Mia's death since she had been there that night and knew the Jordans. She had visited the Jordans on Monday morning and learned several surprising details.

"You know she never told them who the father of those babies was? And she was pregnant before she had the first one."

"Three pregnancies? What happened to the first?"

"A miscarriage in the first three months. She spent several days in the hospital. They hoped she would get better after that, but she just went into a total tailspin."

"Who do they think the father of her babies was?" I asked.

"Well, there was a football coach that was a bit of a perv. Reggie Moreland is his name. He often had girls in his office, and people said they've also seen him at the local teen hangouts acting like he's just one of the crew. Girls have left with him in his car."

"Gross. The Jordans thought it was him?"

"Suspected. But never had any proof. The only person who seemed to help Mia was Pastor Dixon. He spends a lot of time with the youth at Grace. Mrs. Jordan said he always came to check up on Mia and would meet her for counseling sessions at the church or in town."

"How dedicated," I said sarcastically. "Did you ask Mr. Jordan about the lost time on the video?"

"Yes. He said only two people came in during that time and he never left."

"And those two people were?"

"Pastor Dixon ..." My curiosity was aroused.

"... and Daddy." My heart skipped a beat.

"After that everyone else came in for the final part that we saw," Dorcas said.

It didn't look good. If Mr. Jordan were present the whole time, it was hard to see how anyone could interfere without his consent. And, of the two people who did come in, one was my dad. Most people would suspect him over Eric Dixon. And could we really rely on Mr. Jordan's testimony? He might have his own motives for getting rid of his troubled daughter.

"I spent the rest of Monday and part of today with another unsavory task," Dorcas said.

"Which was?"

Dorcas picked up the remote and turned on the TV. She cast YouTube from her phone. Eric Dixon appeared wearing what looked like military-style boots and a camouflage t-shirt.

"Is this a wild game supper outreach?" I asked.

"If only, My Dear. No, this is Sunday morning worship."

"We need men to be strong warriors for the family," Dixon shouted. "We need women to be submissive handmaids of the Lord. Anything less rejects God's design for us all. Too many of you women don't keep yourselves groomed and fit for your husbands like you should. You need to be ready to give him a good restful home when he returns from fighting the battles of the Lord."

"There's a man looking to get castrated," I observed.

"There are reams of it, Diana. Sermon after sermon. He says some icky stuff about what he and his wife do before, during, and after sex."

I suppressed a laugh. Dorcas remained the only thirty-something woman in the world who could say "icky" and it seem perfectly fitting.

"He preached a whole sermon on masturbation," Dorcas said. Her eyes were wide as only she could make them.

"Is he for it or against it?"

"I don't know. I stopped halfway through. I also did some digging into his past. You know his dad was a pastor in town too. Not at Grace. His dad was at Calvary Church. He stayed there for almost thirty years."

I remembered hearing of the Dixons, but I hadn't really known their family well at all.

"He must not have had any brothers or sisters. I don't remember any Dixons in my class."

"He was an only child. His mom worked in obstetrics and gynecology at the hospital. She was a Bertrand."

My eyebrows raised. That name I did know. The Bertrands got rich on oil money in the early twentieth century, invested well, and got out before things went bad in the early eighties. They maintained a lavish lifestyle, coming as close as Picardy had to a country club set.

"The family can't have appreciated her marriage to a minister. Even one as influential as Dixon's dad was."

"That's the kind of thing you have to read between the lines," Dorcas said. "Nothing in the records to suggest there were any serious fights. All this stuff in the sermons bothers me, Diana. We have definite standards for women's conduct and dress, marriage relationships and all that in our church, but women serve and teach, too. All this talk about women being subservient to men is new to me."

"The scary thing is what sometimes accompanies it," I said. "The Bible's a tricky book. There are places where it upholds the dignity and worth of women, of all humans. But there's a lot of misogynist language in other biblical passages that can be used to justify all kinds of abusive behavior toward women."

"I do know the Bible pretty well myself, Professor," Dorcas said. She said it lightly, a mild rebuke with no bitterness.

I realized how condescending I could come off sometimes and was glad she took it well.

"Sorry, Dor. I slip too easily into lecture mode. Professional hazard. We're hearing all kinds of stories right now about sexual abuse in churches. A few people were brave enough to come forward, and now the floodgates are opening."

"That's horrible," Dorcas said. "How do you study all this and not get completely cynical?"

"Who says I'm not?" I replied.

"Maybe you are some. But not like Delilah."

I grinned, "Nobody is like Delilah. Although I should probably be nice to Delilah for a while since she gave me a helpful push with Trey."

Several more clips revealed that Eric Dixon was quite the showman. He dressed up in costumes many Sundays, including a construction worker and Uncle Sam. He took a turn playing bass guitar in the praise band one Sunday. His leadership style was typical of many megachurch pastors I'd observed across the country. Grace Bible in Picardy was in no danger of becoming a megachurch anytime soon, but it seemed like Dixon wanted to play with the big boys. And, given the power of social media, men like Dixon could build an online following far out of proportion to the size of their actual congregation.

"And he was the monitor on the night of the exorcism? I have to say I agree with a lot of his warnings about the dangers of spiritual warfare obsessions, but I find a lot of what he says about women hard to take."

"I find it all hard to take. They need to visit Trinity Assembly and see how it's done."

I didn't want to get anywhere near the topic of Trinity Assembly of God and "how it should be done."

"What's next?"

She checked her phone. "I set up a Zoom conversation with Terence Dearman. He works the nightshift. We planned for nine tonight."

"Look at you being all tech savvy, Dor." She actually blushed a little, and then her face clouded. "There's one more thing I need to tell you. Actually, one more thing I need to show you. I was getting some things for Momma out of her dresser and found this."

Dorcas passed me a document. It was official in style and bore the heading: **OFFICIAL REQUEST FOR EXHUMATION**. I read several lines before it hit me what I was reading. Everything in me rebelled against reading the words in the blanks, all of which were filled in. The date read November 2. The "Subject" line read: DINAH LUCILLE HEBERT. The signature line read: DENNIS WALLACE HEBERT. I'd seen my daddy's handwriting enough to know that it was his authentic signature.

"Dear God," I could feel the color draining from my own face.

"This year, Diana. Just a few weeks ago Daddy filled this out. He wanted to dig Dinah up. Why would he do that? And it looks like Momma tried to hide the document or something? Why would they do that? Either of them."

I thought I might know. "There's one more thing I haven't told you, Dor." I gave her the news about the *Devil's Circle* adaptation.

Dorcas' mouth dropped open and her face flushed. "She can't do that. We've talked about how we would never let them make that one into a movie. We all agreed. I don't know why she even wrote that book. It's the only one I struggled to read. It's too personal and graphic."

Her response mirrored my own. I had nightmares for weeks reliving Dinah's death through Lucille's prose when I finally forced myself to read *Devil's Circle*.

"So why would Daddy want to exhume Dinah?"

"I have all kinds of guesses. But I think we're just going to have to ask them both."

"That didn't seem to help you and Delilah at the hospital." Once again, she was right.

We tried to talk of other things for a while until our Zoom appointment at nine. The two of us gathered around my laptop and opened a room. Soon a notification dinged, and a black man a little older than me materialized on the screen. His face was lined with slight wrinkles. His hair had started to gray at the temples. He started to speak, and a loud crash interrupted him. He gave us a sheepish smile and held his hand up as if to say, "Just a minute."

"Reginald! Deandra! I got a Zoom call going on in here. Keep it quiet."

His wife's voice filtered in from the next room, "Get back in here and leave your daddy alone."

Dorcas and I both grinned at the familiar chaos of a bustling household.

"Sorry, ladies. Kids and all. It's good to see you again. I wouldn't recognize you if I didn't know it was you. You were just little girls when I was growin' up in Picardy."

"Thank you for your time, Mr. Dearman."

"Terence. Mr. Dearman's my dad."

"I saw your dad the other day. He's looking well. I didn't get to talk to him though. Need to go by and see him before I leave town."

"He's looking good and stubborn as ever. Tell him all the time he'd be looking better if he ate more salad and less gumbo."

"Wouldn't we all," Dorcas said.

"Terence," I said. "We understand that the police called you in for questioning about our sister's death. A lot of people around here suspected you for a while. Why was that?"

Terence sighed, bowed his head for a moment, and willed himself to go back to those dark days.

"Well," he began. "I could tell you it's because no good deed goes unpunished. Or I could tell you that it's because I was a young black man growing up in a white world. Both of those are true. The official reason given was that I brought her home that night."

"Brought her home?" I'd never really thought about how Dinah got home that night. We had all been out earlier. I knew she had the station wagon and just assumed she'd driven it back.

"Yeah. I was hanging out with friends along with all the rest of the town. Started back home pretty late. Was probably close to 2:00. I'm riding down the road toward our place, and I see a car pulled off on the side of the road. I realized it was your station wagon, so I pulled over to see if maybe Mr. Denny needed some help."

He grew quiet and reached up to wipe his eye. Dorcas reached over and took my hand. I gripped it hard.

"She had her head on the steering wheel and was moaning in pain. I opened the door. She looked kind of wild-eyed at first, but then she seemed to recognize me. She said, 'Terence, something's wrong with me. I don't know what. Can you get me home or to the hospital?'"

He paused again.

"How much do you really want to know?"

I exchanged a glance with Dorcas, swallowed, and said, "Everything you can tell us."

"I put my arm around her and eased her out of the car. Blood was everywhere. All over the driver's seat. You could see it all down her because of her white skirt. I got it all over me and all over my truck. One of the reasons why they had me come down."

"What was the nature of the wound?"

"Wound?"

"Yes. It was a stab wound?"

He shook his head. "No. It wasn't. It was coming from ... down there."

It took me a second to understand what "down there" meant for Terence. Dorcas seemed a little confused still.

"Terence, I don't mean to be crude. But are you saying Dinah was bleeding from her vagina?"

"Yeah. That's it. Sorry. But it wasn't normal like ladies have every month. I'm no expert, then or now, but even as a kid I knew it was too much. I've been in the room when both of my kids were born, and now I can tell you for sure that it was too much. Something was wrong on the inside, just like they said."

"You got her into your truck?" I had to ask the questions because Dorcas' lower lip was trembling, and I could see she was on the verge of losing it.

"I did. It was very slow going. My old truck didn't have good shocks. We bounced a lot, and she moaned with every bump. I was scared to death that she would die right there in my truck."

"You headed for our house?"

Terence bowed his head. "We did. Looking back, I should have headed straight for the hospital. But your house was less than a mile away. She almost got there herself. And, well, ..."

I could tell how hard it was for him to say, so I said it for him.

"You were a young black man with a bleeding white woman in your car."

"Yeah," he said. "I had nightmare images of what would happen if I brought her in. I figured your daddy could do it or the ambulance would run out and get her. So, I pulled into your front yard. Your daddy was outside and saw me coming with her in my arms. I've never seen a man rocked so hard. He opened the door to the kitchen. She had like a spasm or something, and I almost dropped her. I laid her on the kitchen table for a few minutes while they got a bed ready."

I closed my eyes, fighting to block out the images and voices from that night that were tearing at my mind.

"I think maybe one of you came in while she was on the table. Your momma pulled you out. Then they scooped her up and took her to the bed. She was saying all kinds of stuff by then. Not really making sense. I called the ambulance and headed back up to the road to wait for them. They came flying in a few minutes later, and we all ran inside."

He paused again.

Dorcas was weeping quietly beside me. My own vision was clouding.

"Go on," I said with a shaky voice.

"We heard screaming and crying as soon as we opened the door. Mr. Denny and Ms. Lucille both. And then one of you came down, and I heard feet running back up. Pretty soon we could hear y'all crying upstairs."

Delilah had disobeyed orders, and she paid the price by being the one to tell the rest of us our sister was gone.

"They tried to revive her, but it was too late."

I steadied myself. "How do you think Dinah died, Terence?"

"I'm not a doctor."

"What would your guess be?"

"She was losing too much blood and going into shock. I think they said it was heart failure in the end. I could buy that as the reason she died, but there was something else wrong that caused that. It was like something was attacking her from the inside."

"Do you believe in magic, Terence?"

He laughed, surprised at the unexpected question. "Well, I'm supposed to be a sophisticated city man now. But you know the stories and tall tales we grew up with in those swamps. Who's to say what's out there? My daddy's been known to dabble in a little Hoodoo on the side. All while serving as a deacon at the African Methodist Episcopal Church."

A sudden thought struck me. I could see a black man smiling at us, amused as four girls ran from a grove not so far from where we sat. *Sam.* I laughed, happy to have something to lighten the dark conversation. Dorcas looked at me, and I whispered, "Tell you later."

"But if you're asking if Satanists killed your sister? I think that's a load of bull. Always have."

"Terence," Dorcas returned to the conversation. "Do you remember any of what Dinah said?"

"A little. She didn't talk much at all in the truck. When she saw your daddy, she started asking him to help her over and over. We laid her on the table, and your momma bent over her. She screamed, 'Momma, I need a doctor. Help Momma.' And your momma said, 'It's okay, we're going to get whatever this is out of you.' She panicked then and kept saying she needed a hospital, not an exorcism. Your momma left to get the bed ready. That's when one of you walked in, I think, and she was yelling that they were killing her, letting her die."

I shuddered and tried to block out her screams in my head. Tried and failed as I always did.

"Your momma came in and pulled the sister out. She kept repeating stuff over and over until they came to get her."

"What was she repeating?" Dorcas asked.

Terence searched his memory for a moment. "So stupid ... so stupid ... should have known better ... Pepsi ... Pepsi ... God, please don't leave me."

I wrote the words down as he said them. My brow furrowed as I read over them.

"I know," Terence said, reading my expression even through Zoom. "I could never make any sense out of it. Mr. Denny said he wasn't sure what she was saying."

"You told my daddy everything she said?"

That didn't surprise me at all. What surprised me came next.

"Yeah. About two months ago. He called me. Wanted me to repeat all of it to him like I am with you."

I felt Dorcas' hand tighten on mine. *What was Daddy up to?*

"Thank you, Terence," I said. "It was good to talk with you again."

"You too. You ladies take care. I hope you find what you're after."

We sat in silence after the call ended.

"Diana," Dorcas sobbed, bringing the silence to an end. "I don't know if I can do this."

"Do what?"

"I don't know if I can go wherever it leads. Will we ever see Daddy and Momma the same again? Will we ever see anything the same?"

Good questions. And I didn't have answers to any of them.

"Nothing's ever the same, Sweetie." I hadn't used that nickname for her since she was a little girl, but it seemed right. "Change is scary. It can be painful. But it can also make things better."

Dorcas laid her head on my shoulder, and I put my arm around her. Eventually my head rested on hers, and we sat contemplating the past and the future.

CHAPTER EIGHTEEN

CHIP WAS, WELL, A CHIP OFF THE OLD BLOCK. He didn't resemble his dad as much physically, but he definitely had Trey's witty personality. The two of them together kept us laughing the entire evening. Brandy was a bookish and quieter teen with long brown hair. I could see Trey in her face even better in person than in her picture.

Trey introduced me as his oldest and best friend. Chip took it at face value and ran with it all night. Brandy, older and more perceptive, knew there was more to us than just friends. I noticed her watching me with a probing air throughout the night. She paid particular attention when Trey and I interacted with each other. It struck me at one point that Brandy was approaching the same age Trey and I were the year my sister died. I was nervous around her and felt like I was awkward the whole time, but she seemed cautiously open to me by the end of the night.

We'd gone out for hamburgers and shakes, then stopped by a small bowling alley that had just opened in town. I was rusty to say the least. Trey and Brandy had fun at my expense as I cleaned the gutter for much of the evening.

"That's okay, Diana. Dad says we're all still learning," Chip said.

"Thanks, Chip," I said. "I've got a lot left to learn. Will you teach me?"

"You bet," he grinned. So much like Trey. Always looking out for the underdog, sharing M&Ms with lonely little girls.

We pulled up to my house at about 11 on Saturday evening. I noticed a car I didn't recognize parked in the drive.

"Have a great night, Diana. Thanks for coming," Trey said.

"You too," I smiled and got out. We'd decided against any public displays of affection in front of his kids until we were sure where things were going.

"Bye, Diana," Chip said, "Keep practicing."

"Will do, Chip," I said, "Bye, Brandy."

"Bye, Diana. It was nice to meet you." I was relieved that she seemed sincere. I'd grown up with sisters, but I wasn't sure how good I was with kids anymore.

They pulled away with honks and waves. I heard a click or two from the vultures as they snapped away. One stray flash lit up the yard.

"Really, people," I said, shaking my head at them.

A couple of camera operators standing at the property line shrugged sheepishly.

One brave reporter said, "I don't guess you have a comment."

"Just one. Bill's Burgers has the best shakes in town. You can quote me. That's Bill with two l's."

Several of them laughed as I walked up the steps into our house. It had been a fairly quiet week compared to the one before. Trey had received a call on Thursday from the New Orleans Police saying they had picked up the two men responsible for causing our wreck and chasing us into the cemetery. Unfortunately, they were local guns for hire who specialized in intimidation for a fee. They told a story similar to Selena's. A man contacted them and asked if they would scare two people, further details to be sent under separate cover. Their instructions were not to hurt us, but they did their job so well they had come close. I remembered feeling the car mirror shatter close to my head. Trey's car was also ready, so we had taken a return trip to New Orleans on Friday to pick it up. We'd come back Saturday morning to pick up his kids, giving me my first opportunity to meet them. I was nervous enough on Thursday when I first heard I would see them, and then I made the mistake of texting with Delilah.

TOLD U

I know.

HOW WAS IT

Private.

NO FUN DE-BORE! DETAILS

Riding up for car, picking kids up on the way back.

OMG! YOU COULD BE AN S-MOM

That last one fired my nerves and kept me anxious until Saturday night. Was I really ready to be a stepmom? I'd almost decided that domestic life wasn't in the cards for me. Now it could be right around the corner if I wanted it. So much to figure out.

Dorcas and I had interviewed several people caught up in the aftermath of my parents' quest to find Dinah's killer by purging the town of evil. There wasn't anything new to add to our understanding of what had actually happened to Dinah or Mia. Just a lot of pain. So much pain and loss. We hoped those interviews would give us information to help us face the most difficult interview of them all, our parents. I tried to ignore the nagging voice inside that insisted we were just procrastinating.

We were constantly being reminded of how much trauma our own tragedy brought to our little town. Fear and suspicion had laid deadly roots in Picardy. Stories abounded of false sightings of satanic ritual sites, my parents leading expeditions into the forest to uncover clues, police interviews of suspects, and demonization of those suspects by local gossips. Dorcas and I had been exhausted by the end of the week. Escaping to New Orleans with Trey had been a welcome distraction.

A hearing had also been scheduled for my father's case. The grand jury would start examining the case on December 15 if my dad were ruled able to appear by his doctors. We had visited him twice during the week but avoided raising our questions about the exhumation when he'd shown obvious signs of weakness and a limited attention span. I could tell Lucille was worried. With the Hightowers hovering most of the time, we had lost the opportunity to talk with her about it too.

I entered the living room and saw a woman engaged in conversation with Dorcas. She had long blonde hair tied back in a ponytail. I judged her to be about my age or a little younger.

"Debbie!" She said when she saw me. "Wow! You look different."

"Guess so," I said, giving Dorcas a questioning glance.

"Diana, you remember Stacy Thibodeaux," Dorcas emphasized the last name like I should know it.

I was still lost. Stacy took up the conversational slack.

"Diana. That's a pretty name. I want you to know I don't buy into any of that stuff people are sayin' about you bein' fake and a liar and all that. People got to make their choices, I say."

"Yeah. Thanks for that."

"Anyway," Dorcas said. "Stacy has something for us. Something Daddy requested she find for him a few weeks ago." She was looking at me again with an intense expression.

That's when it hit me. *Thibodeaux! Ron Thibodeaux's daughter!* She attended Picardy in Delilah's grade. Her father was my dad's coroner friend.

"Yeah. Mr. Denny asked if I knew where Daddy might have hidden something extra special. Things were a mess when he died. A lot of it was still in a box we kept in our attic. Just in case any of his official stuff needed to be preserved for the records office, you know. Anyway, I finally found what Mr. Denny wanted."

She handed a manilla envelope to my sister.

"Sorry to stop by so late," she said. "Bingo night and all. Have a good one."

I think we thanked her. We were in such shock I wasn't sure. When her car rolled up our driveway, Dorcas slowly opened the envelope. Two documents dropped into her hands. One read: CERTIFICATE OF DEATH. The other carried the simple description: AUTOPSY REPORT. Dorcas' hands visibly shook as she leafed through the documents. I waited with bated breath.

"Cause of death is confirmed to be heart failure due to massive trauma and what he calls 'abdominal obstruction.' Indications of sepsis.

It's strange that Mia also died of heart failure, but no abdominal issues like he cites here."

She flipped over to the autopsy report.

"Same general conclusions here. There's a list of things found in her system. No indication of illegal drugs or alcohol. No surprise there. Lots of chemical things I don't understand."

I glanced over the list and shook my head. "A lot of these notations are beyond me. And, to top it all off, it's hard to read all this medical script."

We placed a Zoom call to Delilah and shared what we had. She looked at the pictures of the documents Dorcas snapped and sent to her.

"I'm having a hard time reading this too. A lot of the chemical notations look abbreviated."

"Any ideas?" I asked.

"Yes," Delilah said. "Let me send these to Tianna. She's a general practitioner at the Picardy Health Center. I'm hoping she can read these abbreviations and symbols."

"Tell her to keep it to herself," I said.

"Will do."

After we hung up, Dorcas asked, "Bed and then what tomorrow?"

I surprised her by saying, "I think I'd like to go to church."

Grace's little auditorium was filled to capacity for the Sunday morning worship service. Their youth ensemble led worship. Their young faces radiated joy in some cases and communicated abject boredom in others. One girl was texting while she was on stage with the worship team. Dixon bounded on stage when his time came and delivered a resounding call from the Gospel of John 15:9 to be "in the world but not of it." He spent much of the time listing the usual array of satanic avatars, which consisted of pretty much anyone who didn't gel with the white lower middle-class "down home" congregation eating up his words.

Dixon was greeting congregants when we merged into the crowd moving at a snail's pace toward the back sanctuary doors.

"There's his wife," Dorcas said as a blonde woman joined him. "You can meet her too."

It's incredible how ingrained biological responses never quite leave you. Pavlov's dogs taught us a lot about how we respond to both stimuli and trauma. The sight of Dixon's wife sucked the moisture from my mouth and throat. My palms produced a sheen of sweat. Every flight or fight mechanism in my body sent a burst of adrenaline roaring through me. My body prepared to fight in obedience to programming set in place over twenty years ago.

"Well. Hello, Dr. Chambers. I would introduce you to my wife, but I'm not sure which name to use for you." Dixon presented this comment as friendly banter. The subtext was clear from the edge in his voice.

"No need. We're old friends," Crissy Hines Dixon said. "Can't believe I didn't recognize you at the coffee shop, Little Debbie."

Another reason I'd changed my name.

"Surprised you noticed me at all, Crissy."

"I like to go by Christine now. See, you're not the only one who can play with names."

Dorcas noticed the tension that laced the conversation. "I didn't know you two knew each other."

"Crissy and I went to school together," I said, "My sister, Dorcas."

"Oh, we know Dorcas," Crissy cooed in syrupy tones. "How are you, Honey? You were always so cute followin' Dinah around at the basketball games. I was really torn up when she died. She was so smart and sweet."

I fought to keep from clenching my fists as images of Crissy taunting me about Dinah and Mr. Francis ran through my mind.

"So, Dr. Diana, will you be leaving town soon, or do you plan to stay through Christmas?" Dixon tried to make it look like he was just defusing the tension. He almost succeeded, but his eagerness to know the answer slipped through his façade.

"I've got permission to be remote until the January term begins. We'll see."

"Well, good for you. I hope you can be some comfort to your parents. I'm afraid they're going to need it. We'll be praying for them."

I nodded, not trusting myself to speak. Nothing I wanted to say would help us. We moved along so that the people behind us could speak to the Dixons.

The youth were clustered in the foyer. I motioned for Dorcas to follow as I approached several teenage girls.

"Hi, Ladies," I said. "You did a great job this morning."

One red-haired girl's jaw dropped, "Oh, wow! Are you the Heberts?"

"We are. I'm Diana, and this is Dorcas."

"Sick! I've seen all the *Demonologist* movies. The *Christine* ones too!"

"That's nice," I said. I tried not to let it bother me that Christine got her own blasted franchise. *Someday Christine.*

We started talking with the girls about church, youth group activities, and eventually got around to Pastor Dixon.

"Oh, he's great," a preteen named Melody gushed, her silver braces flashing. "We're not really big enough for a full-time youth minister. He and Ms. Christine spend a lot of time doing activities with us, counseling people, stuff like that."

Before we knew it, the crowd had thinned considerably. Crissy walked out with her two small boys, waving at us and the crowd of girls. Both boys had full heads of blond hair inherited from their mother.

"Well, we should go. It's been fun to talk to you," I said. The others said their goodbyes and started breaking up. The red-haired girl, Bethany, walked us to the front door. Just as we were about to leave, I looked back into the worship center and saw Eric Dixon talking with a tall teenage girl with dark hair. They were standing near the back entrance that led to the administrative offices.

"Who is that with Pastor Eric, Bethany?"

Bethany looked and wrinkled her nose. "That's Chelsea. Chelsea Whitmer. Senior basketball player. She's kind of his favorite right now."

"His favorite?"

"Yeah. He always seems to have a favorite. Theresa, Thomas, Natalie, Mia ..."

"Mia?" Dorcas and I both snapped to attention.

"Yeah, Mia Jordan," Bethany paused. Then her eyes widened. "I'm sorry. I forgot about your daddy. She was a regular here for a while. I don't remember it much, but my big brother was in the youth group at the same time as her. Sad what happened to her. I hope they decide your daddy didn't do it. She was always drugged out. It was just a matter of time before something happened to her."

I avoided commenting on the last part and thanked Bethany for her help. Dorcas opened the door and started out. I took one last look over my shoulder. Dixon smiled and gave Chelsea a hug. The hug lasted a beat longer than it should have. I felt my skin crawl. She returned his smile and started back across the worship center. Dixon turned and caught me watching him. For just a second, menace flickered across his face. Then it was gone, and his amiable exterior fell back into place. The transition happened so fast I wasn't sure I'd seen it at all. He nodded in my direction and headed for the office area.

Monday was spent catching up on classes. Final exams were approaching. I felt an acute ache as I zoomed with my students. Home-sick for them and for Nashville, I wished I could be there in person as we had our final class sessions. A cluster of them stayed after my graduate course to talk about our infamous family and what it was like growing up as an Hebert. I was surprised to find myself enjoying the conversation. Even more so when several students admitted childhood traumas of a similar nature. After I signed off, I thought about how much my fear of owning my past had cheated my students. I'd worried that they would see me as less of an authority if they knew everything. The truth was just the opposite. My story humanized me for these students in a way few other things could.

I opened another window and contacted Pedro. We chatted for a while about how things were shaping up for the end of the semester. I shared the news I'd just received that afternoon from the Nashville Police. They had traced the burner phone from my apartment to a Louisiana dealer but found no information on the purchaser. All roads, it appeared, led back to Picardy.

"Thank you, Pedro."

"You bet. I hope things go well this week."

"Pedro, can we talk for a minute?"

"Sure. I don't think I'm going to like this conversation."

"What makes you say that?"

"When someone asks if I can talk after we've already been talking for an hour, I expect the next part's going to be heavy."

Ever the expert shrink.

"You said before I came here that maybe my time with my family would help me think about what I want moving forward."

"I don't know if those were my exact words. But, yeah, I hoped that might be the case."

"You were right. In more ways than I expected. I need to tell you ..."

"It's Trey, isn't it?"

I blinked in surprise. I'd told Pedro a lot of stories about Trey when we first met. But I didn't remember mentioning him much over the last five years.

"Yes."

"You love him?"

"I do. I love you, too. You will always hold a special place. But, with Trey, it's ... different. I'm sorry."

"You don't need to apologize, Diana."

"Are you okay?"

"Hell, no. It sucks!" Something about the way he said it caused us both to break out in laughter. His expression turned serious again, and he said, "It does suck for me. I hoped when you made peace with your past and moved forward it would be with me. I always knew that might not be the case. I can't say I expected you would start things up with Trey, but I also can't say I'm surprised. I always knew you still cared for him, even when you didn't want to seem like you did."

"Thank you."

"So, are you coming back?"

"I think so. For sure I will for the spring. After that, I don't know. We're still figuring things out."

"I hope it goes well, and I look forward to seeing you again soon. Always know that I'm here for you."

"Me too. Pedro, we had some good times. I'm better for our years together."

He touched the screen and nodded. "Me too. May you find the answers you're looking for, Diana."

The evening was spent with Trey and Dorcas. Dorcas worked on a scrapbook she'd been preparing of our parents' cases over the years. Trey and I sat on the couch grading for our respective courses. At one point, Trey looked up and said, "Look at us all grown up and dull."

"Grown up, yes. Dull, never," Dorcas said.

I logged into Zoom the next morning and finished yet another class. After giving them some pointers on preparing for the essay final, I wished them a good holiday break. I'd just signed off when Dorcas entered the room. She was clasping and unclasping her hands in a nervous frenzy.

"What's up?"

"Tianna."

"Did she find out anything?"

"I think so. Diana, she wants us to come down to her office."

I closed my laptop cover slowly. That didn't sound good.

We drove there in silence and maintained it as we walked into the sanitized white walls of the clinic. It was bustling with all manner of patients. Tianna was waiting for us in the reception area. She removed her hands from the pockets of her long white coat and hugged us both. Her hair spilled down over her coat in curly rivulets, and silver spectacles gave her an air of sophistication. She led us into her office and closed the door.

"It's so good to see you both. You especially, De ... Diana. It's been way too long. Let me get the rest of the posse here."

She sat at her desk and typed on her laptop. In a few minutes, the sound of a Zoom window opening peeled through her speakers.

"Hey, Girl! Lookin' good," Tianna said. "You turning blue on me?"

"Just the hair, T," Delilah said.

"Your sisters are here," Tianna said, scooting back and turning the screen toward us. We waved to Delilah.

Then Tianna's expression turned grave. Very grave. She produced the copies of the death certificate and autopsy report that Delilah sent her.

"I wanted to talk to you all together. Sorry you can't be here in person, Delilah."

I felt a knot form in my stomach. Tianna had the air of a doctor preparing to deliver difficult news to a patient.

"I went over this report several times. It's crap because Thibodeaux was a typical small-town coroner for his day. Lots of things missed or glossed over that we would highlight today. He was long obsolete by the time he filled this out, out of step with the times for even 1995. But he did do some good basic chemical analysis."

She stopped and looked at us, including a glance at Delilah on the computer screen.

"I don't know how to ask this tactfully, so I'm just going to ask it. Did any of you know that your sister was pregnant when she died?"

Our startled silence answered the question for her.

"I didn't think so. You see these notations here."

She pointed to two abbreviations. Tianna had highlighted them and spelled out the full terms in ink beside the abbreviations: Mifepristone and Misoprostol.

"What are they?" Dorcas asked.

The name "Mifepristone" did ring a distant bell in the back of my mind. I looked at the laptop, and my heart stopped. Delilah never showed real emotion if she could help it. Tears were streaming down her face, carrying a black flood of mascara with them. She knew what they were.

Tianna projected a look of pure empathy toward Delilah's image on the screen and reached over to take both of our hands.

"Mifepristone and Misoprostol are powerful abortifacients. You might know Mifepristone as RU-486. They are the base components for legal abortion pills. Taken together, they facilitate an abortion in the early stages of pregnancy."

Things were moving too fast to keep up. Dorcas was starting to cry. I was still stunned.

"Do you mean to say that Dinah was pregnant and took an abortion pill to terminate the pregnancy? That just doesn't sound like Dinah."

"Lots of women do it for all kinds of reasons, Diana," Tianna said. She seemed to be watching to gauge my reaction.

"I'm not judging. There's no firmer advocate for a woman's right to choose than me. I just can't see that being Dinah's choice. It's just ... the way we were raised ... what we were taught to believe. I've never known any woman who would have been a more natural and willing mother than Dinah. I can't see her doing it."

Delilah looked down, subdued for once and unsure what to think.

Tianna locked eyes with me for a moment. She seemed reassured by my description of Dinah.

"There's more. I wanted to see what you would say before revealing the rest. There are two things that are curious about Thibodeaux's findings here regarding Mifepristone. First, Mifepristone was not legalized in the United States until 2000. It was developed in the eighties and started being used in France in 1987. Whoever obtained the dose Dinah took obtained it illegally. It was not sanctioned for use in the United States in 1995."

Dorcas dabbed her eyes with a handkerchief and willed herself to stop crying. "How would Dinah obtain an illegal drug like that?"

"I don't think she did," Tianna said. That caught our attention. Her audience was in the palm of her hand. "The second curious thing about Thibodeaux's finding is the dosage of Mifepristone. It's off the freaking charts! This medication, even today, is meant to be taken in a controlled environment, preferably a doctor's office, with emergency tools at the ready and in conjunction with other drugs to prevent infection or reactions. We've only just started allowing people to take them at home without supervision over the last four years. Now that practice could be up in the air along with every other aspect of reproductive care after the

Supreme Court overturned *Roe v. Wade* this summer. At the very least, the patient needs to consult with a physician and follow the dosage instructions to the letter. The patient is given Misoprostol to take at home within seventy-two hours after the Mifepristone dose. They are not meant to be taken at the same time, and their dosage is carefully regulated. It's considered routine today under the right conditions, but it carries serious risks. There can be severe uncontrolled bleeding. If the fetus is not eliminated successfully, fetal material and other substances can collect in the birth canal. It's the same effect as when complications arise in childbirth, necessitating a C-section. If the fetal material is not removed through suction or surgery, the patient can get septic and die."

"And you think this is how Dinah died?" I asked.

"I'm sure of it," Tianna said. "It can happen too fast. Especially if people don't know what's happening. If she'd gotten to a hospital, they might have moved fast enough to stop it. But even when Terrance found her, it may have been too late. From what Delilah told me about her final words, she didn't know what was happening either until close to the end. How can that be if she took the drugs on purpose?"

Dorcas and I both leaned forward. Delilah was listening with rapt attention. "What do you think happened, Tianna?" I asked.

"Dinah was always the most disciplined person I knew. Remember when we tried to estimate ingredients for that cake we made? She wasn't having it. Made us throw out the glob we made, took out the measuring cups, and had us redo it all."

She and Delilah attempted a smile at the memory.

"There's no way anyone takes this kind of dose unless they want to hurt themselves," Tianna continued. "She was not the kind of person to do this and make careless mistakes. It's far too much. No surprise she had fatal complications. That's also why it happened so fast. Whoever did this didn't know what the hell they were doing, and Dinah paid the ultimate price. Based on the dosage and how she was acting right before her death, I think someone slipped her the drugs."

One word snapped to the center of my brain. *Pepsi.* In that stream of nonsense final words that Terence repeated, the one that stood out the most to me was "Pepsi." An odd word for Dinah to say given how rarely we were allowed to enjoy soda. It hadn't seemed to fit. Now it did.

"Pepsi," I whispered. "She said she should have known better, and then she said something about Pepsi. She figured it out."

Tianna had cleared up so many mysteries, yet so many more beckoned. Foremost among them, how did our pure as the driven snow sister end up pregnant? There was no one in the picture as far as I knew. Very casual boyfriends at best. She spent too much of her time taking care of us to really date. Second, how much did our parents know? Dinah must have told them that night we heard her arguing with them in the barn. How far would they go to "remove what was inside her" as Lucille wrote in *Devil's Circle*? I read that line as a reference to demonic oppression. What if it was code for something else?

We thanked Tianna for everything, still numb and shell-shocked.

"Please let me know if I can do anything for you," Tianna said as she escorted us out.

"Well, hello there!" a voice called to us. It was Crissy Dixon with her son Samuel. She noticed our red eyes. "Why, is something wrong?"

"We're fine," I said. "Just a touch of allergies."

"In December?"

"We're weird that way. Are you okay?"

"Oh, yes. Just came in because little Samuel might have an ear infection."

"I'm sure they'll get to you soon," Tianna said, ushering us toward the door.

"I should hope so. I've been here for an hour. At least it seems like it. Bye, y'all!"

Dorcas thanked Tianna when we made it outside. "She's more than I can take normally. Much less today."

Tianna nodded. "Are you going to hell if you say a pastor's wife is a bitch?"

I laughed. "I think the accepted expression in religious circles is 'she can be a bit of a trial sometimes.'"

"Well, bless her heart," Tianna said. "She doesn't bother me as much as her husband. He's always been a mean little prick. Even when we were in high school."

"You knew the Dixons back then?"

"Just saw him occasionally when Daddy went to pick up feed for the hogs. He worked there after school stocking and carrying feed out. That was enough seeing him for me."

I started to follow Dorcas to the car when my addled brain processed what Tianna had said. I had to call her back from the front entrance of the hospital.

"Yeah. You need something else?"

"Tianna, where did your daddy buy his feed?"

"Johnson's Feed and Seed."

CHAPTER NINETEEN

DECEMBER 31, 1995

"Trying to feed this crew is like slopping hogs," Momma moaned as Dorcas upended the basket of rolls stretching to get more chicken.

"Sorry," Dorcas said. She didn't sound at all sorry as she devoured the chicken leg.

Daddy looked at his watch. "You girls better hurry and clean your plates if you want to make the New Year's Festival tonight."

"Fireworks! Fireworks! Fireworks!" Dorcas screamed.

"Only for little girls who finish their supper," Momma insisted.

Picardy's annual New Year's celebration in Beauregard Park stood second only to the Fourth of July community picnic in importance. Everyone who was able gathered for free food and games in the park. At midnight the city fireworks shattered the night sky with explosive color. I was thrilled to be going this year. Last year, we had been ready to go when a deliverance session changed our plans. I prayed nothing would stop us from going this time. Trey said he would be there at eight, and I was determined to spend some time with him. We hadn't seen each other much since Christmas.

"Can you shut up about those fireworks?!" Delilah said.

"Delilah, don't be cruel to your sister. A lot of lonely girls wish they had sisters."

"Tell them I have one to spare," Delilah grumbled.

"Delilah!"

"It's okay, Momma. Debbie said Delilah's mean because it's her month time."

Delilah glared at me. I shrugged and turned my attention back to my plate.

"Dorcas! Deborah! We do not discuss such things. Especially at the table."

Daddy rolled his eyes and pushed back from the table. I could only imagine what it was like to live as the only man in a woman's world. He checked his watch.

"You finished, Deborah?"

"Yes, Sir."

"Why don't you go up and let your sister know we're almost ready?"

"Okay."

I hurried up the stairs and eased up to Dinah's door. The change in Dinah over the last two days encouraged me more than anything else during this confusing Christmas break. I thought after Christmas morning that she would never be herself again. But something about that fight with Momma and Daddy reignited a spark in her. She still looked sad on occasion, but the fire was there again. Dinah seemed more like my sister. Capable, confident, and ready to lead. I was glad to have her back.

I knocked and peered around the corner. Dinah was standing in front of her mirror in her bra and panties. She was looking at herself as if conducting an inspection. Her hand rested on her stomach. She looked up when I knocked. I found it strange. My sister never indulged in vanity. She was sparing with makeup and lipstick. I never remembered her checking herself out in the mirror like that before.

"Daddy said we're about ready to go."

"Okay," Dinah said. "I'm just getting dressed. I think I'm going to take the station wagon if all of you don't mind taking the truck. I have a couple of things to take care of tonight. You can ride with me on the way if you want."

"Sure."

I lay on her bed while she dressed. She finished and ran a brush through her long dark hair.

"What do you think? Christmas gifts. Thought I would give them a first run tonight."

"You look beautiful as always, Dinah. The top matches your eyes and hair really well."

She grinned and posed like a model on the runway, giving me a better view of her new purple top and white skirt.

CHAPTER TWENTY

An Excerpt from

DEVIL'S CIRCLE (1996)

by Lucille B. Herbert

Deadly threats were mounting. Lucille received several messages bearing images of pentagrams stuffed into the mailbox or on the fencepost outside. Lewd threats and blasphemies scattered throughout made them noxious to read. Even worse, the senders promised to do horrible things to her girls. Torture, sexual perversions, and death were all outlined in horrific details. Lucille was thankful that she managed to find these before the girls did. Until the day Dorcas came into the kitchen with a disturbing message.

"Look, Momma. Someone left a picture for us."

Lucille looked down and had to grab the table to steady herself. Dorcas held a crude drawing showing an altar with goat heads on either end. Four little images with dark hair lay across the altar. Blood dripped down the sides and pooled on the ground.

"Lord help us," Lucille said. "Dorcas, where did you get this?"

"It was on the porch under a rock."

Lucille realized too late that Deborah and Delilah were looking through the kitchen door.

"What's that, Momma?" Deborah asked.

Lucille tried to think of a convenient white lie. She decided in the end to tell the truth.

"Girls, we've been getting some messages from people who don't like the way Daddy and I try to help people."

Dorcas continued grinning, oblivious to the weight of what was being shared. The older girls paled and glanced at each other in fear.

"I don't want you to worry. But we do need to take precautions."

"Are we still gonna get to go to the New Year's fireworks tonight?" Deborah asked.

"Yes. But you are going to have to stay close to Daddy and me. And Daddy will also give you something special that you will need to hang onto. Understand?"

They nodded, subdued and quiet.

That evening, they ate supper and put away the dishes. While Lucille and the girls prepared to leave for Beauregard Park, Denny worked feverishly in the artifacts room. Lucille had put the final dishes away when Dinah entered the room.

"Momma, I'm going a little early to hang out with some friends. Can I take the station wagon?"

Lucille watched her closely. Dinah showed no signs of the demonic influence that had gripped her on Christmas Eve. Denny and Lucille had conducted several tests on her including having her dip her finger in holy water, read out loud from the Bible, and say the Lord's Prayer. No signs of possession. A search of her room had revealed no hex bags or other items used to levy a curse. A special blessing of her room by their pastor should have warded off any influences from the use of a Voodoo doll.

"You don't want to wait and go with us?"

"Momma! I'm eighteen! How long do you expect me to go everywhere with my family?"

Lucille considered and said, "That's fine. But I want you to wait for your daddy before you go. He has something to give you."

"Okay. Thanks!"

She skipped out. Lucille smiled, glad to see Dinah acting more like herself than she had in a while. Lucille dried her hands and walked to the artifacts room. Denny was bent over the coffee table finishing his work on four small pieces that looked like tea bags.

"Are you almost done?" she asked.

He looked up and nodded. "Just about. They took longer than I thought."

"What's in them?"

"Holy water. But not just any holy water. Gathered from the Jordan River itself according to Cyrus Beeman. Cyrus also gave me some soil collected from the Temple Mount in Jerusalem. And, of course, a cross as well. They're just objects in and of themselves, but combined with prayer, I'm hoping they will create a hedge of protection stronger than anything we've seen before. Only thing is I don't have time to make any for us."

Lucille smiled and took his hand. "I'll watch your back if you watch mine."

Denny grinned and pulled her into a tight hug.

"I love you," he said.

"I love you too. Always."

"We're going to make it through this. God will protect us even when we walk through the valley of the shadow."

Lucille pressed her face into his chest and prayed that it would be true. They walked out into the living room holding hands. Delilah, Deborah, and Dorcas were sitting on the couch waiting for them. Lucille looked around in confusion.

"Girls? Where's Dinah?"

"She got a call from Ashley asking if Dinah could pick her up early, so she left."

"Denny," Lucille said, gripping his arm.

"It's okay," he patted her hand. "I'll look for her when we get there and make sure she has her bag."

He squatted in front of the girls and held out the bags for their inspection.

"You see this string, Girls? These bags are meant to go around your neck. They have powerful objects in them that will aid you in your prayers and defend you against evil."

"Are people going to try to hurt us tonight, Daddy?" Dorcas asked.

"They may try," Denny said. "But God is our defender and protector. We have to trust in Him. You wear these, stay in constant prayer, and look for us at all times."

The girls nodded solemnly. "We will, Daddy," Deborah said.

Denny smiled and gathered them all into his massive arms for a hug.

"Come on! Let's go enjoy some fireworks!"

The girls squealed and raced out of the house to the truck.

"Denny? What about Dinah?"

CHAPTER TWENTY-ONE

"WHAT ABOUT DINAH?" Lucille asked.

"Did you know she was pregnant?" I was done being subtle or polite.

Lucille paled and looked over at my daddy sitting up in his bed.

"Don't look at him!" I shouted.

They both looked startled. Delilah yelled at Lucille all the time, but I never had except for that one time right after Dinah died.

"Deborah. The Hightowers."

"Damn the Hightowers! And damn your stubborn insistence on calling me Deborah. It's Diana if you ever expect to get a response from me again!"

"De ... Diana. Let's calm down and talk this out."

"Calm down, Angel," Denny said.

"Did ... you ... know... that ... Dinah ... was ... pregnant? That is the only answer I want to hear from you right now."

"Yes." Lucille said.

"When?"

"She told us on Christmas Eve in the barn. Child, don't look at me like that."

Dorcas was standing behind me with her eyes brimming, confusion and anger manifesting in equal parts.

"What did she tell you?"

"She'd gotten pregnant and needed to make plans."

Daddy looked down at the bedsheets.

"Daddy, what else?"

"Angel …"

"Daddy, if you ever want to speak to me again, you will answer my questions."

Anguish was written in his eyes and all over his face. "She told us somebody raped her."

I heard a moan from Dorcas behind me. I wanted to be shocked, but part of me already knew. The scalding shower and the compulsive motions Dinah displayed that night would have alerted me instantly if I saw any of my students do it. *If only I had been older and knew what I know now. Poor Dinah. Dealing with it all alone.* Except she had tried to tell someone.

"What did you say when she told you about it?" I asked.

I thought I was beyond the capacity to be surprised when it came to Lucille. But Lucille held depths even I hadn't plumbed. She looked at me, and I saw it on her face. Shame and regret. "No. Please don't say …"

"It happens all the time. Especially in our world with such high moral standards. Girls get themselves into a situation and go too far. And then they confuse it with rape. I just thought …"

"Girls get themselves into …" I thought seriously about returning Lucille's childhood slap with interest. "Can you even hear yourself?"

"It happens a lot to young Christian ladies, and she had been hiding things from us. She'd been working a job we didn't know about until that night."

Tears of anger were running freely down my face, and my hands were balled into fists. Daddy's face was covered with tears too. Seeing him cry any other time would have broken me. Right then it seemed like he could never cry enough tears to atone for the sins of the past. Dorcas sobbed behind me as well. Lucille wasn't crying, but her tortured expression conveyed how much she was breaking inside.

"You're comparing not telling you about a part-time job to lying to you about a rape! You're sick! You were sick then, and you're sick now."

"Diana?" Lucille reached and touched my arm. I slapped her hand away viciously. Pain and shock rippled in equal parts across her face. *Good.*

"Dinah came to you for help. She was feeling broken, ashamed, scared, and God knows what else. And you blamed her! No wonder she left that night. I wouldn't blame her if she hadn't come back. Maybe if she hadn't, she would still be alive."

Lucille had nothing left to say. No excuse to offer.

"Who did it?" Dorcas' voice was edged with an anger I'd never heard from her before. They always warn you about when the quiet ones get angry. Dorcas sounded as if she could deal out deadly vengeance to whoever was responsible.

"We don't know," Daddy said. "It's the truth. I wanted to believe her that night." He tried not to look at Lucille, and she didn't look at him, but I could feel the tension.

"After she died, you decided you did?"

"Yes."

"Timely."

"Diana ..."

"She didn't tell you who did it or when?" Dorcas asked.

"No." Lucille said. "We didn't get that far. It was my fault. I reacted badly to the news about the baby, and then she said she was raped. I ... told her ..."

"Told her what?"

"Too many girls use that as an excuse for fornication."

"Momma!" Dorcas wailed.

I didn't have words left.

"It had to be about three weeks before Christmas Eve," Lucille continued. "Long enough to know for sure she was pregnant."

"Did she ever say anything about an abortion?" I asked.

"No," Lucille said. "She never said anything about the pregnancy to us again."

"And you dealt with it the Hebert way," I said. "By shoving it down and not talking things through."

"We thought she would come to us again when she was ready," Daddy said. "After what happened the first time, we were afraid it would blow up again. It was hard for us too, Angel. We didn't know what to think or how to process it."

"Well, at least you had each other," I said. "Dinah was alone. What you should have done is believe your daughter and process it by supporting her in every way you could."

"We know that now, Diana," Lucille said. Miracle of miracles, Lucille was crying real tears. "She was my baby, my first one. You have no idea how many nights I have cried out to God in anguish to let me die if only she could live again. I hope you never know what it's like to hold your firstborn's broken bloody body."

"But that's not how it works, is it? No do overs and no resurrections. You don't know who did it?"

"No," Denny said. "We had thoughts. Suspicions about people who may have been involved. We tried to investigate."

"You tried to frame the whole damn town!"

"Diana, la ..."

"If you say language, I swear I will knock you across this room, Lucille. Did it ever occur to you to start with her job?"

"They were covering it up," I'd almost forgotten Dorcas was there. "They were ashamed to admit the pregnancy. Weren't you?"

"Dorcas ..."

"No, Momma. I always trusted you. I always take your side. How dare you abuse that trust! How could you do that to Dinah? She would have done anything for us. How could you ever be ashamed of her?"

"We tried to work with the sheriff's department. Ron Thibodeaux told us that she died from some kind of abortion drug," Daddy said. "The police interviewed people, but they decided in the end that she must have taken it herself. We tried to keep going, but there was pressure."

"Pressure?"

"The ministerial association in the parish started getting involved. Saying that we were into crazy stuff and that we killed Dinah ourselves as part of some exorcism ritual. They used passages in *Devil's Circle* to support their claims."

Lucille shook her head. "I wish I'd never written that book."

That was the last thing I expected her to say.

"Then why did you greenlight it for film production?"

Her head snapped up. "What?!"

"Trey and I talked to Selena, the actress who plays Dinah. She's the one who's pretended to be Dinah all this time. She said you greenlit a film adaptation of *Devil's Circle*."

"I would never. I ..." Hurt seeped into her eyes and comprehension into mine at the same instant.

"I did," Daddy said.

Of course, he did. Daddy might be old school, but he shared my appreciation for the value of internet sleuths. You do a *Demonologist* film, and every YouTuber and TikToker would take a deep dive into the backstory. The odds of someone uncovering new information were increased exponentially.

"Because you wanted to reopen the investigation. Get people nosing around again. That's also why you filled out the exhumation paper."

"How did you know about that?" He asked.

I looked at Lucille. "Someone may have fished it out of the mail."

"Lucille?" Daddy said.

"I didn't see any point in bringing this up again, Denny. It almost destroyed us before!"

"I want justice for my little Angel before I die," Denny said. "I don't care if it destroys us. Our ministry is not worth more than these girls. They are my life."

"Our life," she insisted.

He hesitated, and I was amazed to see genuine tears welling up in her eyes for a second time. His silence spoke volumes.

"You started a satanic panic in this town, and then you got a taste of your own medicine when they went after you, all of us, as crazy demon chasers and you as filicidal parents."

Lucille nodded. "The ministerial association, somebody in it, found out about Dinah's pregnancy. They threatened to go public with it and portray it as a good girl gone bad. We just couldn't."

"Why?"

"We were ashamed."

"Of Dinah."

"Of how we handled it," Lucille said. "Of what it would do to Dinah's reputation and memory. Of the impact it could have on our ministry. I know you don't agree with me, Diana. But we do help people. Why sacrifice all that when Dinah was already gone? Why not continue to do it in her honor?"

"You asked Ron to remove the death certificate along with the autopsy report. You agreed with the ministerial association to a ceasefire if they didn't disclose what happened to Dinah."

Both of them nodded.

"How did you know the ministerial association knew?"

"They sent the president of the association to talk with us several times."

"And who was that?" I already knew. The pieces were clicking into place.

"Todd Dixon. Eric's father, in fact."

My daddy knew me well even after all these years. He could read it in every fiber of my being.

"Diana?"

"He did it, Daddy. Eric Dixon. He raped Dinah and slipped her drugs the night of the New Year's fireworks. He slipped her enough to cause a fatal reaction and kill her."

"Pepsi," Lucille whispered. "I thought she was just hallucinating."

"But when would he have had the chance, Angel?"

"He worked with her at Johnson's Feed and Seed. After hours." It would be a simple task to probe what Eric Dixon drove in his high school days. I expected to find a red Honda Civic at the end of our search.

"So that's where she worked," Daddy said. "At Johnson's."

"I can't believe Mr. Johnson never told you."

"If Dinah asked Arliss Johnson to keep a secret, you can bet he would take it to his grave. He probably never associated her death with her work."

"He had to wonder why she quit so soon," I said. "She left to get away from Dixon. Then she learned she was pregnant. I saw her the night it happened. The rape. I didn't know enough to recognize it then, but I do now. She looked so scared and confused."

My composure dissolved. I felt Dorcas' tender arms around me.

"But I don't understand. Why would he have to kill her?" Daddy said.

I raised my head from Dorcas' shoulder.

"I can only guess, but I think because he was afraid she would tell. And I think she planned to keep the baby."

"What makes you say that, Angel?"

"She changed in those last couple of days. It was like the fight had returned to her. She was always at her best when she was fighting for someone else. And you should have seen the way she was looking at herself in the mirror. Holding her stomach. She told me she had things to take care of that night. I think they agreed to meet up and talk. When he realized she was going to keep the baby, he spiked her drink."

Dorcas shuddered. "Even if she promised not to tell anyone, that baby would forever be a living genetic link between them. He might try to say it was consensual, but would people believe him?"

I nodded. "And there was no physical evidence beyond that because Dinah didn't know what she should do or where she should go. Her first impulse was to wash away what happened and push it down inside. We weren't taught anything about sex except that you weren't supposed to have it until you were married. Imagine her trying to process the assault with what we knew. The only thing her culture equipped her to be was ashamed and afraid when she was violated and traumatized."

"Her culture and her parents," Lucille said.

"I didn't say that."

"I know, Diana. I did because it's true. We were so afraid of your innocence being corrupted that we never taught you how to live in this world. The very things we did to protect you were the things that hurt you and drove you away."

I didn't know what to say. It was all too much at once.

"We have these theories," Daddy said. "But we're still stuck in the same place. We have no definitive proof."

"We have this," I said, holding up the autopsy report. "Thanks to you. And I don't think that we really need to exhume her body now based on what we have here."

Lucille said, "Please no. Let's let her rest in peace if we can."

"I also want to ask for the Mia Jordan autopsy report. They need to look for any kind of drug in her system that specifically causes heart failure."

"You think Mia was ...?"

"I think he groomed her, raped her, carried on a relationship with her that resulted in two other children, and then enlisted her to frame you for her murder."

"But why?" Dorcas said. "And why would she agree to do it?"

"The movie. The adaptation of *Devil's Circle*. If he heard Daddy greenlit the adaptation, he might have suspected that Daddy was looking into Dinah's death. And we know from Selena that he has connections within the production company strong enough to enlist her and several others for his ghost stunts."

Daddy groaned.

"What?"

"He came by the day I filled out the exhumation request. It was lying on the table. He could have seen it."

"Did you see him look at it? Or you, Lucille?"

"He always comes when I'm gone. It's like he can't stand to be around me." Lucille said.

"That's weird." *Although I had to admit he was not alone in that sentiment.*

"We don't know that he saw it, but he could have," Daddy said.

"He did come by once when you were home, Momma," Dorcas said. "That morning of the Jordan exorcism when I was preparing your coffee. You were out in the barn. He hovered in the kitchen and talked a little bit."

A thought came to me. "Dor, was he alone with the coffee?"

"No. But, I mean, I was moving around the kitchen not paying attention."

Lucille's jaw was set hard in what Delilah called her "Momma gonna shut that down" expression. "He didn't want me there. That's why I got sick the evening of the exorcism."

"Yes," I said. "Who knows why, but maybe he feared you'd notice something other people wouldn't. People fake demonic possession all the time. A little makeup, a voice changer, some drugs to induce vomiting, amateur theatrics, and you have the exorcism of Mia Jordan live and uncensored."

"That's why she goaded Daddy about Dinah," Dorcas said. "They wanted to get him so upset that he wouldn't be looking for inconsistencies or evidence of a fake."

"That may be what he thought you would notice," I said to Lucille. "You tend to stand back and observe. And I think all of us would agree you're pretty cold-blooded even when everyone else loses their mind. He couldn't risk you seeing through Mia's deception."

"I might prefer the word 'stoic' to 'cold-blooded,'" Lucille said with a sigh. She seemed in agreement about the rest.

"And Mia?" Dorcas asked.

"He slipped her a drug either orally or through injection during that skip in the video while he was praying with her. And she didn't know that was part of the deal. Or she thought he would just be faking her death."

"But she realized at the end," Dorcas said. "When she told her dad that something was going wrong. She realized Dixon had betrayed her."

Silence settled over the room for the first time in a while.

"So, what do we do?" Dorcas asked.

"We should take this to Lester Owens, my attorney." Daddy said. "He can take it to the D.A. and see if there is any way we can reopen Dinah's case. At the very least, it can help us argue for further inquiry into the nature of Mia's death. It might be the key to clearing us."

I agreed. "It's a thin trail at best, but at least we have something more to offer them now than we had before."

"It could be very dangerous," Lucille said. "Dixon is a popular and powerful man here. He's demonstrated that he's willing to kill to cover up this transgression. All his transgressions. If what Diana says is true, we have no idea how many girls there have been over the course of his career. He's probably dodged accusations before. Maybe we should let it rest."

"Why are you so opposed to settling this?" I asked.

"Because I will not survive if I lose another one of you."

"That's not going to happen," I said, wishing she'd been able to say those words to all of us twenty-five years ago. And hoping I was right.

CHAPTER TWENTY-TWO

THE SUN WAS SETTING AS WE DROVE toward home. I tried to call Lester Owens, but his phone kept going to voicemail. I didn't leave a message, deciding something this sensitive needed to be handled face to face.

"We're just going to have to go see him tomorrow morning," Dorcas said.

"First thing," I agreed.

I'd called Delilah to tell her about our conversation with our parents. Her phone went to voicemail too. *Strange.*

"Nobody's answering tonight."

My phone played Bryan Adam's "Heaven." I smiled and answered it. Dorcas shot me a "I bet that's not your ringtone for everyone" grin.

"Hey!"

"Hey, Beautiful. How're things in your juke joint?" Fake Humphrey Bogart asked.

"Going great, Rick. I got this handsome heartbreaker on the line, and I just can't quit him."

Dorcas put her finger in her mouth and made a gagging motion.

"How did things go today?"

"It was the day from hell. But I think we know the truth about Dinah's death."

"Seriously?"

"Yes."

"Tell me."

"It's a lot. Come over to the house, and we can talk face to face."

"Will do. Let me stop by my place and change. Then I'll be right over. See you in a few."

"Love you."

"Here's looking at you. And love you too."

Dorcas tried her best to look disgusted and failed. "I'm glad one good thing came out of all this tragedy."

"Two," I said, reaching over and touching her shoulder. "I got to know my sister again."

We pulled up in front of our house and stopped on the edge of the property line. Given the devastating news of the day, we were hungry for a little levity. I rolled down my passenger's side window and leaned out of the car. "Hey! Did you guys know that Elvis is in our living room right now? Right now!"

Those with a sense of humor laughed. They'd started to look forward to our banter. Less patient reporters just groaned and shook their heads.

"What's in the artifacts room tonight, Dor?"

"Well, I'm glad you asked, Diana. Tonight, we'll be featuring the wig of actress Jayne Mansfield, killed in a tragic car accident on our own U.S. Highway 90. Ms. Mansfield cultivated connections with Anton LeVay, founder of the Church of Satan. Some say LeVay placed a curse on Mansfield's attorney and boyfriend, Sam Brody." Dorcas leaned out her window and projected her best scary voice at the crowd. "A curse which backfired when Brody was killed in the car also carrying Ms. Mansfield."

I almost lost it when the crowd actually got hushed for a second. One eager preteen, probably hoping for Delilah's return, had her phone focused on us. "This is so going on TikTok!"

"Have a good night, Vultures," I called as we rolled down the road.

"So, Dor, do we really have Jayne Mansfield's wig in the collection?"

"I think Daddy actually bought it at Dirt Cheap."

I walked into the living room more exhausted than I'd been in a long time. Dorcas went into the kitchen to fix us some microwave dinners. I paced the room, trying to process all the crazy revelations of the day. Finally, I heard a car in the driveway. *Trey!*

I hurried to the door and was surprised to see Crissy Dixon standing there holding a covered dish.

"Hello," I said, trying not to show my surprise.

"Hey, Debbie! I mean, Diana. Shoot, that's so hard to get used to."

"Tell me about it," I said. "Would you like to come in?"

"Sure would. I brought a green bean casserole for you. Thought you girls might need some help what with you being so busy trying to help your parents."

"Thanks. We appreciate it."

"Christine!" Dorcas said when she entered the living room. "I didn't realize you were here."

"Sure am. Got a casserole for you, Dorcas."

No one invited her to sit. But she did. We politely took seats on the couch across from her. I wasn't sure how well I really wanted to get to know her again. First, all the baggage from the past loomed over us. Second, relationships get awkward when you have to tell someone that their husband was a rapist and a sexual predator. Oh, and a murderer too. Knowing something about how tragedy upended lives, I felt for her despite our personal issues and even more for her kids.

"Sorry, Crissy. We weren't expecting company. Do you want some water or sweet tea?"

"No! No! No! Heavens, you girls don't need to wait on me. So, tell me, how's looking into your sister's death going?" *Weird conversation starter.*

"You know," I said. "It's hard. We're not really making much progress. But we're hopeful still."

"Really? Because I was talking to Stacy Thibodeaux at the store this afternoon and, you know Stacy, she tends to take a nip or two in the day. Gets pretty wasted in the afternoons. She told me this interesting story about how she brought you two a death certificate for your sister. And an autopsy report. Imagine those turning up after all this time!"

I tensed and felt Dorcas do the same.

"And then," Crissy continued, "Those nosy reporters said they heard you spent some time at the Hightowers' after you left the clinic. Who's at the Hightowers'? Well, besides the Hightowers, of course."

"Well, we can't really say much about that," I said.

"I wouldn't think of invading your privacy. But I hope you would think about all the trouble something like that could stir up. Good folks doing good things could get hurt if all this rot got stirred up. You'd think about that, wouldn't you, Little Debbie?"

I didn't like where this was going at all.

"I think I hear Trey," I bluffed. "Let me check and see." *If I can get to the porch, I might be able to attract the vultures. They'd love to step foot across the threshold.*

I'd just placed my hand on the doorknob when I heard Crissy say, "Stop right there, Debbie, Diana, or whoever the hell you are. Trust me, Trey ain't here."

I turned to see her aiming a .45 caliber handgun at me.

"He's with my husband. And, if I don't leave here with those papers, he's dead."

CHAPTER TWENTY-THREE

DEC. 31, 1995/JAN. 1, 1996

Dinah pulled into Beauregard Park just in time for my 8:00 rendezvous with Trey. I was glad she'd let me come with her or Trey would've been left waiting. She put the station wagon in park and looked down at my fidgety hands.

"It's going to be okay, Debbie."

"What?"

"With Trey. Don't worry."

I hadn't burdened her with my problems because I knew she was carrying something. I just had no idea what. It didn't feel fair to push my troubles on her when she had her own problems.

"I know. I didn't want to bother you with it. I know you have your own stuff."

Dinah turned to me and cupped my chin with her hand.

"Look in my eyes and hear this. You will never be a bother to me, Sweet Little Sister. You mean more to me than I can ever say. You are beautiful, smart, kind, and fierce. I see it. Trey sees it. He knows you're worth the wait. It will be okay. You will be okay. We will be okay."

I threw my arms around her and hugged her tight. The wetness and warmth of her tears moistened my neck. When we separated, she reached out and gently smoothed my hair.

"Go have fun tonight. I want to talk to you tomorrow about something. Something amazing."

"What is it?" I asked.

"Not tonight. When we have more time. Go see Trey."

I got out of the car and heard Trey calling me from near the bandstand. I hurried toward him. Just before I reached him, I turned back. Dinah was locking the station wagon. She saw me looking at her and waved. Then she started toward the picnic area. Her new purple top and white skirt melted into the crowd.

The night went well. Better than I feared. It wasn't the same as normal, but Trey and I were more comfortable than we had been for several weeks. We sat with Delilah when the fireworks began and heard Dorcas screaming in delight from my daddy's arms as each one exploded in the night sky. I watched the fiery plumes plummet back to earth, wondering what 1996 held for each of us.

We drove home packed into the old truck. I was full and content. Delilah and I even sat on our beds and talked for a little bit, a rare thing for us, after we got home. We settled into bed about 1:30, and I dropped off to sleep almost immediately.

Loud banging in the kitchen awakened me. I lifted my groggy head. Delilah was still asleep. I rubbed my eyes and checked the clock. It read 2:20. More bangs and shouts came from downstairs. I threw my covers off and stumbled to the stairs. It sounded like Dinah and Momma. I hurried downstairs and turned into the kitchen. And screamed.

Dinah lay on the kitchen table, her feet hanging off the end. Her beautiful purple top was in disarray and had dark stains on the front. As my eyes traveled down her, I saw what those stains were. Her white skirt was stained dark red from her waist to her ankles. As I watched, her face contorted and she contracted in pain, gripping her abdomen.

"No ... exorcism .... hospital ... Oh, God!"

"Dinah? What's wrong?"

"Debbie?" Dinah turned her pale and sweaty face toward me. "Help me, Debbie! They're killing me!"

I reached for her hand, and she reached for mine. Before we touched, I felt myself being pulled back.

"What are you doing here, Child? You don't need to be in here." Momma shut that down.

"Debbie! Don't leave me! Oh, God, please don't leave me!" I wasn't sure whether that last phrase was a plea or a prayer. Or both.

Momma shoved me toward the stairs.

"Momma, what's wrong with Dinah?"

"Deborah, go upstairs and stay with Dorcas. Don't let her come down here. Keep Delilah up there too."

"But, Momma! What's wrong with Dinah?"

"Deborah, please," Momma had never pleaded with me before. It scared me. "Help me, Deborah. Help Dinah by staying with your sisters."

I realized that she needed to be with Dinah, and I was only slowing her down. I nodded and ran upstairs. Dorcas was sitting up in bed when I opened her door.

"What's happening, Debbie?"

"Dinah's feeling bad. Momma's with her. She sent me to stay with you."

I jumped in the bed with her. She immediately grabbed me and buried her head in my chest. In spite of what I said, she knew something was horribly wrong. Delilah walked in a few minutes later. We sat together on the bed, all three of us, listening to the chaos below. Finally, Delilah had enough of waiting. It had gotten strangely quiet downstairs.

"I'm going down."

"No," I hissed. "They said to wait."

"I'll just take a look. Be right back."

Delilah was gone before I could protest further.

"I'm scared, Debbie." Dorcas whined.

I hugged her tighter.

"It's okay, Sweetie. She'll be okay. We'll be okay."

Just at that moment we heard a primal sound from downstairs that chilled me to the bone. The noise resonated somewhere between a yell and a drawn-out moan. The sound itself was terrifying enough. The real horror set in when I realized that my daddy was making it. Then I heard Momma crying. Sobbing. Loud enough to be heard upstairs. I sat there not wanting to hear or see anything else. If only we could just close the door and I could inhabit a world of continuing hope with Dorcas for a little longer.

That option ended with Delilah's return. She staggered into the room and looked at me with a stunned expression.

"Delilah?"

"She's gone."

"Who?"

"Dinah."

"Where did she go? Did they take her to the hospital?"

Delilah looked miserable. "Debbie, she's dead. Dinah's dead."

"No. She's sick. They're going to help her. You heard wrong."

I wanted to throw up when Delilah started to cry. Then someone started screaming. It went on for what seemed like forever. I thought at one point that someone probably should tell them to keep it down. Then I realized that it was me screaming.

CHAPTER TWENTY-FOUR

An Excerpt from

DEVIL'S CIRCLE (1996)

by Lucille B. Hebert

Denny returned at about 2:00 in the morning. Lucille peered out the window as his truck pulled into the yard. She threw on a housecoat and picked up a flashlight.

"Did you find her?" Lucille called as she hurried out to the truck.

Her world collapsed when she saw Denny struggling to pull Dinah from the passenger seat. Her face was deathly pale as was his. Lucille screamed as Dinah's legs cleared the doorway and she saw Dinah's white skirt stained with red.

"What's wrong with her, Denny?!"

"I don't know. I can't find any reason. These cuts are just appearing." Denny ran across the yard cradling Dinah in his arms. They reached the kitchen.

"Lay her on the table while I get our bed ready for her."

He nodded and eased Dinah gently onto the kitchen table. She moaned and gripped her chest.

"It's okay, Angel. We're going to help you."

Dinah pushed herself up with supreme effort to grab his arm. Her face contorted with the pain.

"Daddy! I hear them chanting in my head. They're killing me! Help me!"

Dinah screamed and fell back on the table. She held her abdomen again. Denny reached down and pushed the front of her purple top up enough to see her stomach. His mouth dropped in horror. Lines of red, subtle strips piercing the flesh, slowly formed on her stomach. They were drawn as if by an unseen hand. Denny recognized the shape before it took complete form. A pentagram. Small wounds were appearing now on her forehead and arms. Someone somewhere was cutting into his daughter remotely, magically.

"Lucille! Hurry!"

By the time Denny carried Dinah to their bed, blood was everywhere. Her hair was matted with it. Her face covered. Tiny cuts seeped all along her arms and legs. Lucille lit candles as Denny called the ambulance.

As they joined hands to pray, Lucille looked at their nightstand. There sat the protective bag Denny had made for Dinah. They never found her at the fireworks display that night. All their searching had led nowhere. She must have gone somewhere else. Someone had cast a curse, and there was no hedge of protection. Their eldest had entered the world vulnerable, and evil had seized its opportunity. Lucille pictured the little pink bundle that had been placed in her arms eighteen years ago and thanked God she hadn't been able to look forward to this night.

"Daddy! I'm scared!"

"Hang on, Angel. Hang on!"

"They're chanting! I hear them!"

Denny produced a missal and started reading in Latin. He was rusty, but desperate for any remedy. Dinah's head sank on the pillow, and her eyes started to close.

"Dinah! Dinah!" Lucille screamed. "Stay with us."

Dinah looked one last time at her through slitted eyes. And then opened them wide. Lucille started to breathe a sigh of relief when she realized that Dinah's eyes were unnaturally open. They stayed open, unblinking.

"No! No! God, no!" Lucille screamed.

Denny dropped the missal and slammed his fists on the bed. He threw back his head and howled like a wounded wolf howling at the moon. Through her pain, Lucille heard running feet. The girls would know soon. Seconds later, hysterical sobs from above confirmed that they knew.

As Denny and Lucille sat in the wreckage of their greatest failure, the distant sound of an ambulance siren reached their ears. They looked at each other across the bloody bed in stunned helplessness. Dinah lay there silently, beyond help and beyond pain.

CHAPTER TWENTY-FIVE

CRISSY MOTIONED WITH THE GUN for me to rejoin Dorcas on the couch. I moved reluctantly away from the door. My heart was beating far too fast. Her threats against Trey affected me more than the gun pointed at me. Every nerve in my body was firing, and it was taking supreme effort to hold myself in check.

"What do you mean? Trey went to his house."

"Eric was waiting for him," Crissy said. "Lured him away by saying that you'd just discovered new information and needed their help. Eric knocked him out and secured him."

"Secured him where?"

Crissy smiled with no humor in her eyes whatsoever. "I don't think so, Diana. You are a smart lady. I'll give you that. All of you are. But it's time for this game to end."

She shifted the gun to Dorcas beside me. Dorcas glared back at her, her gaze unshifting. I knew she had to be terrified, but she was hiding it well.

"I was sitting here just five minutes ago feeling sorry for you," I said, "Dreading the moment I would have to shatter your world by telling you your husband was a lying predatory scumbag. Looks like you already got the memo."

"Little Debbie," Crissy said. "Got that big vocabulary and the best you can come up with is scumbag. Maybe you're not so high and mighty after all, Hebert."

"If the word fits ..."

"You don't know anything about my husband."

"I know he killed my sister. That's all I need to know."

Crissy rose and paced around the room. She made sure to keep the gun pointed in our general direction. I stole a quick glance at Dorcas to see how she was faring. She met my gaze and blinked as if to signal to me that she was okay.

"Everyone is so narrow and small," Crissy said. "They don't understand great men, men of destiny, and what they need. They hunger more than the rest of us. Sometimes they feed that hunger in ways that cause pain. But what is that pain weighed against the good that they do in the world?"

I was sick of hearing people justify hurting others in the name of the "greater good." The argument crumbled when my parents had made it earlier, and it sounded equally hollow in Crissy's mouth.

"You're a woman. You should know how it feels to go to someone you trust for help only for them to prey on you. To want to be loved as a whole person only to discover that all too many men care about is your body and how you can satisfy them. How could you abandon those girls to that kind of manipulation and abuse?"

"I'm a woman who's a mother and a partner with my husband in a greater work than you can understand or appreciate. I'm not unsympathetic to what you're saying. But our family comes first."

"You can say it's about preserving your family, and you may even believe that," I said. "But at the end of the day, it's about holding on to power and privilege no matter who it hurts or what it costs the rest of us. There's no justification for that."

"You knew?" Dorcas said. "You knew he killed Dinah, and you still married him?"

Crissy shook her head. "I didn't know about your sister until a month ago. Eric told me what happened and that your parents were about to authorize production of a film that could expose what happened. We needed to stop it."

"By destroying my parents?" Dorcas said.

"Your parents are two-bit circus hucksters fighting an imaginary war. We help people every day in the real world. My husband will be the executive director of our denomination's state convention in a year and of the national convention in five. I love him. I believe in him. Helping him contain his demons is the least I can do. It's my calling. It's my duty."

A wave of nausea washed over me as I considered the full implications of what she was saying.

"You may not have known about Dinah. But at some point after your marriage, probably not long after, you started to realize that Eric was abusing women and young girls. You're not a counselor, restrainer, or protector. You're an enabler. You've not just looked the other way. Every one of those girls was abused with your active support."

"That's not fair," Crissy said, glaring at me. "I hate it! I wish he would stop it. He keeps promising me he will. And he really tries. It's gotten longer and longer between each instance. I care about those girls. But he's my husband. The father of our boys. Our life and our ministry yield so much good. Good that outweighs the cost."

"You sound like Lucille. And I will tell you the same thing I told her. People are the point. Not a cause or creed or ministry. Any belief system or movement that discards human beings like disposable collateral damage rests on sick foundations."

Crissy's eyes flashed. She raised the gun and pointed it straight at my head. Dorcas' eyes widened and her body tensed. I eased my leg closer to hers, hoping she would catch my signal to stay still.

"You've got a big mouth and a lot of opinions, Hebert. I would love to shut you up for good. Before that, we have business to conduct."

I gazed steadily at her, trying to look past the gun barrel to her face. She held the gun like she knew how to use it, but I sensed the tiniest uncertainty in her eyes. *How far is she willing to go?* Our lives depended on the answer. And probably Trey's too. I wanted to believe she was bluffing about him, but she didn't seem to be.

"How do I know you're telling the truth about Trey?"

Crissy pulled out her phone and pushed several icons on the screen. She held the phone out. As I moved to take it, she pulled it back slightly.

"Don't get any ideas about tryin' to call anyone. I know how to use this thing and I will."

I nodded and accepted the phone. Trey was slumped in the passenger seat of a car. His head was tilted against the headrest. Anguish gripped me at the sight. I fought to keep my composure and stay steady as I passed the phone back.

"Trey Laurence is the best man I have ever known. He's a better man than your twisted husband can ever hope to be."

"That's sweet," Crissy said. "Not sure why that matters right now."

"It matters because I want you to know that if anything happens to him while we conduct this 'business,' I will make sure both of you pay a heavy price. No matter what it costs or how long it takes."

Crissy smirked, "I'm the one with the gun, Honey. Where are the papers?"

"This is so stupid!" Dorcas said. "You have any idea how many images of those documents we've shared trying to interpret them? The originals don't matter."

"Eric says we can dismiss the others as fraudulent if we have the originals. Believe me, people buy all kinds of lies when they have an interest in believing you."

"You should know," I said. "You've made a career or 'ministry' exploiting people's trust."

Crissy moved the gun closer to Dorcas.

"Where are they?"

Dorcas stared back in defiant silence.

She shifted the gun back to me.

"How about you, Diana?"

"I forget."

She seemed genuinely upset. "I don't want to hurt either one of you. You're giving me no choice. How about we try this?"

Crissy walked around the couch behind us and rested the gun against Dorcas' temple. "Are you willing to tell me now, Diana? Because I'm very prepared to blow her brains all over you right now."

Dorcas swallowed and tried to look straight forward, refusing to make eye contact with me. My mind raced back to that night I had tried so hard to block out over the years. My throat was raw when I finally stopped screaming and yelling. That feeling of my sister being ripped from me seared my soul and burned my heart once again. *Not again!*

"Please leave her alone," I begged. "You can kill me if you need to hurt someone."

"That's what I thought," Crissy said. "Like I said, I don't want to hurt anyone. Where are the papers? Now!"

My mind struggled to focus. If we gave the papers to Crissy, we might still make the case with the copies. I couldn't know that for sure. We could lose the opportunity to gain justice for Dinah, Mia, and who knew how many other women on a technicality. The alternative meant losing Dorcas. I knew what Dinah would choose.

"Okay. Please just take the gun away from her. I'll tell you."

"Diana, no!" Dorcas cried.

"Shut up, Dorcas!" Crissy barked, pressing the gun harder against her head.

"The barn! We took the papers out to the barn and put them in a special secure case in the loft."

Crissy frowned. "You better not be lying to me, Diana."

"I'm not. We were keeping them there until Lester Owen's office opened tomorrow morning."

Crissy backed up and looked at Dorcas. "How could you tell her, Diana?" Dorcas said.

"I'm sorry. We're out of options."

Dorcas's frustration seemed to satisfy Crissy that I was telling the truth. She moved to the window and looked out at the reporters gathered beyond the property line.

"Okay. We're going to take a little trip."

She motioned for us to rise. We obeyed and filed toward the kitchen door.

"Open it slowly, Dorcas," Crissy said. "Don't try to pull any tricks or run. I'll empty this gun into your big sister's back."

Dorcas eased the door open and led the way to the barn. Crissy slipped the gun into the pocket of her green cardigan. But we knew it was still trained on us.

"Let's take a leisurely stroll across here. Don't give those reporters any reason to get stirred up."

The walk from our house to the barn had never taken so long. The dead grass crunched beneath our feet. The sounds of the night were awakening all around us. The barn loomed ahead like a malevolent sentinel. Just a matter of yards away lights flickered and conversations were audible. Help was that close and that far away at the same time. I gained a new appreciation for our "vultures" and wished I had a way to contact them without alerting Crissy.

Dorcas turned on the barn lights. The two fluorescent bulbs flickered to life with a loud buzz. She walked slowly toward the narrow ladder leading to the loft.

"Are you kidding me?" Crissy said when she saw the ladder. She backed up and swung the gun back and forth between us. "This is a trick! You think you're getting away while we climb this ladder!"

"It's up to you. You don't have to trust us. But you're not getting those documents unless we go up that ladder."

Crissy stared at me, trying to weigh my sincerity. Her gaze flicked to Dorcas to do the same. She deliberated for a moment, then exhaled and motioned with the gun toward the ladder.

"You first, Dorcas. Then me. Diana, you stay on the ground until we reach the top. Then you come. You scream, yell, or do anything else to attract attention, and I will kill your sister. Got it?"

Both of us nodded. Dorcas stepped to the ladder and gave me a quick look before she started to ascend. Delilah joked about having a "sister radar" when she had found me in the woods. There was, of course, no real sister radar. On the other hand, I was hoping our sister intuition was synching as well as I thought. Our lives depended on it. I was lying. Dorcas knew I was lying. When she supported my lie inside the house, I trusted that she knew what I had in mind. We were about to find out if we really were on the same page.

Crissy had confiscated our phones immediately after putting us back on the couch. No hope of assistance there. We were going to have to help ourselves and Trey as well.

My daddy was a child at heart. That's one reason he did so well with kids. Many conservative Christians had objections to celebrating Halloween, among them Lucille. Daddy never actually celebrated Halloween because there were too many people in his circle opposed to it. He instead channeled that love for horror and spooky tricks into his museum of curiosities. We never had huge crowds, hence the humble housing of the artifacts. It didn't matter to Daddy. He delighted in taking groups of any size into the loft to show them his haunted treasures, especially around Halloween.

I remembered two years ago sitting across from him in a Jackson, Mississippi diner while he gave me an animated description of his latest trick. He'd engineered it just in time for Halloween and to coincide with the release of the blandly titled *Christine Returns*. It was based on my own experience with my least favorite doll in the artifacts room. We'd told my parents about mine and Trey's foray into the room because they'd noticed the intrusion. Lucille had even used the episode as part of *Devil's Circle*. We'd, of course, omitted the part where Trey gave me my first kiss. What Daddy didn't know and all that.

Dorcas reached the top of the ladder and disappeared into the loft. Crissy slowly followed her. She kept the gun trained upward in case Dorcas tried to throw anything down the opening. I watched her reach the top and slip through the square opening. I glanced around one last time looking for any safer option, I saw none and followed them up.

They were waiting for me at the top. Dorcas stood on one side of the opening while Crissy planted herself on the other with her gun trained on Dorcas. I stepped off the ladder and joined Dorcas.

"Where are they?"

"In that box," I nodded toward Christine's wooden box inside the homemade china cabinet. She sat where she always had, pouring disdain our way through her artificial eyes.

"Are you serious?" Crissy eyed Christine with distaste.

"Hey, it's our most secure place on this property. Daddy gets too much mileage out of that doll to leave it out here unprotected. We put the papers under the folds of her dress."

Crissy rolled her eyes and groaned. "I've said it all my life and will say it again. You people are weird. Okay, you're going to open the case and get the papers from under the doll, Dorcas. Diana, you will stand back and wait. Anyone tries anything, and I will shoot. Got it?"

We nodded. Dorcas produced her key to the cabinet and stepped toward it. I backed up a couple of feet. There were actual papers in Christine's box under her dress. Daddy put them there at a loss for where else to keep them. They were certificates of provenance detailing the history of her ownership. I carried doubts about their authenticity. Daddy's claim that Christine dated to the early nineteenth century rested on those certificates.

Dorcas opened the cabinet and reached beneath the folds of Christine's dress. Crissy's eyes shone with new light when her hand reappeared gripping the certificates.

"Give them to me!" Crissy commanded.

Dorcas handed her the certificates and eased away from the door. Crissy moved into her spot, flipping through the documents by the dim light seeping through the roof and the hayloft door. Dorcas slipped her hand around the side of the case and looked at me. I nodded and took a tentative step toward Crissy.

"Hey wait! This is not ..."

Crissy's complaint was cut short by her own hysterical scream as Christine launched forward into her face. Dorcas removed her hand from Daddy's improvised trigger and slammed the open door of the cabinet into Crissy. She stumbled and lost her grip on the gun. I jumped forward and kicked it, hoping to knock it down to the first floor. It came close but stopped to rest on the edge of the opening. Crissy unleashed a cry of rage and leaped toward the gun. She was already on the ground and closer. I knew I couldn't beat her to it.

Reaching into the cabinet, I yelled, "Run, Dorcas!" I grabbed my tool and disappeared behind the cabinet just as Crissy recovered the gun. We crawled through the sea of artifacts.

"Not funny, Ladies! This doesn't change anything! I know where you are!"

It was obvious she didn't by the way she scanned the room.

I looked across the room to where I could barely see Dorcas crouching behind a Native American totem. I put my finger to my mouth and held up my companion. Dorcas nodded in comprehension. I touched my head and Dorcas nodded again. She pointed subtly toward the right. I sank lower and crawled in that direction.

"Diana! Dorcas!" Crissy was losing it.

I could tell she wanted to fire a shot, but she was worried about alerting the press. I wasn't sure they would even hear it with all the noise at their makeshift camp. I was glad she, at least, thought they might.

"Diana! Think about Trey. Is it worth losing him over all this? Come out!"

A noise to the left attracted her attention. She moved that direction. Dorcas had thrown one of Daddy's voodoo dolls to distract her. Crissy reached the spot and picked up the doll.

"Getting tired of this, Girls! I'll set fire to this whole damn place if it means the papers will go with it!"

No, she wouldn't. She didn't want to alert the press outside, and she was no longer sure the papers were in the barn.

Dorcas tossed another doll, this time toward the hayloft window.

"Stop it and come out!" Crissy screamed, aiming in the direction of the sound. She swung back to the right and caught a glint of blonde in the moonlight. A smile played across her lips.

"Diana, I see you. Stand up and let's get this over with." No movement. Crissy strained to make out the hint of white just beneath the blond hair. "Diana, I don't want to make any noise, but I will if I have to. Don't doubt me." No movement and no response. "Stubborn Bitch!"

Crissy said. She pointed the gun and fired. Her target exploded into a million porcelain pieces. Christine's head and fibers of "Jayne Mansfield's wig" scattered across the loft.

"What ..." Crissy never finished her sentence. I jumped her from behind while Dorcas lashed at her feet with a small pitchfork. Crissy went down. All three of our hands fumbled for the gun, but it was beneath Crissy's body.

"You can't get the gun! Get off me!"

"I'll settle for this then," I said, delivering a deeply satisfying punch to her face. "Go, Dorcas! I'll hold her." My mistake was taking my eyes off her to see if Dorcas had gone. Dorcas was shaking her head. "I'm staying with you," she insisted.

My response was cut off by the butt of the gun striking my shoulder. Crissy had managed to pull it out and get just enough room to swing.

"Diana!" Dorcas screamed.

The blow was enough to knock me off balance and allow Crissy to scramble to her feet. She retreated to the ladder and took a step down to the second highest rung. She pointed the gun at us again with triumphant disdain. *All that for nothing.*

I looked up to see Dorcas beside me. She'd tried to get to Crissy but was not fast enough.

"I'm sorry," she said as she extended a hand to help me up.

I stood unsteadily, nursing my throbbing shoulder while Crissy tried to reassess the situation.

"I want to know where those papers really are right now. And then we're going to Beauregard Park to give them to my husband. Any further delays or foolishness will end in your deaths. In fact, I may just go ahead and lighten my load right now."

Crissy pointed her gun at Dorcas. I scanned the distance between us, calculating if I could push Dorcas away before she fired. Then we heard the sounds outside. Crissy glanced uneasily toward the unseen property line, wondering if her shot had been heard. As much as I wanted it to be the case, I doubted it. Random gunshots in rural Louisiana were not as rare as they might be in other places. And the vulture camp was a noisy place.

"What are those crazy reporters doing?" Crissy said. She was trying not to look as nervous as she felt.

I listened closer. It wasn't the reporters. Another demographic in the vulture camp had been thrown into a frenzy. There could only be one reason why. A smile spread across my lips as new hope surged through me.

"We're not going anywhere with you," I said. "This is your last chance to take that gun off my sister and talk this through reasonably. You won't get another one."

My newfound confidence scared Crissy more than my words. She looked uncertainly back and forth between us. She opened her mouth to respond when the ladder tipped slightly to the left and back toward the right. Crissy reached a hand, the one not gripping the gun, out to steady herself. I'd gotten the message. As Crissy reoriented, I jumped forward and kicked the ladder, separating it for a moment from the support notches it locked into to give it stability. Crissy pivoted toward me. As she did, the ladder slipped backward as it was pushed from below. Crissy screamed and fired a second shot that went wild. I heard the bullet embed itself in the roof above us. She tumbled off the ladder and fell to the first floor. We heard her strike the ground hard.

Crissy moaned in pain but forced herself to rise.

"You crazy bitches! When I get up ..."

Before she could finish her sentence, Delilah's steel-toed boots slammed into her face. Blood, along with three of Crissy's teeth, spewed across our barn. She tried again to push herself up and speak. This time Delilah's fist knocked her back down. By the time Dorcas and I reached the ground, Delilah's heavily tattooed right arm was a blur as she hammered Crissy in a frenzy of wrath.

"Delilah!"

Delilah ignored me. One look at Crissy told me Delilah could easily kill her if she didn't stop. I jumped forward and threw my arms around Delilah.

"Stop! We need her. They have Trey. He's in trouble."

Either Trey's name or my touch pierced the feral part of Delilah's brain. She dropped Crissy and backed away. She squeezed my arms and then turned to wrap me up in her own embrace.

"Are you okay?"

"We're fine," I said.

She detached herself from me and swept Dorcas up into an equally tight hug.

Dorcas winked at me over her shoulder and said, "Who knew that all it took was getting held hostage to get some Delilah love."

"Shut up," Delilah said as she released Dorcas and wiped her eyes.

"You have the best way of turning up when I need you lately," I said. "How did you get here?"

"I took Taylor's private plane as soon as we finished with Tianna this afternoon. I just couldn't wait to come back after everything we learned about Dinah today. My staff is rescheduling performances for a few days."

"Okay," I said. "This is extremely low on the list of things to care about right now. But Taylor?"

"Yeah. Sweet kid. She's cool. A little vanilla sometimes, but we've all gotta start somewhere."

Crissy moaned and rolled over on her back.

"Speaking of haters who gonna hate," Delilah picked up Crissy's gun and trained it on her.

There was no need. One look at Crissy's battered face confirmed that she was spent for now.

"What now?" Dorcas asked.

I wished I had a good answer.

CHAPTER TWENTY-SIX

WE CARRIED CRISSY FROM THE BARN to the house. Screaming fans from the road shouted Delilah's name, not noticing or caring that their idol was moving a woman's inert body. She waved with one hand once or twice and then focused on the work at hand. We settled her into a kitchen chair. Dorcas produced a rope she'd brought from the barn. We tied and gagged her.

Crissy started to wake up. Her hostile eyes shifted to each of us in turn as we looked down at her.

"Should we clean her wounds?" Dorcas asked.

"I'll pour a whole bottle of peroxide down her and see how she likes that," Delilah said.

"Seriously."

"She'll live," I said. "We can't waste time with that right now."

"So how do we help Trey?" Dorcas said.

The song "My Savior Lives, My Savior Loves" by Casting Crowns filled our kitchen.

We looked at each other.

"Sure as hell not mine," Delilah said.

Our eyes rested on Crissy. It was coming from her pocket. I reached into her pocket and produced her phone.

"How do I unlock it?" I said, pulling the gag down slightly.

"My anniversary. August 15, 2001."

I slipped her gag back and entered the numbers.

"Hello?" I said.

"Where are you, Crissy? You're taking too long!"

I pushed speaker so the others could hear.

"Crissy's a little tied up at the moment."

There was a pause.

"Dr. Chambers. You never cease to amaze. There's more than a little Hebert left in you. Where is my wife?"

"Here with me. Where is Trey?"

"With me. He's starting to come around a little bit. He's going to be furious when he realizes what's happening."

"You have Trey, and I have Crissy. Let's trade and be done. No harm, no foul."

"We're not on equal terms unless you're okay killing my wife. Somehow, I don't think you are. I like Trey, but I have no such handicap."

I looked helplessly at my sisters. Their anxious faces suggested no way out.

"Okay. What do you want?"

"I want those papers brought, along with my wife, to the playground at Beauregard Park. We can exchange them there. I will leave Trey at a remote location and release him once the papers are safe in my hands."

"The playground at Beauregard Park. Is that where she met you? That night?"

"Yes. She wouldn't be alone with me after we were together."

"You mean after you raped her."

"I loved her. You may not believe me, but I did. I watched her all through high school. I couldn't believe it when she started working at the store. I even drove back after work a couple of times to give her a ride home. We were alone one night after hours. I stayed a little longer to help her with her work. Maybe I misread the signals. I thought she loved me too."

I fought to keep the contents of my stomach from spilling on the counter. Delilah and Dorcas looked equally sick.

"She was just being nice and helpful. Dinah never thought you would interpret it as anything more than friendship in your sick little mind. You assaulted her in the store that night?"

"Call it what you want."

"Dinah quit and thought she was done with you. Then she discovered she was pregnant."

"She told me," Eric said. "Dinah asked me to meet her at the mall, and we talked in the food court. She always met me in public places after we were together. I begged her to marry me. She said no. Why couldn't she just start a family with me?"

"Because she didn't want to spend her life with the sick son of a bitch who raped her," I said.

I was trying to remember that I didn't want to antagonize him too much until we had Trey back, but it got harder the more he talked about Dinah.

"She planned to tell your parents and have the baby. When it became clear that she wouldn't marry me, I begged her to have an abortion. My mother was a gynecologist. She had access to drugs, including experimental ones not yet approved in the United States. I told her it would be easy."

"Why couldn't she just have the baby? What did it matter to you if she had the baby and went off to school?"

"I couldn't take the chance that she would someday revive her accusations of rape. And there would be the baby. Everyone would know something happened between us. My father had already planned a path for me that would give me a great platform and ministry."

"So why did you meet that night?" I asked, grateful for once that the long-winded preacher liked to hear the sound of his own voice. Dixon was entering Bond villain levels of disclosure.

"I'd kept sending her messages and calling. She asked me to meet during the fireworks at Beauregard to tell me once and for all to stop."

"You secured the abortifacients with the hope that she would agree to take them to get rid of you?"

"Yes. I stole them from my mother's office. I asked Dinah to do it, and she refused. Told me she was going to have the baby and give it up for adoption. I was desperate. She'd brought a drink with her from the snack area. Someone stopped us to talk to her, and she sat her drink down. I took the opportunity while she was distracted to pour the medicine into her drink. I was nervous. And it was dark. I was in a hurry. I poured too much in. It was an accident!"

Our kitchen was dead silent. Tears flowed from all our eyes, but no one sobbed. The expressions on our faces were set and hard. Crissy peered anxiously at us, real fear gripping her as she watched us brought to the edge. Eric Dixon sensed what our silence meant even through the phone.

"I loved her! She was the most amazing woman I've ever known! I didn't mean to kill her! I would have given anything if she had agreed to marry me."

"I'm sure that's great comfort to the woman who just earned herself a prison sentence for you," I said, relishing Crissy's devastated look at her husband's declaration of love for Dinah more than I should.

"If I'm not mistaken, you love someone too. And time is running out for him."

Score one for Dixon. I felt my balance eroding and put my hand on the counter to steady myself.

"Where is he, Dixon?"

"Tucked away for safekeeping. Like I said, I'll come back and release him after you get me those documents at Beauregard Park."

"Okay," I said as my sisters nodded.

"Good. No one has to die here if you play it smart. Beauregard Park in two hours. That will allow some time for any lingering people to go home. Diana, do not call the police and come alone. If I see your sisters or any cops, I will leave immediately and end Trey. Understood?"

"Yes," I said bitterly.

The call ended.

I made the mistake of picturing my first kiss with Trey in the artifacts room and our more recent first in New Orleans. New tears filled my eyes, and I covered my face with my hands. Dorcas hugged me tight as I sobbed into her shoulder for a few minutes. She cried with me while Delilah pounded the countertop in frustration.

Through my sobs, I heard my ringtone.

"I didn't think you liked the *Demonologist* theme," Delilah said.

I released Dorcas and snatched the phone from my pocket. Excitement raced through me as a familiar voice spoke.

"Diana, is that you?"

"Yes! Yes! Selena, where are you?"

"I'm in New Orleans. I got another call from ... him. He wants me to drive down and be ready to play Dinah in two hours at Beauregard Park in Picardy."

My shoulders slumped. Besides testifying to how truly sick Dixon's love for the theatrical ran, Selena's news told us nothing new about his plans for us or Trey, but we knew the real reason Dixon planned the meet for a full two hours away.

"He expects you to be at Beauregard in two hours?"

"Yes. I'm supposed to stop off at the old Picardy school to pick up my tools."

My sisters were thinking the same thing I was.

"Selena, you have no idea how much you've just helped us. Just stay put and we'll take if from here. I will never forget this. You've honored my sister's memory tonight."

We could hear the emotion in her voice.

"Thank you. The honor is all mine. Please let me know if there is anything else I can do."

"We will."

"Say what you will, he has a strong sense of irony," I said after she hung up.

"You think he has Trey at the school too?" Delilah asked.

"He has to," Dorcas said. "He's on the local historical preservation board, and they have access to the building. Where else? He wouldn't take Trey to his house or the church."

"Selena's given us an advantage if he does have Trey there," I said. "We can surprise him ahead of the meeting time. We might be able to save Trey without having to give up the documents."

"We should bring them just in case," Dorcas said. "Trey's more important than holding onto them."

She walked over to the stove and opened a drawer next to it. Dorcas removed the two documents, taking special care to shoot a triumphant look at Crissy. Crissy glared at her.

"Trey will never forgive himself if we give up our chance to stop Dixon in exchange for him," I said. "Still, I'd rather let him live with that than live without him."

"It was that good, huh?" Delilah said.

The return of her snarky comments encouraged me. We were still in the wilderness, but the path out was beginning to unfold.

"No details!"

"Yeah, we'll see how long you hold out. Inquiring minds want to know."

"Do we call the police?" Dorcas asked.

I shook my head. "I don't want to risk their alerting Dixon before we have Trey."

"I can call Momma and have her on standby to call them when we're ready."

Neither of us looked excited at the prospect.

Dorcas insisted. "We have to tell them. Dinah was their daughter. They have a right to know. And to help."

"Daddy can barely get out of bed still," I said. "Lucille could jump the gun and let them know too soon."

Delilah nodded her agreement.

"Maybe you should go see if you can find Trey. I can take Emily Gantry here to the police station, and then we can meet you there.

Dorcas, you can go stay with Mom and Dad. Coordinate things from there. You can call us when you know if Trey is at the school, Diana."

"No!"

We all flinched, including Crissy. Dorcas' shout echoed through the house and commanded our full attention. She reached out and took our hands.

"Don't you get it? Don't you understand?"

We obviously didn't, and neither of us knew what to say.

"We are surrounded by cruel people who want to destroy us and everyone we love," Dorcas continued. "They have power and resources beyond our reach. What we have is this!" She held our linked hands up for emphasis. "Dinah faced her struggles alone because we were too young to understand or help. If she were here, she would remind us we don't have to do that. I'm not staying with Momma and Daddy. We're not separating. You're my sisters. Your blood is my blood. Trey is like my brother. I'm going with you. I will die beside you if I have to. But, Diana, no sister of mine is ever facing the darkness alone again."

A hush fell over the room.

"The kid has a point," Delilah said softly.

I gripped Dorcas' hand tighter and reached over to take Delilah's. She slid her fingers through mine and squeezed my hand. Our eyes instinctively swept to the space between Delilah and Dorcas. None of us said it, but all of us felt it. The sense of Dinah's presence was so powerful I almost expected to see her standing there with us, her hands linked to ours and her smile warming us all.

"I love you both," I said.

"I love both of you," Dorcas said.

Delilah nodded. She was fighting to hold back her tears.

"Me too. I mean, you too. You know."

"We know," I said.

"We go together?" Dorcas said.

"We go together," I said. "We can call Lucille and Daddy on the way."

"What about her?" Delilah asked. Crissy looked questioningly at us.

"We can't risk her alerting Pastor Pervert," I said. "Let's lock her in the artifacts room.

We'll send Deputy Gorman out to pick her up once we deal with Dixon."

The three of us dragged Crissy, chair and all, to the artifacts room. After checking her bonds, Delilah lowered her gag to give her a drink of water.

"You'll never get away with this. Eric will figure out what you're doing. You're condemning your friend to death!"

"You better pray not. I'll be back to take my frustrations out on you if anything happens to him."

Delilah shoved the gag back into her mouth rougher than necessary.

Dorcas slammed the door and locked it.

"Let's go get Trey," Delilah said, as she threw a reassuring arm around me. "I worked too hard to get you crazy kids together to let anything happen to him."

CHAPTER TWENTY-SEVEN

IT TOOK US FAR TOO LONG TO LOSE the vulture squad. Dorcas pulled out every trick and still had a couple of cars tailing us. She finally lost them three miles north of Bayou Mystère. We circled back and picked up my car from Trinity Assembly of God's parking lot. We'd tried this car change trick several times. I thought it worked when we went to the Hightowers', but Crissy's knowledge of that trip meant someone had traced us then. I hoped nobody would follow us now and accidentally alert Eric Dixon to our presence.

We enjoyed two advantages. Surprise gave us an opportunity to get close to Trey before Dixon knew we were there. Catching Dixon at the school before he could lead us onto his chosen battlefield, Beauregard Park, meant that we were choosing the field of play and setting it in a place that we all knew well.

"Absolutely not! You need to call the police and let them handle it."

"I wasn't calling to ask your permission, Lucille. We're on our way. Dorcas will text you when we need you to contact Deputy Gorman."

I heard a thump and a groan.

"Denny!" Lucille's image shook as she hurried to Dad's bedside.

He was trying to get up and failing. He lay on the floor beside the bed. I watched as he tried to push himself up again and pounded the floor in frustration when he failed to rise.

"Tell them to wait. I'm ... I ..."

Lucille set the phone down on the dresser where I could still see. She pulled a nitroglycerin tablet out of her pocket and held it to my Dad's mouth. He swallowed it and sat on the floor with his back against the bed.

"They can't go. Don't go, Angels. Please."

Lucille glanced back at the phone. I could see the worry etched on her face. I did the only thing I could. I lied to my dad.

"You're right, Daddy. Get back in bed. We'll call the police and let you know when we have Trey back."

He nodded, still trying to catch his breath.

Lucille walked back to the phone and said, "Thank you, Diana. Let us know what the police say."

The window closed. I was about to put the phone back in my pocket when a text came through. It was Lucille:

Let me know when you're ready for the police. Will be waiting. Prayers for Trey. Be careful.

Relief swept through me.

Thank you.

The darkened carcass of our school loomed ahead of us. I pulled around the building, and we parked across the street behind the hardware store. I noted the broken windows at various points along the main building. It was possible we might have to crawl through one of those windows if Dixon locked the door behind him. We slipped across the street and tried several doors before the service door near the gym opened for us.

The smell of hardwood greeted us as we entered the darkened court. Memories of physical education classes and basketball games filled my mind. Phantom smells drifted from the past. My nostrils stung with the stifling aromas of sweaty bodies and leather balls. All three of us stopped and stood in rigid silence when Dorcas' shoes squeaked on the gym floor. We resumed our silent parade after it was clear that no one was coming to investigate.

Dorcas activated her phone light, and we crept along the hallways. They hadn't even bothered to remove the lockers. They stood like silent sentinels, some with their doors still open, waiting for their students to return. No one would ever use them again. Their watch had ended.

Emptied classrooms prompted memories of long days spent in classes waiting for the bell. The thrill of pouring out into the hallways at the end of the day had kept us going. Except of course, for those poor souls destined for detention. They stayed after school. *After school!* Given Dixon's sick fascination with irony, I guessed where he was keeping Trey.

I touched Dorcas' shoulder and leaned over to whisper in her ear. "Mr. Francis' room." She nodded. I signaled for Delilah to follow. We entered the high school wing. Mr. Francis' room sat nestled in between Mrs. Estrada's home economics class and Mr. Tyler's chemistry class. I noted the ghost of an American history bulletin board. Frayed images of George Washington and Abraham Lincoln hung beneath a rotted heading that proclaimed "esidents' Day."

A voice was coming from Mr. Tyler's old room. *Eric Dixon!*

"Selena, I hope this is going to voicemail because you're driving. Time is wasting. I left the items you need at center court in the old Picardy High School gym. You can enter through the service door at the back of the gym."

We all flattened against the wall behind the lockers as Dixon emerged from Mr. Tyler's room carrying two items. One was a duffle bag that I guessed contained Selena's tools. The other was an old portable Bunsen Burner from the chemistry classroom. He paused and looked down the hallway. Satisfied that no one was there, Dixon stepped to the door of Francis' classroom, looked in, and continued down the hallway toward the gym. I didn't dare breathe. Thankfully, there were several ways to get to the gym, and he chose to go the opposite direction from the way we had come. We all stepped out once he was out of sight and hurried to Francis' old classroom.

Trey was tied to the teacher's chair behind the big brown desk. Dixon had knotted two thick nylon cords around him in addition to the regular rope that bound him. His mouth was gagged with a red handkerchief. He looked up at the sound of my approach. I loved that there was someone who looked at me like he did. I reached around his head and untied the gag. My fingers lingered over a nasty bump left by Dixon's surprise attack. It seemed to be swelling in the right direction and hopefully wouldn't pose any serious issues.

"You are the most beautiful sight I have ever seen," he said before I stopped his words with a deep kiss.

"And she's not even the one with the switchblade," Delilah said.

"Delilah!" Trey laughed as I moved back so she could examine his bonds. "How's my favorite inappropriate sister?"

"I'm good, Romeo," Delilah said with a wink. "You'll be glad I'm the inappropriate sister when you see what I brought. I bet Juliet there doesn't have one of these."

Delilah was indeed the proud owner of a switchblade which she produced and used to start sawing at his ropes.

"I'm not even going to ask why you carry that," I said.

"Just be glad I do. It works underwater too."

"I'm sorry I didn't tell you about Dixon on the phone. If I had, you would have known not to trust him."

"It's not your fault." A shadow passed over his face. "I heard enough of his conversation with you on the phone to get the gist. I'm so sorry, Diana. I could kill him for what he did to Dinah. She deserved so much better."

Dorcas hissed from the doorway, "I think I hear him coming!"

Delilah sawed faster. I wished we had a second knife so I could help her. One rope snapped. Then a second. Delilah got the last one started enough to weaken its structural integrity. Trey flexed and stretched with supreme effort. The last rope snapped.

"That's the closest I'll ever come to feeling like Superman," Trey said.

"I hope you've got a bulletproof ass too," Delilah said. "These people like guns."

Trey leaped from the chair and wrapped me in his arms.

"I was so scared when he said Crissy went to your house."

"We're okay," I said, savoring the feel of his arms around me and his chest against me.

"Let's keep it R-rated, people," Delilah said. "As much as I would like to get the sexy details De-Bore-A has been denying me, I'm afraid we don't have time for X right now."

Dorcas nodded feverishly. "He must have gone the other way earlier, but he's coming back now."

"Let's go," I said. "We don't want to get trapped in this classroom."

The four of us rushed out of Mr. Francis' old room. We could indeed hear Dixon's footsteps coming back our way. We started down the hall in the opposite direction, but it was obvious we couldn't get down the hall fast enough to beat Dixon's pace. Dorcas and Delilah flattened themselves against the wall behind the lockers on the right side of the hallway. Trey and I took the left. I felt Trey tense up beside me when Dixon appeared around the corner. Every muscle in his body was screaming to rush Dixon. I touched his hand and mimicked a gun with my thumb and index finger. He got the message, though I could tell he didn't like it.

Dixon reached Mr. Francis' old room and walked in. A minute later, a very unpastoral stream of obscenities issued from the room. Dixon emerged with gun in hand, one the same make as Crissy's, and looked wildly down the hall both ways.

"You think you're clever, don't you! Let me guess. Selena! This is not a game, Ladies. I'm a very serious man."

We stayed silent as he ranted, his words echoing off the walls and reverberating through the metal lockers. I made eye contact with Dorcas and drew an invisible shield over my heart. She nodded. I eased my phone out and began to type:

Police now

I checked to be sure that my phone was on silent. A minute later, Lucille's reply flashed on my screen:

Done. On their way.

Dixon was pacing now in both directions, first down one side of the hallway and then the other. He was too smart. He knew we didn't have enough time in the period he was gone to get far.

"Come out and we can do this fast! No one gets hurt. I just want the documents."

He was getting closer. Almost on top of us now. Dixon was closer to Delilah and Dorcas on the right, which meant he would see us first on the left. The locker beside Delilah was one of many that hung open, its empty maw crying out for books to fill it. As he approached us, I felt Trey readying himself to charge. Dixon took two steps forward. We made eye contact. A humorless smile spread across his face, his cheeks raising his wide-rimmed glasses. He started to raise his weapon.

Delilah slammed the open locker door into his face. He stumbled backward. His crooked glasses wobbled for a moment and tumbled to the floor.

"Damn you!" Dixon shouted.

He braced himself against the wall to regain his balance. His gun hand waved back and forth with random inaccuracy.

"Run!" Delilah yelled.

Dixon fired wildly twice. Fortunately for us, he couldn't see without his glasses. I looked over my shoulder to see him fumbling on the ground for them.

We were losing track of each other in the darkness. I reached out and grabbed Trey's hand. I heard Delilah and Dorcas' footfalls but couldn't see them. We entered the cafeteria just in time to see Delilah disappear through the opposite doorway. The room itself was a jumbled mess. It staggered me how much raw material the school board had just discarded in the consolidation. Tables and chairs were strewn across the room, many of them upended so that the legs stuck up. Tables standing properly were scattered throughout the cluttered room. The two of us started navigating through the debris field of Picardy's cafeteria. We both stumbled several times. Trey swore as his foot caught on an overturned chair. He dislodged himself, and we crept toward the center of the cafeteria. I reached the halfway point when we heard someone coming. Dixon was moving again, and I guessed he had recovered his glasses.

"There's no way we're going to stumble through this trash heap before he gets here," I said.

"These tables look like lily pads to you?"

"What? You've got to be kidding."

"I never kid, Sweetheart," Fake Bogart said. "Well, at least I'm not kidding now."

Trey leaped onto the nearest tabletop and extended his hand to help me up. We jumped across a series of exposed tabletops in the most bizarre game of *Frogger* in Picardy High School history. Our feet had just hit the floor on the other side when Dixon came bursting through the opposite door. He fired a shot. A bullet embedded into the door frame near us. We ducked and ran through the open door.

"Glad this guy's got Stormtrooper aim," Trey gasped as we picked up the pace.

Then we were back in the darkness. The lockers flew past as we ran for the gym service door. I didn't see Dorcas or Delilah anywhere. It worried me, and though he tried not to show it, I could tell it worried Trey too. The service door appeared ahead. We drew on our reserves and reached it without complications. Trey kicked it open, and we stepped into the cool night air.

Delilah turned to meet us. I was thrilled to see her until I realized that she was alone.

"Where's Dorcas?"

"I thought she was with you," Delilah said, her brow creasing with concern.

Even though Dorcas' ankle had recovered mostly from Thanksgiving, it was still a little tender.

"We should have stayed with her." I moaned.

"I'll go back and look for her," Trey said. "You wait for the police."

"I didn't just get you back to send you back in there alone," I said.

"No time to argue!" Delilah said, grabbing both our hands and pulling us back into the building.

We didn't have to go far. Dixon heard the door opening again. He called to us from the gym.

"Come say hi to your sister."

We exchanged worried looks all around. Delilah made a sweeping motion and pointed down the hallway. I nodded, signaling that I understood. She hurried down the hallway toward the main gym doorway as Trey and I entered through the service doors.

Dixon was standing at center court with his arm wrapped around Dorcas' chest and his gun aimed at her head. Dorcas' expression looked more apologetic than afraid.

"I'm so sorry! My ankle gave out."

"Don't worry, Dor. Are you okay?"

"Yes. I'm just tired of Dixons pointing guns at my head."

Dixon smirked. I wanted so much to wipe that smirk off his face permanently.

"Well," he said. "It seems that we're here again. I'm perfectly fine trading one hostage for another. Now, the papers please."

I noticed that the portable Bunsen Burner was lit, its purple flame illuminating the gym. It stood next to Dixon and Dorcas. Its flickering light gave the scene an eerie psychedelic feel.

"You planning on doing a chemistry experiment?" I asked, trying to buy Delilah time.

"Not exactly," Dixon said. "I plan to consign those documents you're carrying to the flames where they belong. Then we can leave this behind once and for all."

"How do we know you won't just shoot us when you have the documents?" Trey asked.

"You don't," Dixon said. "You do know for sure that I will shoot her if I don't get them."

He pressed the gun tighter against Dorcas's head. She winced.

"Your plan is nuts from beginning to end," I said. "We've got digital copies of those papers, and we have Mia Jordan's body. Any competent medical examiner will identify the drugs in her corpse now that we know what to look for."

"There's no way to prove I administered those drugs," Dixon said. "It could just as easily have been your father or hers."

"DNA tests of Mia's kids and all the information about what you did to Dinah should help. Plus, I'm sure other women will come forward once they hear about Dinah and Mia. I don't know if Dinah was the first, but we know she wasn't the last. I believe there's no statute of limitations in Louisiana for murder or sexual assault."

"Manslaughter," Dixon insisted, tightening his grip on Dorcas, "I didn't mean to kill her."

"If you say so. We'll see if the jury agrees. Even if you kill us, my parents know everything now and will pursue it to the bitter end this time. More so if you hurt another one of their daughters."

"Which is why I'm leaving the four of you locked up here, collecting my wife from your house, and getting out of town with my family. We'll start over somewhere. You know a thing or two about how that works."

"Not going to work, Dixon," Trey said.

"And you know it," I finished.

"Shut up!" Dixon's scream shook the silent gym.

The echo struck me as even more terrifying because it mimicked in audio form the flickering visual effect. My stomach lurched as he pressed the gun tighter against Dorcas' face. Her lip trembled, and the hint of a tear trickled out the corner of her eye.

"Shut the hell up with your judgmental nonsense, you self-righteous Bitch!" Dixon was descending into a full-blown screaming rant. "You had one role in all this. You were supposed to be the skeptic, the spoiler. I brought you down here to help me, not them!"

His trick in Nashville finally made sense.

"You wanted me here because you thought I could help you destroy my family," I said. "That I would believe they caused Mia's death. Maybe even that Dinah was calling me from beyond the grave to get justice for her."

"It's what you do all the time," Dixon said. "How many times have I seen you on the news exposing spiritual con artists and supernatural fakes? You know you're not comfortable with what your family does.

How can you justify condemning me when your parents prey on people's vulnerabilities too?"

Anger burned through me. Not just because of his hypocrisy. He'd struck a nerve. I wasn't free of hypocrisy myself.

"It's rich to hear you talk about exposing spiritual con artists."

Our time was up. I hoped Delilah was in position. My last challenge brought him back to the present. Dorcas whimpered as Dixon's arm crushed her chest and the gun pressed so hard into her temple it had to be leaving a bruise.

"Papers now!"

I reached in my jeans pocket and produced the papers.

"Here they are. Let my sister go."

"Not until I have them in my hands. Bring them over here and lay them on the floor. I want to authenticate them before I let Dorcas go."

I hesitated. *Surely Delilah must be close now.*

Dixon's exasperation was getting the best of him.

"Over here! Now!"

I stepped forward slowly. My steps were measured far below my normal gait. Dixon could tell.

"Hurry up!" He shifted the gun away from Dorcas' head toward Trey. "Not so fast, Hero. I see you."

Trey stepped back. Dixon extended the gun further and motioned for Trey to take another step back.

I was preparing to take another step when something whizzed past me with the sound and fury of a million buzzing bees. Dixon screamed in agony. His gun clattered to the ground. Dixon released Dorcas and doubled over. Dorcas stood still for a second before her mind processed what was happening. She hobbled across the court toward Trey. He ran to meet her and placed himself between her and Dixon. I had dived for the fallen gun and now stood aiming it at Dixon. A wicked-looking miniature throwing knife ran through Dixon's hand. Blood spurted from the open wound. Dixon's face twisted with pure hatred, a look I was only too happy to return.

"Great throw, Delilah!"

I saw Delilah's head peek around the corner. She hadn't reached the far side of the gym yet. Her mouth was hanging open and she was staring past me, utterly amazed. I turned to see who had thrown the knife.

Dixon's face followed mine. His eyes widened, and he bit his lip.

Dixon trembled and said, "No! You know I didn't mean to! I loved you!"

My blood chilled, and I turned slowly to look behind me. For a split second, I thought Selena had come to help us. Then I almost believed my dead sister had really returned from the grave. A figure was walking toward us in the semi-darkness. The long wavy hair, her height, her gait, her facial structure, all were so familiar. Selena's performance paled in comparison to the resemblance born of blood and genes. She hadn't had time to put her hair up. With her long locks down like I remembered them as a child, I realized for the first time in a while how much Dinah had resembled Lucille. She had looked more like her than any of the rest of us. *That's why Dixon always felt uncomfortable around Lucille. He saw Dinah every time he looked at her.*

Dixon had been seeing her tonight too. He thought it was Dinah for that split second before the moonlight revealed the steaks of gray in Lucille's long hair. We'd long lampooned "Warrior Lucille" from the *Demonologist* films. The fictional version was adept at several skills we had never seen Lucille demonstrate. One of them was knife throwing. Dorcas told us once when we were having fun at Lucille's expense that we "didn't give Momma enough credit."

Now that Dixon recognized her, he recovered some of his bravado.

"You come to cast the demons out of me, Ms. Hebert?"

"There's no exorcizing your demons, Eric," Lucille said. "You're beyond help. Your character has been twisted and deformed since you were a child."

She looked over at the three of us.

"Are you okay?"

We nodded. Even Dorcas didn't know what to say. Lucille looked around the room.

"Where's your sister?"

"I'm here," Delilah said. She appeared from her hiding place and joined us at center court. "That throw was amazing!"

Lucille allowed herself a tiny smile. "Comes in handy sometimes."

Blue and red lights flashed outside the building. Dixon stared at them in rage.

"You didn't have to get the police involved."

"We should have kept them involved twenty-five years ago," Lucille said. "It was wrong of us to let your father intimidate us into submission. I should have known then that you were responsible somehow."

"You are sacrificing me without thinking about what it will cost."

Lucille stepped beside me. She was trembling with barely contained fury. *Momma's about to shut that down.*

"You stole my beautiful daughter's innocence. Then you stole her life. You killed my grandchild. You tried to kill my other daughters on multiple occasions. You almost killed my husband. And, finally, you kidnapped and threatened to kill this man who is like my son. You are not being sacrificed. You are going to face justice for your crimes. And after you have paid the full earthly penalty, I can only hope and pray that you will burn in hell."

We were silent. No one had anything to add. Trey looked particularly moved when Lucille called him her "son." She'd never done that before.

Dixon glared at her, but he was out of clever commentary.

"Everyone okay?"

Jim Gorman entered the room with two other officers. I breathed a sigh of relief and handed the gun to him.

"We're good now. Thank you for coming!"

Gorman studied Dixon.

"Well, Pastor. This sure is a disappointment."

Dixon growled like a feral animal ready to rip Gorman's throat out. Gorman produced handcuffs and approached Dixon.

"His wife is tied up at our house," Delilah said.

"Reggie, you go wait for the others outside," Gorman said. "Bring them to the gym. Ben, drive out to the Hebert place and fetch Mrs. Dixon. And get the lights on in here."

"Not sure where the switches are," Officer Reggie said.

"Well find them, dammit!"

"I can help with that," Trey said. "I used to open up before night games."

"We used to open up sometimes, and you never could find the right switch fast enough," Delilah said, rolling her eyes and shaking her head at me.

"Well, show us then, all-knowing Master of Song," Trey said.

I smiled as I watched them walk toward the breaker box, squabbling all the way, with Officer Reggie in tow. Officer Ben nodded to us and left to provide Uber service for Christine Aurora Hines Dixon, criminal mastermind and failed hostage taker.

Lucille wrapped her arms around Dorcas, stroking her hair with one hand while she checked Dorcas' temple for signs of swelling. Satisfied that she would be fine, Lucille kept holding her close. Dorcas rested her head on Lucille's shoulder. Lucille looked over her head at me, and we exchanged a warm smile. Our first warm smile in decades.

"Thank you."

"You don't ever have to thank me, Diana," Lucille said.

She didn't hesitate or struggle as she said my name. "I hope you know I would do anything for you. No matter what else may be between us, you'll always be my baby girl."

"It's good to be on the same team for a change," I said.

She detached herself from Dorcas but left one arm around her.

Lucille gazed at me and said, "That day, that day I regret so much. I asked too much of you because I always ask too much of myself. I love you all so much, more than I have ever been able to show. You're all special and gifted in so many ways. But you ..."

She paused.

"Are better taken in small doses," I teased.

She smiled and finished, "Are the most like me."

I swallowed and tried to find the right words. None came. I settled for returning her smile with a slight nod. I had never admitted it to myself, but I knew it was true.

"What's taking so long with the damn lights?" Gorman asked. "I'm having trouble getting these cuffs tight. Can't see a thing."

"You have the papers, Diana?" Dorcas asked.

"Yes."

Just as I reached to hand the documents to Dorcas, I heard a shout behind me. I was turning to see what was happening when the documents were snatched from my hand. Eric Dixon stood free with a maniacal look in his eyes.

"We'll see if the charges stand without these," he tossed the documents toward the Bunsen Burner. They fell short, but close enough that they threatened to catch fire anyway. A breeze from the open gym door stirred them and inched them closer to the blaze.

"Trey!" I yelled as I dove for the documents.

I knew there was no way Trey could reach us in time. *I have to save these documents! For Dinah, for Mia, for every woman he's hurt or might hurt in the future.*

"Diana, he's got Gorman's gun!" Dorcas shrieked.

I ignored her. My hand wrapped around the papers, and I snatched them back from the brink of destruction.

The rest happened so fast I had no idea what was going on until it was over.

Dorcas screamed, "No!"

A gun shot erupted in the gym. At the same instant, I felt a weight drop on top of me. A thud like two bodies colliding on a football field came from behind me. Metal clattering on hardwood told me the gun was again in play. Grunts and vicious blows echoing behind me told the tale of someone receiving a brutal beating.

"Ease up, Trey. I think you got him." *Delilah! Delilah urging restraint no less.*

I searched my body for signs of pain and felt none. Nothing except the weight resting on me. I started to move it off.

"Oh, God! Diana, don't move yet! Be careful." *Trey!*

"Trey, what's going on?"

Then I smelled it. Lucille's lavender perfume drifted into my nostrils. And I knew what the weight was on top of me.

As my senses returned to normal, I heard Dorcas sobbing hysterically nearby. Trey's feet appeared, and he gently lifted the weight off my body. I rolled over to see him cradling Lucille in his arms.

Dixon lay on his face, hands cuffed behind his back, with Officer Reggie sitting on him. Jim Gorman struggled to his feet, nursing a bruised face and a swelling eye.

Delilah was holding Dorcas and looking apprehensively at us. I crawled to Trey and looked down at Lucille. He wordlessly passed her to me so that her head was resting on my lap. An ugly red spot darkened his pants where she had been lying. The bullet Dixon meant for me had gone into her back and failed to exit. Blood was already soaking her shirt. With no time to find a weapon or prevent Dixon from firing, Lucille used the only tool she had left. She'd thrown her body over me, taking the death sentence that should have been mine.

"Why do we have her on her back? Shouldn't we turn her over, so the bullet doesn't do more damage?"

Trey reached and brushed his fingers against my cheek. His sympathetic eyes gave me my answer.

"No. We can't give up. We ..."

Lucille's eyes flicked open. Flecks of blood on her mouth told me that the bullet had damaged her lungs. Her breaths came in shallow gasps. She couldn't speak, but I could tell from the brightness and focus of her eyes that she recognized us. A smile of satisfaction crossed her face when she saw me looking down at her.

"Can you hear us?" I asked. "We're going to take care of you. You're going to make it."

She shook her head slightly. Her hand traveled up to my chest and settled on my heart. She looked into my eyes and mouthed a single word. "Proud."

I could feel my sisters gathering around us. Her eyes traveled our little circle, settling on each in turn. They started to close. I lost all sense of time and place.

"No! Don't go! Momma, don't go!"

Her eyes flicked open, and a smile spread again across her face. Tears trickled down her cheeks.

"Momma," I said. "The ambulance is coming. Hold on. We love you! Momma!"

She exhaled and stared beyond us at the rafters. It took a minute before we realized that she was seeing far beyond the rafters. Her eyes widened with wonder and joy. As the light faded from her eyes, her lips moved to form one last word. "Dinah."

Dorcas broke down completely, sobbing and heaving. Delilah held her in shocked silence. In the distance, we heard the wail of an ambulance siren piercing the night.

"Momma!" I called. "They're here. Hang on!"

I kept calling her until Trey pulled me into his arms, and I surrendered her to the waiting paramedics. I felt Dorcas and Delilah putting their arms around us. We sat there for twenty minutes, the four of us, huddled together at center court.

CHAPTER TWENTY-EIGHT

JANUARY 4, 1996

We buried Dinah on a cold winter day with the wind stirring our hair and chilling our bones. The pastor spoke beautiful words about how Dinah was "full of life and an inspiration to all who knew her." Her senior picture stood on an easel at the front of the church. She looked so happy and ready for life. I stared at the picture throughout most of the funeral service.

The moment I dreaded most came as the final prayers were said and all our friends filed past the gray casket. They'd opened the lid according to custom so that everyone could get one last view of their loved one. I sat in my spot on the front pew, trying not to look at the casket or people's reactions to seeing Dinah. When the last friends were outside, the funeral director closed the doors and beckoned for us to come forward.

Daddy and Momma rose. Daddy carried Dorcas. Delilah shuffled behind them with her head down. She'd actually agreed to wear a blue dress for the occasion. I thought she cleaned up pretty well. I watched them walk down, rooted to my seat. Daddy began to cry as soon as they reached the end. Dorcas joined him. It was awful. Momma and Delilah were stoic but shattered as they gazed down at Dinah.

I sat there staring at my hands in my lap. I just couldn't do it. Did I really want to see her like that? I felt a hand touch mine. Funeral directors maintained lax security. Through my tears, I saw Trey standing beside me. He looked handsome in his black suit. It was the first time I'd ever used the word "handsome" in connection with my friend.

"Come on, Debbie," Trey whispered.

"Are we leaving?" I asked hopefully.

"No. We're going to see Dinah."

I recoiled. "I can't, Trey. I can't!"

"You have to," Trey said gently. "You'll always wish you had if you don't. I'll go with you."

I struggled at first. Then I thought of Dinah leading us through the dark with Daddy's flashlight. Dinah throwing me the keys. Dinah telling me it was going to be okay in the car that last night. Somehow, I found the strength to rise. Trey wrapped his arm around me, and we made our way to the front.

Daddy and Momma had backed away and were holding each other. Dorcas stood near them and away from the casket, not knowing what to do. Delilah stood beside the casket, still looking at Dinah. Trey and I slid in beside her.

I looked down at Dinah's face one last time. She was still beautiful. Her black hair was arranged around her like a silky pillow. The expression on her face was peaceful. Momma had picked one of her favorite green dresses. It brought out the black of her hair and would have the blue of her eyes if they'd been open. People always said that the dead looked so "good" after the mortician got done with them. I decided that was just polite talk. Dinah did look nice, but not like herself. There was so much makeup that she looked more like a wax effigy of my sister.

I moved closer to Delilah. I touched her shoulder, expecting some sharp retort about getting "fresh." Instead, she turned and hugged me tight. I held on to her. A few seconds later, Trey wrapped his gentle arms around us both. We sniffled and held each other. I felt motion beside my legs and looked down. Dorcas was pushing her way into our little circle. I lowered my arm and pulled her in. The four of us stood there, wrapped in each other's arms and huddled together until they came to shut the casket and carry my sister to her final resting place.

CHAPTER TWENTY-NINE

WE BURIED MOMMA ON A WINTER DAY much like the day we buried Dinah. The wind whipped us at the graveside just like it did on that other sad day. We were gathered at the exact same spot. Momma's plot lay beside Dinah's with one reserved for my daddy when his time came.

Daddy was doing better than we feared. We all three tried to go in and tell him that night. None of us could do it. Trey spared us by volunteering to tell him. The heartbreaking sounds coming from his room told us Trey had done what he promised. For all our disagreements over the years, I always appreciated the way Momma served as Daddy's constant rock. I hoped he would be able to carry on without her.

I was impressed by the people who came. People from town my parents hadn't seen for years flocked to express their condolences. Several members of Delilah's roadcrew and fellow musicians showed up. I confess to considering more than once whether it was proper to solicit autographs at a funeral. Flowers arrived from several colleagues at Vanderbilt, including one huge arrangement from Pedro.

The Jordans arrived early and made a point to catch us as we were entering the church. Mr. Jordan gripped Daddy's hand while Mrs. Jordan hugged each of us in turn.

"I'm sorry we blamed you, Denny," Mr. Jordan said.

"I know what it's like to lose a daughter," Daddy said. "I understand. There are no hard feelings here."

"We trusted him," Mrs. Jordan said. "Mia trusted him. And he ..." She couldn't continue.

Mr. Jordan put his arm around her and nodded to us.

"Thank you for uncovering the truth. Especially at such a terrible cost. It hurts. I guess it will always hurt. But at least we understand now what she was going through. I just wish we'd been able to see it when we could help her."

We knew that feeling all too well.

Trey helped Daddy navigate with his cane and sat beside us on the pew. The dreaded moment came when everyone else stepped out and we stood gazing down at Lucille. This time there was sadness but also a sense of completion and triumph. Momma was gone. She had made so many mistakes, and there was still so much emotional weight to unpack from those difficult years. She gave her life to protect her family in the end. To protect me. *She had a good run, Sweetheart.*

"Are you okay?" Trey whispered to me.

"No," I said, squeezing his hand. "But I'll get there."

Several people met us outside to offer sympathies. One of them was Erin, Trey's ex-wife. I'd never met her and braced for an awkward conversation. There was no need. Erin was kind and friendly. She clasped my hand with warmth. We talked for several minutes. It felt more comfortable and natural than I would have expected. Chip stood to one side. His red curls matched Erin's and complimented the blue of his suit. He gave me an eager fist bump. Brandy lingered behind him in a pretty, yellow dress with her brown hair French braided. She watched me closely as I talked to her mom. She looked away when I tried to make eye contact. *Oh well, baby steps.* When we finished talking, Erin said goodbye and ushered the kids out of the way so that other people could step up.

"Bye, Diana!" Chip called as they moved down the line.

I waved and turned to the next person in line, Mrs. Fields, Momma's old friend. I had just finished talking with her when I felt someone beside me. I turned to see Brandy standing there, her eyes brimming with tears.

She hugged me and said, "I'm sorry, Diana. I'm so sorry!"

I started crying again and held her tight.

"Thank you, Sweetie," I said.

Maybe being an "S-Mom" wouldn't be such a bad thing after all.

Daddy did well as the pastor preached the graveside sermon. He leaned on his cane during the standing portions and sat quietly until the prayers at the end. Dorcas stayed at his side. We'd already talked about the future, and she'd been adamant that she was staying with Daddy. I hoped someday she could start a life of her own, but I suspected they would continue doing their thing for the foreseeable future. Rushing from one deliverance crisis to another.

The *Demonologist* series would continue and probably gather more steam than ever with Momma's death. If Delilah's musician friends had not been enough to cause a stir, several members of the cast, including Selena, appeared at the funeral to show their support. I'd already been contacted by a couple of people asking if I would write something telling the true story behind Dinah's death. Academic publishers had been asking for years if I would be willing to produce a memoir of my years growing up in the Hebert household. Maybe now it was time. Lots to consider. I never wanted to be defined by my family's legacy, but I was ready to own it in a way I hadn't been before.

That resolve grew as I noticed a couple of figures standing at the edge of our crowd of mourners. I couldn't place them at first and had to lean slightly forward to see them from my seat between Dorcas and Delilah. The tall girl looked like an Olympian athlete, a fitting human representation of the goddess Athena in her flowing black dress and long black hair. She could almost have passed for an Hebert sister except for her impressive height. A woman with auburn hair stood by her side, obviously her mom from their resemblance, and clutched her arm with a palpable ferocity as if she feared her daughter would float away if she let go.

My cognitive gears broke through the fog of memory as I recognized Chelsea Whitmer, the high school basketball star I'd noticed talking to Eric Dixon the morning we visited his church. Her face was stoic and set hard. Then she noticed me looking at her. For just a moment, the disciplined exterior melted. Her eyes communicated pain, sadness, and resolute hope all in a series of quick expressions that disappeared as fast as they'd come, leaving behind only a slight mist. Chelsea gave me a swift nod and forced her eyes forward.

Her mother followed her gaze. Tears ran down both cheeks as she gazed at me. She slipped her arm around her daughter's waist and pulled her tighter. Mrs. Whitmer mouthed the words, "Thank you." I smiled at her and looked away before I teared up again too.

We had already received two messages of thanks from women who had been sexually, emotionally, and spiritually abused by Dixon when they heard the news of his arrest. Based on my experiences with other cases, I expected we would hear of more victims in the days ahead. Deputy Gorman had stopped by two days after that tragic night at the old high school to tell us that not only would Dixon be charged with the murders of Mia, Dinah, and Lucille, but he and Crissy would face multiple charges of assault. I felt sorry for their kids. On the other hand, they had a better chance of growing up healthy away from the Dixons' influence.

I knew Eric Dixon's downfall would produce quite the stir in little Picardy and ripple throughout the national evangelical world. The usual spin machine had kicked into gear almost immediately after he was arrested. Some conservative Christian leaders on social media insisted that we shouldn't judge Eric Dixon because "all of us are sinners." Some even dared to call his victims women with "loose morals." I dreaded how bad those attacks could get. Religious institutions tended to victimize the victims all over again in their quest to protect themselves from the ugly hypocrisies committed right under their noses. So much potential to heal existing alongside equal potential to hurt. The capacity of religious belief to inspire and devastate lives in equal parts remained one of the things keeping me committed to exploring faith in all its mysteries and ironies. For our own sake and for the women seeking healing, I hoped pledges of support for us and condemnation for Dixon's actions came louder and from farther afield.

Daddy and Dorcas turned to me at the end of the graveside service, bringing me back to the present. He was leaning on her still, but less and less as the days went by. His strength was returning. With exercise and a better diet, the doctors said he stood a good chance of living many more productive years. They both hugged me for a few minutes. When we separated, Daddy reached into his suit pocket and produced a small brown envelope.

"This is for you, Angel."

The name DEBORAH was printed in Lucille's bold script across the front.

"We found it in a little safe she kept at the back of her hope chest," Daddy said. "I'm sure we'll find more as we sort through the rest of her things. I wanted to give it to you before I forgot."

"Thanks, Daddy," I said, giving him another hug and a kiss on his cheek.

"You coming?" Dorcas asked.

"I'll be there in just a few minutes."

Dorcas understood. She nodded and started guiding Daddy toward the main gate.

I studied the envelope for a moment. It felt light in my hand. The aged appearance it carried suggested Lucille had prepared it years ago. There was nowhere in my black dress to store it, so I decided to open it if I had to hold it anyway. I broke the seal and shook its contents into my hand. A silver pendant, an antique brass key, and a slip of paper slid into my hand. The silver pendant sparkled in the brilliant sunlight. Shaped like a circle, it held a pentagram in the center. Not an accessory I would expect Lucille to possess. The antique key could open a chest or maybe even an old door lock. I unfolded the slip of paper.

"You will know what to do with these if the time comes. Protect them all if I can't. You may not believe me, but there is no one besides your Daddy I trust more than you. You are the one most like me."

What is this? What are you entrusting to me?

She could no longer answer. I'd spent most of my life ignoring her advice, and when I finally wanted it, she was gone.

As people started to melt away, I lingered. Momma's newly minted gravestone wouldn't be in place for another week. A temporary placeholder stood where it would rest. I stepped in front of the nearby tombstone engraved: DINAH LUCILLE HEBERT, BELOVED DAUGHTER AND SISTER.

"I'm so sorry we couldn't save you," I said. "We love you so much. We miss you. I've tried so hard to make you proud. I'm going to keep trying. I hope you knew what you meant to us."

"She did," Trey's voice said, as he put his arm around me. "She was proud of you when we were small and causing hell for her after school. How could she not be now?"

We stood at Dinah's grave. Sweet memories of the past filled our hearts and minds. It hadn't been all bad. Some of it was so good. Trey's hand wandered up to my neck. As he rubbed it, he felt something and stopped.

"What's this?" he asked.

I smiled. "I haven't dressed up much since I've been down here. I wear it all the time in Nashville. I have for twenty-five years."

Trey pulled on the tiny gold chain just enough to expose the gold heart-shaped locket at the end. The word FOREVER glittered in the bright sunlight.

"Whoever gave you this must be a classy guy."

"He has his moments."

"How long is forever?" Trey asked.

"As long as we want it to be," I said. "I won't pretend it's going to be easy. We've always been two sides of the same coin pulling in different directions. I don't want to pull away anymore. I know what I want. I want you in my life. Every day. Every night. Always."

For once, Trey didn't have any clever quips or a Bogart quote.

"Me too. Every day. Every night. For as long as we live."

Our lips met. As we kissed, I heard Dinah's voice saying, "It'll be okay."

As we made our way toward the front gate, Trey reached into his pocket and produced a familiar black candy packet.

"Bracer for the road?"

"You are such an enabler," I said as I held my right hand out.

My other hand still gripped the envelope with Lucille's mysterious legacy. I decided to wait and show it to Trey later.

"So how does this work?"

"Let me finish up at Vanderbilt this spring, and then maybe we could meet halfway? Definitely not in Picardy. Maybe not in Louisiana. But close enough that we can still be involved in the kids' lives."

"You see yourself being involved in my kids' lives?" he teased.

"Face it. You're not gettin' rid of me, Sweetheart."

"That was a terrible Bogart impression."

"I have other skills to compensate," I said.

We walked through the cemetery gates where my family stood waiting for us. Daddy, Delilah, and Dorcas beckoned for us to join them. A feast waited for us at home provided by friends and neighbors. As Trey and Daddy loaded the car, I stood with my arms around my sisters and looked back to where my sister and Momma lay at rest beneath all the floral arrangements.

Once again, I heard Dinah's voice saying, "It'll be okay." The Demonologists' daughters were going to be fine.

ACKNOWLEDGMENTS

Most books carry only one name on the cover, but they are never the product of one person alone. No person is an island, and no book is produced in absolute isolation. We all benefit from networks and communities of supporters who encourage us when the going is tough and help us in those places where their gifts can come alongside us and complement our own.

I want to thank my amazing cover designer, Brandi Doane McCann, who captured the heart of this story and the Hebert sisters' personalities so well. Thanks also to Mark Spencer for his editorial assistance. Mark is an amazing teacher of writers as well as an accomplished author himself. Appreciation to Katherine D. Graham, who also provided helpful edits and feedback on the story, genre, and structure. I've had the benefit of some great teachers along the way, both near and far. Thanks to Abbie Emmons for her informative design course that guided us during some challenging final design phases. Joanna Penn has created a vibrant community of authors through her *Creative Penn* podcast and website. I'm one of many who has benefitted enormously from her advice. Barry Hankins modeled intellectual honesty and fair-minded approaches to researching every topic in his history classes at both Louisiana College and Baylor University. I'm indebted to him for helping me discover the incredible journey that is the life of the mind. Appreciation also to Connie Douglas and Fred Downing, who impressed on me as an undergraduate in their "Values Studies" course at Louisiana College how profoundly storytelling can bring us into engagement with the deepest questions in life and, in the words J. R. R. Tolkien, provide an "escape to reality."

We live in "interesting times," as the old Chinese curse reads. New voices are emerging daily to tell heart-wrenching stories of abuse in religious communities. Deepest respect to these courageous people who speak truth to power and seek to set others free from the pain they have endured. I can't begin to imagine what you've been through, but I hope it helps to know that so many of us see you, we hear you, and we want to join with you to help all of us do better.

I'm blessed with both an amazing support system and an in-house production team in the form of my incredible family. Hannah Culpepper excelled as always in redesigning my website and other social media platforms as well as planning promotional events. Josiah Culpepper applied his professional skills to producing my professional photos, consulting on videos and social media, and answering design questions for us. Micah Culpepper shares my love for writing and reading and is an incredible writer who provided excellent editorial suggestions and a solid sounding board for processing story ideas. One of the greatest joys of being a parent is watching all three of them grow into incredible humans who make the world a better place just by being in it. Love and appreciation to all three of them as well as to Maggie, Hunter, and Andrew. I couldn't do it without all of you. Thanks also to my amazing parents, Ann and Kenny Culpepper, who thankfully gave us a much calmer place to call home than the Heberts did.

Most of all, thanks to my wife, my love, and my life, Ginger Culpepper, who brought her keen professional editorial eye and design skills to the daunting task of editing this text. She has been instrumental in every phase of this project, including keeping the author well and happy. The dedication at the beginning doesn't begin to do justice to the many ways she has helped make this a better book and me a better person. Love you always and forever, every day and every night, Mon Amour! We did it, and now it's time for everyone else to enjoy it.